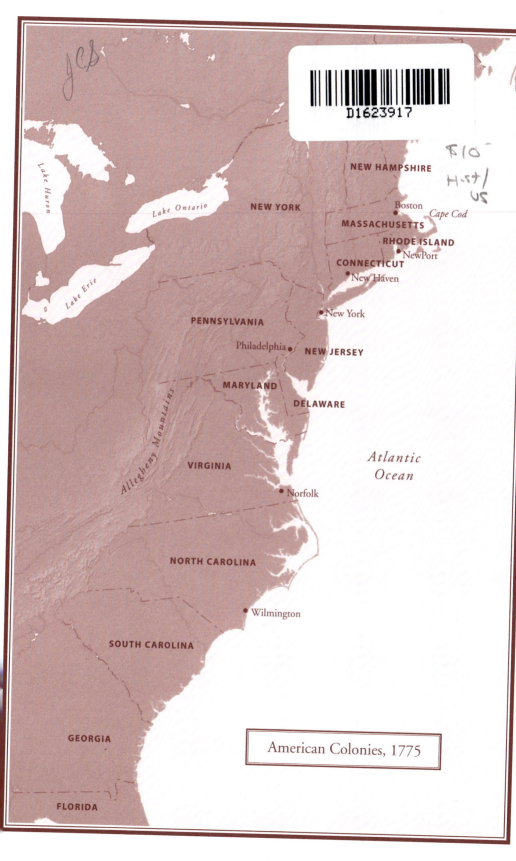

American Colonies, 1775

Unlikely Heroes

Unlikely Heroes

Ordinary Men and Women
Whose Courage
Won the Revolution

RON CARTER

SHADOW
MOUNTAIN

Visit us at ShadowMountain.com

Library of Congress Cataloging-in-Publication Data

Carter, Ron, 1932-
    Unlikely heroes : ordinary men and women whose courage won the Revolution / Ron Carter.
        p.   cm.
    Includes bibliographical references and index.
    ISBN 978-1-59038-797-9 (hardback : alk. paper)
    1. Heroes—Fiction.   2. United States—History—Revolution, 1775–1783—Fiction.   I. Title.
    PS3553.A7833U66 2007
    813'.54—dc22   2007018574

Printed in the United States of America
Publishers Printing, Salt Lake City, Utah

10   9   8   7   6   5   4   3   2   1

★　★　★

*For the legions of unknown people
whose unsung heroism has, from the dawn
of time, served us all*

CONTENTS

★ ★ ★

CONTENTS

THE PETTICOAT THAT SAVED PAUL REVERE

APRIL 18, 1775

BOSTON

★ ★ ★

T HE ABRUPT KNOCK AT THE FRONT DOOR of his comfortable Boston residence brought Dr. Joseph Warren to his feet. He laid aside the book he had been reading in his spacious library and looked at the clock on the fireplace mantle. It was ten minutes before nine o'clock in the evening. His eyes narrowed as his mind leaped ahead.

Near nine o'clock. Past the time the British have ordered the streets cleared. Who could it be? The redcoats? Have they finally come to arrest me?

Only too well was he aware of the nerve-wrenching tension between the rebellious Americans and the British, tension that had risen to catastrophic proportions in Boston. The burning of the tax stamps sent by King George III, the shooting of American colonists in the streets by panicked British soldiers that had become known as the Boston Massacre, the dumping of three hundred forty-two chests of tea into Boston Harbor by colonists disguised as Indians—all had widened the division between the colonies and Mother England until Boston was a tinderbox, waiting for the single spark that would ignite the fragile peace into full-scale war.

It was he, Dr. Joseph Warren, respected and beloved by Boston, who had spoken loudly and eloquently for the independence of the colonies, in public meetings, on the streets, and in the Boston town hall meetings, to become the leading citizen in the rising rebellion. It was he who had defied the British, openly demanding that King George grant the Americans their independence. An infuriated King George had responded by giving direct orders that Dr. Joseph Warren was to be arrested and punished for his treasonous attacks on England. And it was the fearless patriot Dr. Joseph Warren who freely walked the streets of Boston and thundered back at King George, "The day you arrest me, ten thousand Americans will rise in arms to my defense!"

His passionate defiance had the British befuddled. Dare they arrest Dr. Joseph Warren and risk an open war in the streets of Boston? Caught between the necessity of bringing the Americans under control and the equally strong desire to avoid a war, the British brought battleships into the Boston Back Bay to surround the peninsula with heavy cannon, capable of blasting to rubble both Boston and Charlestown, the small town across the Back Bay on the mainland. The huge battleship HMS *Somerset* had dropped anchor directly between the two towns. Then the British issued an ultimatum. Persons found in the streets of Boston after dark would be arrested on the spot and imprisoned. There were to be no public gatherings in Boston—not in churches, homes, the town halls, or any other location. In the late evening, all lights in all buildings were to be extinguished. The British were determined to humble the defiant Americans.

Dr. Joseph Warren took a deep breath and set his jaw. *If they've come to arrest me, so be it! Let's get on with it!*

He strode from the library, through the parlor, and opened his front door to face two patriots. Instantly he saw the strain in their eyes, their faces.

Quickly he stepped aside. "Samuel! Jonah! Come in before you're seen."

They stepped quickly into the room, and Warren closed the door. For ten seconds he stood stock still, ear to the door, listening to hear if the men had been followed. There was no sound. He turned to them and spoke with quiet urgency.

"What brings you here at this time of night? You know the risk."

Samuel, the taller of the two, thrust his head forward and the words came spilling: "Doctor, sir, we was down on the Back Bay and we seen some things. The British are gathering on the beach of the Back Bay. Hundreds of 'em. They got knapsacks and muskets and bayonets and they're wearin' full uniforms, like for battle. We can't figger out what they're doin', but the longer we thought on it, the more we got worried."

Warren's mind leaped forward. *Concord! The British have found out about all the cannon and muskets and shot and gunpowder and food we've stored in Concord! They're going to get it! They know that without guns and munitions and food we can't fight them!*

Eyes narrowed and flashing, Warren asked, "When did you see them?"

"Twenty minutes ago. It's goin' on right now! We snuck away and come straight here. Figgered you needed to know."

Warren nodded and for long moments stood with his head bowed while he organized his thoughts and made instant decisions.

"All right," he said softly. "I'll need two men. Paul Revere and William Dawes. Can you get them and bring them here right now?"

"Yes, sir. We'll get 'em."

"Do not tell them a word of what you've told me. Just tell them I must have them here, now."

"Yes, sir."

Warren bobbed his head. "Now, follow me," he said and led them through the kitchen to the back door. "When you've got both of them, bring them to this door. We've got work to do."

Both men nodded, Warren opened the door, and they slipped out into the faint light of a nearly full moon to disappear at a run.

Within fifteen minutes, a muffled knock came at the back door. Warren opened it instantly and stepped aside to let the four men slip silently into the kitchen. All the window blinds in the house were drawn. Warren led them into the dining room where one small lamp burned on the dining table with the wick turned as low as possible. In the dull, shadowy yellow light, the five men took their places, and four of them turned their faces to Warren, waiting. Warren did not hesitate, nor did he waste words as he spoke to Revere and Dawes.

"A short while ago, Samuel and Jonah watched British regulars in full battle dress gathering on the Back Bay. Hundreds of them."

Revere and Dawes both jerked straight in their chairs, eyes

wide in the yellow light, and in the same instant both men exclaimed, "Concord!"

Warren nodded. "There is no other explanation! If it's true, we've got to get word up to those people tonight, and we've got to give notice to everyone we can between here and Concord that the British are coming. We don't know yet if they're going to go by land or take longboats across the Back Bay and up the Mystic River. So we'll have to prepare for either event."

Both Revere and Dawes leaned forward, eyes narrowed, waiting for Warren to continue. Warren spoke directly to Revere.

"Across the Back Bay in Charlestown there is a man named Larkin. He owns the strongest horse in town—a brown mare named Beauty. Do you know Larkin?"

Revere nodded. "I know of him. I can find him."

"Get over there as fast as you can. Larkin will loan you the mare. You ride north from there as fast as you can. There'll be British patrols out in the night. You'll have to outrun them. Stop at the farmhouses on the way and tell everyone you can find that the British are coming. Be certain to give notice in Lexington."

Warren paused, then continued. "As soon as we are certain whether they're coming by land or by sea, we'll mount lanterns in the belfry of the Old North Church. One lantern if by land, two if by sea. As you start your ride, be certain to look for the lanterns. Am I clear enough?"

"Yes. I understand."

Warren turned to Dawes. "You get your strongest horse and go the opposite direction. Get off the Boston Peninsula through the narrow neck to the west that connects us to the mainland, and you also head north. Do the same as I've instructed Revere. Look for the lanterns in the church belfry. With two of you working, one is bound to get through, whether they go by land or by sea. Am I clear?"

Dawes bobbed his head emphatically. "You are."

"We don't have a moment to lose. Do not tell a soul in Boston what you're doing, not even your wives. Get to those horses as fast as you can, and don't stop until you're in Concord."

All five men stood and for one brief moment they looked into each other's eyes. There was a quiet, electric feeling as Warren spoke.

"Our prayers are with you. Go."

Warren led them through the kitchen and held the back door while Revere and Dawes stepped out into the still, moonlit night and disappeared.

Revere, short, stocky, trotted through the narrow, winding streets, watching everything that moved, listening for every sound. Twice he heard British patrols moving in the street and stopped and became invisible behind fences and bushes. Minutes later he opened the gate into a fenced yard and knocked softly on the door of a house.

"Who's there?" came the whispered voice from inside.

"Me. Revere. I've got to talk with Joshua."

The door opened enough for Revere to slip inside, where he faced a surprised Joshua Bentley.

"Joshua, I've got to have you and your boat tonight. You've got to get me across the Back Bay to Charlestown."

Joshua Bentley straightened in surprise. "What? Tonight?"

Revere raised a hand. "Don't ask me why. I can't tell you. Will you do it?"

Joshua peered at Revere for a long moment. He had known him for years as a close and trusted friend.

"Yes."

Bentley followed Revere into the night, and the two worked

their way silently a short distance to another home where Revere stopped and rapped on the door.

"Who's there?"

"Revere and Bentley. We must talk with you, Tom."

Thomas Richardson opened the door, and the two men quickly entered his darkened house.

"Tom," Revere confided, "I've got to get across the Back Bay tonight to Charlestown. Joshua is here and we can use his boat. But we need one more man to row it back. Will you come?"

Tom asked no questions. If Paul Revere and Joshua Bentley said they had to cross the Back Bay at night, that was all he needed to know.

The three men turned east and were soon at the docks where Joshua's boat was tied. They stopped and peered out over the black waters of the Back Bay to study the outline of the huge British warship, HMS *Somerset,* which was anchored dead center on the course they would have to take to reach the docks in distant Charlestown. The lights on the ship glowed dully in the moonlight. Even at three hundred yards, all three men could see the British pickets marching on the decks, watching for any American boats that might be moving on the Back Bay. And all three men knew that if they were spotted on the water, those British pickets were under orders to shoot to kill.

To get from where they were to where they were going in Charleston, they had to get by the huge warship, and they did not have the time to go miles out of their way to avoid it.

"We'll have to take our chances," Revere said through gritted teeth. "Are you ready?"

Both men nodded, and Joshua reached to loosen the ropes that held his boat to the dock.

"Wait a minute," Richardson whispered. "As quiet as it is,

those British pickets are bound to hear the oars rattling in the oar-locks. We've got to do something to silence the sound." They stood in silent thought for two seconds, until Richardson said, "Give me a minute."

He left at a run, up the old cobblestone street half a block, where he stopped before an ancient, two-story house. Bending, he plucked two or three tiny pebbles from the ground and tossed them rattling against the dark second-story window. After a moment, a light came on inside, the window opened, and the silhouette of a woman's head appeared.

"Who's there?" came the call.

"Me. Richardson. We need something to quiet the sound of oars in oarlocks. Can you help?"

The silhouette disappeared for a few moments, then reappeared, and a large piece of cloth came billowing down to Richardson. He caught it and held it up in the moonlight to see what it was. It was a woman's petticoat, still warm!

He grinned up at her. "Thank you," he said as he turned and ran back to the waiting Revere and Bentley. Quickly, strong hands tore the garment into two pieces and wrapped the oarlocks. Then Joshua jerked the tie rope free and the three men stepped into the boat and pushed it from the dock. With Revere on the front bench, the two men settled onto the middle bench, seized the oars, inserted them into the padded oarlocks, and began the steady, deep strokes that propelled them silently across the still, black water of Boston's Back Bay.

They had gone but a short distance when Revere pointed without speaking, back to the Old North Church belfry in Boston.

"Two lanterns," he whispered. "The British are going by sea—across the Back Bay."

Bentley and Richardson, both experienced oarsmen, held the

steady rhythm with the oars, silently dipping the blades in the water. In the quiet stillness, they made no sound as they moved eastward, toward the looming outline of the great British battleship. Their course would take them directly beneath the overhang at the stern of the ship. To them, the moonlight seemed brighter than the noonday sun.

Richardson whispered, "Keep your heads down so they can't see the moonlight reflecting off our faces."

They went on, the only sound the soft whisper of the bow of the rowboat slicing the water, waiting for the shout from the pickets on the warship that they had been discovered. When that happened, their only chance would be to capsize the boat and swim for shore while the pickets tried to kill them with musket fire. Hardly breathing, they continued on, expecting the shouted alarm with each stroke of the oars.

Then, in a clear sky filled with endless stars and a nearly full moon, casting the entire Back Bay and Boston in silvery light, a small cloud appeared. Within minutes additional clouds gathered, moving in the heavens. As the small craft drew closer to the HMS *Somerset,* the clouds reached the moon and covered it completely. The silvery light dwindled and then was gone, and the world was cast in utter blackness. Bentley and Richardson continued their silent stroking as their rowboat came within fifty yards of the huge ship looming above them, and they could hear the boots of the pickets on the wooden deck and the men talking among themselves. They held their course, and in blackness, passed soundlessly, directly beneath the stern of the great warship. They hardly dared to breathe as they came out on the east side and continued on, undetected. They had nearly reached the Charlestown shore when the clouds passed from before the moon and once again moonlight flooded the world.

They tied the boat to the Charlestown docks while Revere spoke.

"I'm to find a man named Larkin. He has a horse I can borrow."

Richardson pointed. "I know him. Come on."

Within minutes they were at the back door of the Larkin home, where Revere explained the plan Warren had conceived. Without a question, Larkin saddled his brown mare and handed the reins to Revere. "She'll get you there," he said, "if you can avoid the British patrols. They're thick between here and Concord. Good luck."

Revere raised foot to stirrup and mounted. "I'll be all right. I'll get the mare back as soon as I can." He turned to Joshua Bentley and Richardson. "Will you two be all right?"

"We'll wait for daylight and row back to Boston. There's no British rule against crossing the Back Bay in daylight."

For a moment the four men exchanged glances, each sensing the drama of the moment.

"Good," Revere said. "I'll be back."

He reined the brown mare around and raised her to a trot in the narrow, crooked streets of Charlestown, iron horseshoes ringing and raising tiny sparks on the cobblestones. He had nearly reached the outskirts when a shouted command came from behind: "Stop! In the name of the King. Stop or we'll shoot!"

Revere could not suppress a grin as he drove his heels into the flanks of the big brown mare and felt the surge of power as she lunged forward at a high gallop.

"Catch me if you can," Revere muttered to himself and was off on the mission and the ride that ushered in the American Revolutionary War.

Hard to Keep a Good Man Down

April 19, 1775
Menotomy, Massachusetts

★ ★ ★

It was well past noon when a pounding came at his front door. Sam Whittemore laid down his towel on the kitchen cupboard and came shuffling through the parlor. Seventy-eight years of age, widowed years earlier, old Sam lived alone in his small, modest home in the tiny village of Menotomy that clustered about the road connecting Boston to Concord. He had heard the British marching toward Boston in the morning, and later someone in the village had shouted there had been shooting between the redcoats and the Americans. Now someone was hammering on his front door.

He swung the door open and instantly his neighbor Lucas Fordham exclaimed, "Sam, they're coming! The British. Back from Concord. The Americans over there met them and there was shooting, and our people drove them out. Shot many of them. The British are in full retreat back to Boston and they're furious. They're shooting at people and smashing into homes! You've got to get out! Hide somewhere until they're gone!"

Without another word Lucas bolted from the door and ran to the next house to pound on the door.

Old Sam paused to listen, and in the warm sunshine of a clear spring day, could hear the faint staccato of musket fire coming from a distance to the west.

Run? Hide? He shook his head. *Not from my own home!*

He limped into his small dining room and lifted the little square dining table to carry it to the parlor where he set it squarely before the front door. Then he went to the wardrobe in his bedroom where he reached behind his clothing to draw out an ancient musket and two aged pistols. He carried them to the table, then returned to the bedroom for the small box of gunpowder and musket balls, which he set on the table beside the musket and pistols. He returned to his bedroom to lift his old saber from the place he had mounted it on the wall above his bed and laid it on the table beside the other weapons. Then, with old, gnarled hands, he patiently tapped gunpowder into the barrel of each weapon, then the patch, then inserted the musket ball, using the ramrod to seat them. He opened the frizzen on each in turn, tapped gunpowder into the pan, closed the frizzen, checked the flints in each hammer, and laid them on the table. Last, he brought a chair from the dining room, set it at the table, and sat down facing the front door to wait.

Soon enough the sound of muskets became louder, and then Sam could hear the British soldiers in the streets, running in full retreat, cursing the Americans, smashing windows and doors, shooting, damaging, and destroying everything they could in their wild, disorganized retreat. He heard them flatten the picket fence to his yard, and as the butt of a British musket smashed into his front door, he reached for both his pistols. Sam cocked the heavy weapons and calmly brought them to bear on the center of the door. A British soldier struck the door once more, then kicked it open, and two redcoats barged into the room, sweating, wild-eyed.

Sam pulled the triggers of both pistols at the same instant, and both the British regulars staggered back and slammed into the wall, to slide down, finished. As Sam laid the pistols down, a third redcoat came sprinting up the walkway, and Sam took up his ancient musket, cocked it, and as the man burst into the room, Sam pulled the trigger. The old musket bucked and roared, and the redcoat went down and didn't move. Behind him came two more, shouting, cursing as they came through the doorway, and when Sam picked up his sword to parry their thrusting bayonets, one of the soldiers fired point-blank at Sam's head. The .75-caliber musket ball struck Sam in the cheek, tore through the flesh, hit and smashed the joint where Sam's jawbone connected to his head, and sprawled Sam backwards. More British soldiers burst through the door, and as Sam was going down, they drove their bayonets into him. When he stopped moving, he had thirteen bayonet wounds in his chest and stomach, and his mouth was hanging open with blood streaming from the gaping wound in his cheek and the broken joint. The British left him on the parlor floor for dead and continued through his house, smashing things as they exited through the back door to continue their headlong rush back to Boston.

Half an hour later old Sam's eyes fluttered open. For a few seconds he lay there, trying to recollect what had happened. He glanced down at his blood-soaked shirt, then realized he could not close his mouth. He reached to feel and remembered the stunning impact of the British musket ball that had torn his cheek and broken his jaw.

Anger rose in his chest to fill him until he was so mad he was trembling. He got to his feet and went out into the tiny kitchen. He took a towel and drenched it in the wooden water bucket filled with drinking water, wrung it out, and wiped the blood from his chest as best he could. Then he cleaned the blood from his jaw and cheek. Last, he looped the towel under his jaw and tied it on the top of his head to keep his mouth closed and returned to the table he had positioned at his front door.

It had been knocked to one side, and his two pistols, old musket, and sword were randomly scattered on the floor. He set the table back on its legs facing the door, gathered up his weapons and the box with the gunpowder and musket balls, and set them all on the table. Within minutes he had reloaded both pistols and the musket and had them laid out on the table, along with his old saber. He set the chair on its legs and sat down once again, facing the door that was smashed and hanging at an angle on its broken hinges. Sam was ready for the next wave of retreating British regulars if they came, but none appeared.

Despite the damage to his cheek and jaw and thirteen bayonet wounds in his chest and torso, any of which should have been fatal, old Sam lived for twenty-eight more years, until he died of natural causes at the age of one hundred and four.

It is hard to keep a good man down.

The Criminal Who Saved Washington

EARLY JUNE 1776
NEW YORK CITY

★　★　★

Isaac Ketcham sat on the thin blanket covering the wood slab that served as his bed in his small, dark cell in the New York City jail. The evidence the sheriff had gathered left no doubt that Ketcham was guilty of counterfeiting American dollars. Six days before, he had been arrested and jailed, and was now awaiting his trial, just four days away. He was slouched forward with his head down and his elbows on his knees as he stared unseeing at the stone floor, terrified at the certainty he would be convicted and sent to prison for ten years, with nothing to do but pace back and forth in a tiny, dark, cold cell, eat miserable food, and sleep on a wooden cot with murderers and robbers for company. He had searched in his mind for every conceivable way to escape, or bribe the guards, or trick the judge or jury into believing him to be innocent, but it could not be done.

He heard the sound of footsteps approaching and turned his head to see two guards stop at the door to his cell, clutching the arms of an average-sized man whose ankles and wrists were shackled. The door clanged open, and the man was pushed roughly into the cell with the ankle chains clanking on the stone floor. The deputies tossed a blanket at the man, removed the ankle and wrist chains, walked back into the hall, slammed the barred door, and twisted the big key in the lock. One of the guards growled, "Here's a cellmate for you, Ketcham. Another counterfeiter just like you."

Ketcham looked at the man for a moment in the dim light— average height, heavy shouldered, young, swarthy—then turned and stretched out full length on his low cot with his face to the wall. Without a word the new man spread his blanket on the floor and also lay down. It wasn't until the jailer brought their meager supper of boiled cabbage and a piece of fatty mutton on wooden plates that Ketcham finally asked, "What's your name?"

The man answered, "Hickey. Thomas Hickey. What's yours?"

"Isaac Ketcham. You in here for counterfeiting?"

"Yes. You?"

"Same. What was your work? What did you do?"

There was a long pause. "I was a bodyguard for George Washington."

Ketcham mouth gaped open. "You were *what?*"

"Bodyguard for George Washington."

Ketcham was astonished. "How did you get mixed up in counterfeiting?"

The young face sobered. "That's a long story."

Ketcham laid his wooden plate on the floor. "We've got time. Tell me."

For half an hour young Hickey talked, haltingly at first, then with a rush. When he finally stopped talking, Ketcham was sitting like a statue, mesmerized in disbelief.

Hickey shrugged. "That's the whole of it. My trial for counterfeiting is in two weeks."

Ketcham slowly shook his head. "I never heard anything like it."

It was well past midnight before Ketcham suddenly sat up on his blanket, eyes wide with a thought that had struck in his sleep. For half an hour he sat in silence, making a plan. The following morning when the guards brought their breakfast of boiled mush, Ketcham quietly whispered to one of them, "Bring me paper and pencil. I've got to write a statement for the judge."

When the evening meal was delivered, the folded paper and piece of lead pencil were delivered. In the dark of the night, Ketcham struggled to print a brief message.

"If you want to save George Washington, I must talk to you in private. [Signed], Isaac Ketcham."

Two days later the guards came to the cell, shackled Ketcham's ankles and wrists, and walked him out of the jailhouse to the courthouse, where the judge was waiting in his chambers.

"Judge, sir," Ketcham began, "I was told things by a man in jail that concern George Washington and most of his staff. William Tryon, David Matthews, Richard Hewlett, and I don't know how many others are plotting to kill him."

For a moment the judge sat stunned, then broke out into laughter. "I don't know what your ploy is, but William Tryon is governor of this state. David Matthews is mayor of New York. And Richard Hewlett is one of the most prominent men on Long Island. You're headed back to your cell, and don't you ever bother me with such nonsense again."

Ketcham raised his hand and exclaimed, "The man who told me is Thomas Hickey. He was put in my cell yesterday. Hickey was a bodyguard to Washington! He told me the whole plot last night! Check your record! Thomas Hickey is to be tried for counterfeiting, but no one knows about the plot on Washington's life."

The judge sobered, then called for his clerk. "Get me the court record on Thomas Hickey. His trial is in two weeks."

One hour later, with Ketcham still in his office, the judge opened the Hickey file and carefully read it. Thomas Hickey, a personal bodyguard for George Washington, was to be tried in two weeks for counterfeiting. There was nothing in the file about a wild plot to assassinate anyone.

He turned a jaundiced eye on Ketcham. "Not a word about an attempt on Washington."

Ketcham was not to be denied. "But does it say he is a personal bodyguard for Washington?"

"Yes, matter of fact it does."

Ketcham leaned forward and thumped the desk. "The assassination is going to happen in the next few days. What will happen if you ignore this warning and then find out it is true?"

For a time the judge leaned back in his chair in thoughtful silence, then called his clerk. "Get the highest ranking officer in the Continental Army you can find over here at once."

Half an hour later a full colonel and a major walked into his chambers with puzzled expressions on their faces. The colonel asked, "You sent for me?"

"Yes." He pointed to Ketcham. "This man is in my court on the charge of counterfeiting. He claims that last night a soldier named Thomas Hickey was put in his cell and told him of an unbelievable plot to assassinate General Washington and his entire staff in the next few days. Thomas Hickey was a personal body-guard for the general."

The colonel said, "I know Hickey. He was caught counter-feiting."

"He's in my court for that," the judge answered, "but a plot to assassinate the general is treason, and Hickey is a soldier. That makes it a military matter, subject to a military court-martial. If this assassination is to take place soon, we have no time to lose. You can investigate this much quicker than I. I recommend you spend enough time with this man to determine if there's anything to this matter."

The colonel spoke to Ketcham. "Are you willing to swear to all this under oath?"

"I am."

The colonel glanced at the major next to him, then back at the judge. "Hold him here for ten minutes. I'll send an armed escort to bring him to my quarters. We'll start the investigation today." The colonel turned on his heel and left the judge's chambers with the major right behind. When the door closed, Ketcham stood and confronted the judge.

"If I help to save George Washington, sir, I demand that you dismiss all counterfeiting charges against me. Is that agreed?"

The judge stared. "So *that's* what you're after."

"Yes."

A sour look crossed the judge's face as he stood, and for a time he paced, then turned back to Ketcham. "I make no promise. I can only tell you that saving General Washington will be given due consideration in your case."

Within minutes, four guards, armed and uniformed, arrived to escort Ketcham back to the colonel's chambers, where the offi-cer confronted the shackled man. Seated behind a huge oak desk, the colonel leaned forward, eyes like lightning. "Before this ridiculous thing goes any further, Ketcham, I have to have solid proof that this plot you speak of is true. If you have such proof, tell me now."

Ketcham took a deep breath. "Right now General Washington's headquarters is at 180 Pearl Street here in New York. Beneath his office is a cellar. In that cellar you should find two barrels marked SALTED COD. Instead of fish, they're full of gunpowder. The plan is to blow them up, and with them, the entire house and the general and his entire staff."

Ketcham paused for a moment, then went on. "Also, less than ten days ago the men with Hickey tried to poison Washington. They put poison in some green peas Washington was to eat for supper. Washington's house cook smelled something odd in the peas and threw them out into the yard, where the chickens ate them. The chickens all died. You can ask the cook."

The colonel called for his adjutant. "Assemble Company B immediately, then have my horse saddled. We leave at once."

Thirty minutes later the colonel, escorted by soldiers with mounted bayonets, was admitted to the anteroom of Washington's headquarters, only to be told the general was away until late afternoon. Five minutes later the colonel descended the stairs into the cellar beneath Washington's office, unlocked the door, and with lanterns held high, entered the dank, dark room. In the center of the floor were two huge barrels with SALTED COD stenciled prominently on the sides. A soldier bashed the top of one barrel open, and the colonel stared in shock at the black granules of gunpowder.

"Quickly," he exclaimed, "get those lanterns out of here, and take these barrels back to a safe place in our munitions store."

He marched upstairs and confronted the startled cook. "Tell me about poisoned peas and dead chickens."

"Yes, sir," stammered the cook. "Last week. I smelled something bad in those peas that was for Gen'l Washington, and I threw them out in the yard. The chickens ate them, and most all of them died. I told my commanding officer, but I don't know what he did about it."

Half an hour later the colonel was back at his office desk facing Ketcham. "All right. Let's hear the rest of it. Who else is involved in this mess?"

"William Tryon. David Matthews. Richard Hewlett. And at least fifty others in this town."

The colonel was incredulous. "The governor? The mayor?"

"Both."

"What part were they to play?"

"Hewlett had merchants poison the peas just before they delivered them to Washington's cook. Tryon provided the gunpowder from the state militia. Matthews had men who secretly smuggled it into the cellar at Washington's headquarters. There's at least fifty other men who are ready to kidnap Washington if the gunpowder doesn't kill him, along with as many American officers as they can. Hewlett and Tryon have agreed to close down and barricade all streets leading into New York after Washington's gone and to cut off the city from any attempt by the American army to save either Washington or his staff, or the other officers."

The colonel bolted out of his chair. "Let's go see this Mr. Hickey!"

Fifteen minutes later the colonel, with his adjutant secretary carrying a pencil and pad of paper, and Ketcham at his side, confronted Thomas Hickey in his jail cell.

"We know about the dead chickens and the gunpowder. We

know about Governor Tryon and Mayor Matthews, and Richard Hewlett, and the plan to kill Washington's staff and the American officers and isolate New York City. You're going to tell us the names of all the other conspirators in this treachery, and you're going to do it now! Start talking!"

For one hour Hickey talked while the adjutant wrote it all down. Then the colonel glared at Hickey. "You are under military arrest for mutiny, sedition, and treason against the American army. You will face a court-martial at the earliest date possible. You will remain here until transferred to a military stockade."

He turned to his adjutant. "We will return to headquarters and immediately assemble every available officer. Our men must find and arrest every conspirator as quickly as possible, before they realize they have been discovered."

Within hours, New York mayor David Matthews was seized in his office, arrested, and taken to jail. Somehow New York governor William Tryon learned that the entire plot had been discovered and instantly fled to the New York waterfront, where he secretly bribed his way onto a British merchant ship anchored in the harbor, the *Duchess of Gordon*, and cowered below decks in hiding for weeks. Richard Hewlett, the rich and powerful merchant, leaped into a carriage and disappeared northward on Manhattan Island.

For the next several days the frantic search for the other named conspirators continued, under direction now of General George Washington. Several of the guilty parties fled into a swamp, where they were surrounded and arrested. Some fled to places unknown and were never found. General Washington was given daily reports, one of which informed him that "we are searching for the conspirators and hanging them as fast as we find them."

With the conspiracy utterly destroyed, it was determined the evidence against New York mayor David Matthews was insufficient, and the charges against him were dismissed.

New York governor William Tryon waited until the British occupied New York in September 1776 before he came out of hiding to become a hero to England and a traitor to America.

Richard Hewlett was never seen again.

Private Thomas Hickey was tried at a military court-martial, found guilty of mutiny, sedition, and treason, and on June 28, 1776, pursuant to written orders of General George Washington, was publicly hanged before a great throng of New York citizens and twenty thousand soldiers of the Continental Army.

As for Isaac Ketcham, the criminal counterfeiter who exposed the entire plot and saved General Washington from the conspiracy to assassinate him and his entire staff, no record could be found regarding whether the charges against him for counterfeiting were ever dismissed.

ADMIRAL SIR PETER PARKER'S DRAWERS

JUNE 28, 1776
CHARLESTON HARBOR, SOUTH CAROLINA

★ ★ ★

BRITISH ADMIRAL SIR PETER PARKER STOOD on the quarter-deck of his flagship, HMS *Bristol,* anchored in the Atlantic Ocean just outside the entrance to the harbor of Charleston, South Carolina. He extended his telescope and for a long time studied the fort that stood on the great sandbar that partially blocked the harbor entrance. With several other British warships under his command, he had been ordered to bombard Charleston into submission and to give general support to British troops that were to invade the southern colonies to put down the American rebellion.

With his ships lined up just outside the harbor, Admiral Parker realized he would have to get rid of that ridiculous American fort stubbornly standing on the huge sandbar called Sullivan Island if he were to enter the harbor.

He spoke to his first officer. "What is the name of that fort?"

The first officer quickly referred to his maps. "Sir, that is Fort Moultrie."

"That fort has to go," Parker exclaimed. "Give orders to take positions to bombard it, and commence firing. Do not stop until the fort is rubble."

"Yes, sir!"

In the heat of the summer sun, the sweating British sailors attached flags to the line and ran them up the mainmast, signaling the other British warships to come within range of Fort Moultrie, drop anchor, and commence a bombardment. One hour later the huge warships, with three decks of heavy cannon, had formed a curved line. With their anchors plunged into the dark green Atlantic waters, their guns began their deadly work, blasting at the fort.

For half an hour, the heavy guns on eight British battleships boomed and bucked, filling the air with great clouds of white smoke while the huge cannonballs flew over the eight hundred yards separating the ships from the sandbar to impact the walls of Fort Moultrie. From inside the fort, American gunners returned fire with their few cannon, more in the spirit of defiance than in any hope of defeating the battleships. Another half hour passed before a frustrated Admiral Parker peered through his telescope in disbelief. Hundreds of cannonballs had impacted the fort, but not one of the walls appeared to be damaged. None of the huge logs was splintered or broken.

What Admiral Parker did not know was that the walls were constructed of heavy palmetto logs. The wood was extremely soft, with the result that when a cannonball struck, the metal simply imbedded itself in the spongy wood. Nothing splintered, or shattered, or crumbled. Those palmetto-log walls were absorbing cannonballs as fast as they hit.

The battle wore on into the sweltering heat of the afternoon, with the British determined to reduce Fort Moultrie to nothing, and the Americans firing back sporadically.

Then an American gunner, stripped to the waist and dripping sweat, took a long look at the British flagship, HMS *Bristol,* where Admiral Parker was on the quarterdeck, shouting his orders to his crew to load and fire. Methodically, the American gunner loaded the twenty-four-pound cannonball into the barrel of his cannon and swung the muzzle slightly to the right to bring it in line with the British vessel. He peered across the open water one more time to gauge the distance to the big battleship, and with a skilled and experienced eye calculated it to be eight hundred yards. Carefully he elevated the muzzle of the cannon to compensate for the distance and pressed the smoking linstock to the powder on the touch hole. The gun roared and bucked, and the American gunner instantly leaned forward, peering through the cloud of white smoke to assess his aim.

The cannonball arched across the water directly toward the figure of Admiral Peter Parker, standing with his left side toward the fort. It whistled past the ship's railing and behind the admiral's beltline, passing so near to him that it severed the admiral's suspenders but did not touch his body. The admiral felt only a slight tug and was unaware of how close he had come to being killed. It was only when his drawers fell down around his ankles that he knew something momentous had happened. One moment he had been standing proudly, shouting orders to his men to load and fire their cannon, and the next moment he was standing there in his white underwear, with his pants puddled on the deck around his feet.

The nearest British sailors saw him stand there for a moment, his mind searching for an explanation as to how he had lost his britches. With the battle still raging and the cannon continuing to roar, the sailors broke into fits of laughter at the comic scene of their commander stooping down to seize his pants and pull them up. With the suspenders cut, there was no way to keep them up, and there he stood, tugging at his trousers, holding them up with both hands. As soon as other sailors heard the uproarious laughter, they turned to look, and within minutes every sailor on the main deck was convulsed with laughter at the funniest sight they had ever seen.

Clutching his waistband, Admiral Peter Parker quickly turned and retreated to his quarters, where he spent ten minutes studying his trousers before he understood what had happened. Then, despite himself, he grinned. A short time later, wearing a second pair of uniform pants, he returned to the battle above decks and issued orders.

"Cease fire! Weigh anchor! We're leaving immediately."

The British naval records detail the essentials of that battle, including the loss of his drawers by Admiral Peter Parker. The one thing that is not explained is why the admiral halted the bombardment and ordered his entire fleet to leave. It is speculated, however, that he decided that if one of those American gunners could shoot his britches off with a cannon at eight hundred yards, Admiral Parker would very much prefer to be somewhere else.

SEVEN WOMEN AND THE STATUE OF KING GEORGE

TUESDAY, JULY 9, 1776
NEW YORK CITY

★ ★ ★

Today was the day!

The rebellion that had been smoldering and building in the thirteen American colonies had erupted in shooting between the British redcoats and the rebels at Lexington and Concord on April 19, 1775. A furious King George III ordered his army to put down the uprising, which only solidified the union between the thirteen colonies and inspired the patriots to total defiance of the king and his mighty army. In an effort to sweep away all doubt and explain to the world why they had risen against England, the American Confederation Congress appointed a five-man committee consisting of Thomas Jefferson, Benjamin Franklin, John Adams, Robert R. Livingston, and Roger Sherman to draft a document detailing all the wrongs the colonists had suffered at the hands of the king and justifying their determination to break free of his tyrannical grasp. The five men had worked for weeks before finally emerging to announce to Congress they had completed their task. The document was finished.

Congress examined the document with growing excitement, then asked each colony to have representatives sign it, to show the king and the world the Americans were united. Famous men from all thirteen colonies attached their signatures, knowing that in doing so they had committed treason against England and the crown and could be hanged. Then they announced the document would be copied and circulated for reading in all thirteen colonies.

And today, July 9, 1776, was the day appointed for the reading of the document to the public in New York City. The event was to take place on the south end of the Island of Manhattan, near the waterfront. It was there the early colonists had laid a great spread of cobblestones and erected a huge statue of King George astride a prancing horse, both horse and rider adorned in royal finery. The monument was made of lead and weighed over two tons.

It was sweltering hot as the people gathered. At the appointed hour a representative stood on the platform, and the crowd quieted as he began to read aloud.

"IN CONGRESS, JULY 4, 1776. The Unanimous Declaration of the thirteen united States of America.

"When in the Course of human events it becomes necessary for one people to dissolve the political bands which have connected them with another and to assume among the powers of the earth, the separate and equal station to which the Laws of Nature and of Nature's God entitle them, a decent respect to the opinions of mankind requires that they should declare the causes which impel them to the separation.

"We hold these truths to be self-evident, that all men are created equal, that they are endowed by their Creator with certain unalienable Rights, that among these are Life, Liberty and the Pursuit of Happiness . . ."

The great throng stood in stunned silence. Never had they heard such thoughts delivered in such simple, crystal clarity.

The reader continued with the body of the document. Obsessed with his own power, the king had denied his subjects these rights. His iron grip reached every part of their lives, and in graphic detail, the Declaration of Independence listed twenty-one violations of rights. The Declaration explained that the colonists had repeatedly and humbly petitioned the king and his Parliament for relief from the unbearable bondage, only to be rebuffed and refused each time. They would take no more of it!

The reader reached the last few lines.

"And for the support of this Declaration, with a firm reliance on the protection of Divine Providence, we mutually pledge to each other our Lives, our Fortunes, and our sacred Honor."

For three seconds no one dared make a sound, and then the entire gathering burst into wild cheering, waving their hats in the air, clapping each other on the back, gesturing, dancing. One of them glanced up at the great lead statue of King George on the high pedestal, pointed, and shouted, "Shall we be rid of him?"

"Aye! Aye!" came the resounding answer. Within seconds a dozen hawser ropes were thrown to catch the great statue, and a hundred men seized them and heaved. For a moment the huge statue held firm, and then one corner broke loose from its granite foundation, and then the statue began to tilt. One more strong heave on the ropes and it tipped and came crashing down onto the cobblestones, to shatter into a thousand pieces. A deafening shout arose. King George was down.

A woman, unknown, unheralded, peered for a moment at the scattered pieces of King George and turned to another woman beside her. "Perhaps we can use King George for our cause," she declared. The two conferred for a moment, then turned to another woman and drew her into their circle to explain. Soon seven women were gathered, and all nodded in agreement. One trotted away to return in a few minutes, driving a heavy wagon pulled by two horses. Quickly they set about gathering the fragments of lead and loading them into the wagon. Others joined in. Before long, they had salvaged all the pieces of King George. Then the seven women climbed into the wagon, two on the driver's seat, and patiently drove through the crowd.

They stopped only to get blankets and some food, then continued on north, then east, and crossed the East River toward Connecticut. For three days they worked their way eastward, sleeping on their blankets, eating their meager supply of food. In the late afternoon of the third day, they stopped the wagon before a smelter located at one end of a small Connecticut town. One woman approached the owner.

"Sir, we have some pieces of a lead statue in our wagon. Could you melt them down?"

The owner narrowed one eye, suspicious. "A statue of who?"

"King George?"

His eyes popped. "Who?"

"King George."

"How big?"

"About two tons."

"What? You have two tons of lead in that wagon? What in the world will you do with two tons of molten lead?"

Carefully she explained her hopes to him.

"Why didn't you say so to begin with?" he asked. "Here. I'll back the wagon up to the smelter doors and we'll get started."

For two days the women waited and watched while the lead was being melted down and the three smelter workers labored to recast the molten metal. On the morning of the third day the owner and his men finished loading sixty-five heavy wooden cases back into the wagon.

"Ma'am, there you are."

The seven women nodded, and one of them said, "We thank you most sincerely. How much do we owe you? We will have the money sent from New York when we get back."

The old owner shook his head. "You owe me nothing. It is we who owe you."

The woman asked, "How many did we finally get?"

"Ma'am, you have 42,038 musket balls in that wagon, sixty caliber, all to be shot back at King George's red-coated troops." He chuckled. "I doubt King George would much approve of what you did with his statue. But America will not soon forget you ladies and what you have done for freedom. God speed you on your way."

The names of the seven women have been lost to history, but their service to the American revolution remains a shining example of the spirit that carried the thirteen colonies to victory.

THE WOMAN WHO SAVED
GENERAL PUTNAM AND THE
AMERICAN ARMY

SEPTEMBER 15, 1776
INCLENBERG, MANHATTAN ISLAND, NEW YORK

★ ★ ★

SUSANNAH MURRAY CLAPPED HER HAND over her mouth and ran from the pantry into the kitchen of the luxurious Murray mansion. Trembling and white-faced, she exclaimed, "Mother, the British are coming! They're after General Putnam and all the American soldiers!"

Mary Lindley Murray, wife of Robert Murray, wealthy merchant with a huge estate in the lush Inclenberg countryside at the north edge of the city of Manhattan on Manhattan Island, turned to face her beautiful nineteen-year-old daughter.

"Where?" she asked. "I have seen no red-coated soldiers. The only soldiers I've seen are the Americans who passed here half an hour ago trying to rejoin General Washington. General Putnam was in charge, I believe. Those poor men were badly beaten in battle this morning, near Kip's Bay. Who told you the British are coming?"

"Sooni! She just returned from town. She's in the pantry right now putting things away. She said the British were there and are marching this way. General William Howe is leading them. They mean to capture General Putnam and all his men, to keep them from joining General Washington."

For a moment Mary stared thoughtfully at her daughter. "I must talk with Sooni," she said. A few moments later she was in the spacious pantry where Sooni, one of the house servants, was busy putting the stored food in order.

"What did you see when you were in town?" Mary asked.

Sooni's eyes grew large. "Red-coated soldiers. So many I couldn't count. I listened. They said they were going to catch Gen'l Putnam and all his soldiers."

"Where are the British now?"

"Marching this way. I came home in the buggy as fast as I could and told Susannah. They'll come right past here very soon."

"Thank you, Sooni. You did well." With Susannah following, Mary walked out of the pantry into the huge kitchen, head bowed in deep thought. For a time Mary stood still, pondering, before she straightened and spoke.

"Susannah, we're going to do what we can to save General Putnam and the American army. Get your sister Beulah and both of you dress in your loveliest party gowns. Fix your hair. I'll do the same. Meet me in the parlor as soon as you're ready."

Susannah gasped. "Party dresses? What on earth—"

"I don't have time to explain," Mary answered. "Now hurry."

Twenty minutes later, Mary was facing her two lovely daughters in the parlor. All three were dressed in classic satin party gowns, white, sky-blue, and delicate purple, with long sleeves and netting and silk ribbons, and with petticoats with great hoops that flared the skirts. In the fashion of the day, their hair was piled high on their heads and held in place by long, pearl-headed pins.

Both young women looked at their mother in utter bewilderment. "What are we doing, dressed for a pavilion ball in the afternoon of a hot summer's day, with the British marching down on us?" they asked.

Mary answered with calm authority. "We are going to delay the British long enough for General Putnam and his soldiers to escape. When the British arrive, follow me. Do what I do, and obey my orders. Do you understand?"

The girls looked at each other, shrugged, and answered, "Yes, Mother."

Within minutes the hired men working in the fields of the Murray estate came running to the great house, breathless, perspiring, some with their pitchforks and scythes still in their hands. "Ma'am," they panted, "there are British soldiers marching this way. They should be here in the next few minutes. What should we do?"

Mary pointed. "Return to your work in the fields and act as though nothing unusual is happening."

"But ma'am," they exclaimed, "they might burn the house and barns and all the buildings."

Mary shook her head. "I will take care of that. Go back to the fields and do nothing that will provoke them."

The men turned and hurried back to the fields, pausing repeatedly to peer south toward Manhattan, New York, and Kip's Bay, where that morning General William Howe and his army had defeated General Israel Putnam and scattered his untrained army of Americans, driving them north in a wild panic, desperately hoping to rejoin General George Washington and his command of soldiers. General Howe intended to catch and capture them. If he succeeded, he would seriously cripple the entire American army. It was possible it would end the war, with the British the victors.

Mary took a deep breath and walked to the great windows in the front of the spacious parlor of the mansion. She stood near the heavy satin drapes to watch the road leading south. Within minutes there was movement, and suddenly they were there—General William Howe and six officers with gold braid on their shoulders and hats, riding tall, high-blooded horses. Behind them in what appeared to be an endless column were marching soldiers in their bright crimson tunics with the white belts crossing their chests, each carrying a large, ten-pound Brown Bess musket over one shoulder. Drummers were pounding out the cadence as the soldiers came on, marching smartly in step.

"Come with me," Mary said to her daughters, and walked from the parlor out through the great, varnished double doors at the mansion's entrance. She stopped on the flagstones between two of the six white marble columns that supported the portico, two stories above her head. When the mounted officers at the head of the column were approaching the white picket fence that enclosed the spacious yard, she walked down the cobblestone paved walkway to the front gate and paused while Susannah and Beulah caught up with her. When General Howe was approaching the gate, she opened it and stepped forward to speak to him. Her voice and demeanor were the personification of the perfect hostess.

"May I presume you are General William Howe?"

For one split second General Howe gaped in total surprise. Before him stood an absolutely beautiful woman of mature years accompanied by two devastatingly attractive younger women, one on each side of her, each stunning in resplendent finery. The three were smiling cordially.

General Howe called his column of men to a halt and swept off his hat. "Yes, ma'am. I am General William Howe. May I have the privilege of knowing to whom I am speaking?"

"I am Mary Lindley Murray, mistress of this estate. My husband is Robert Murray. He is away on business at the moment." She gestured to the younger women. "These are my two daughters, Susannah and Beulah."

The six officers flanking Howe instantly jerked off their hats and bowed to the two girls, who peered up shyly at them, then at the ground, then back at them, smiling demurely.

General Howe bowed in the saddle. "I am honored." He paused for a moment. "Did you have a purpose in coming to meet us?"

"Yes," Mary said. "I need to know if you intend burning this estate. If you do, I beg of you to give us time to remove some of our family heirlooms. They are our treasure. You can have everything else, or burn it as you wish, but we would so appreciate your allowing us to keep the things that have been in the family since 1607." Then Mary smiled her most humble, feminine, beguiling smile. Susannah and Beulah glanced at her in amazement, and then the same smile was instantly on their faces.

General Howe looked wounded. "Oh, no, Missus Murray. Rest assured. We have no intention of harming you or your family or your estate in any way. Our business will take us past your property, but you have nothing to fear from us."

Mary clapped her hand to her chest and exhaled mightily, smiling broadly. "Oh! How kind of you. I had hoped you would be a perfect gentleman."

She paused for a moment, then her eyes opened wide, as though a new and startling thought had occurred to her.

"Oh! General! Would you and your officers consider granting us the honor of your presence by coming into the house for a moment? You must be a bit weary and thirsty on a day such as this. We have tea or lemonade and some absolutely marvelous cinnamon muffins. Surely you can take a few minutes to accept our thanks and gratitude."

The six officers forced their eyes from Susannah and Beulah, each turning to stare at their commanding officer, waiting, hoping.

Howe drew a deep breath and exhaled it, then nodded his head. "It will be our pleasure, ma'am."

All six of his junior officers grinned and instantly dismounted, then waited for Howe to step down from his tall brown mare. Howe gave orders to the column to stand down, and the British officers tied their horses to the hitching rail just outside the gate to follow the three women up the cobblestone walkway, through the great double doors, and into the parlor with its huge mural paintings on two walls and the ceiling two stories overhead. The three women smiled bewitchingly as they took the men's hats and invited them to take seats in the large leather-covered armchairs and on the overstuffed sofa, near the fireplace and mantle that dominated one wall.

Mary turned to General Howe. "Would you excuse me for just a moment? I must go to the kitchen to arrange for the refreshments. Would you prefer tea or lemonade? We have ice in the ice house, so it will be most refreshing."

Howe glanced at his officers. "Tea?"

"Yes, sir."

He turned back to Mary. "Tea with ice will be fine."

Mary gestured to all seven of the British officers. "Are cinnamon muffins acceptable?"

The officers did not take their eyes from Susannah and Beulah when they answered. "Yes. Oh, yes."

Mary turned on her heel and disappeared into the kitchen and hurriedly gave Sooni her instructions. "We need two pitchers of iced tea and a tray with cinnamon muffins. Do not serve them until I come back into the kitchen and tell you. Do you understand?"

Sooni raised an eyebrow in surprise. "Wait for you?"

"Yes. Wait. No matter how long it takes, wait," Mary replied.

She walked back into the parlor and took a seat near General Howe. "The refreshments will be ready shortly," she said. "Would any of you care to use the wash basins and towels in the room just down the hall?"

"No, ma'am," General Howe replied. "Just the refreshments. That will be fine."

Mary moved forward in her chair, sitting attentively on the edge. "Tell me, general. What part of England are you from? I have first-generation ancestors from London and Liverpool."

"My family resides at Hertfordshire."

Mary nodded. "I know where that is. How long have you been an officer in the British army?"

"Since I was sixteen."

"Oh, my! As young as that. That is extraordinary."

She continued, "Did you volunteer for service here in the colonies?"

"No. I was ordered here by His Majesty, King George."

Mary smiled. "How interesting."

Nearby, Susannah and Beulah listened for a few moments, then followed Mary's lead. They turned to the six younger officers and launched into question after question.

"Do you like being a soldier?" "Have you ever been in battle?" "Oh!—isn't it just terribly, horribly frightening when the cannon are shooting?" "Are you afraid?" "Have you ever been wounded?" "Do you ever wish you were home in England?" "Don't your mothers worry about you?"

After forty minutes had passed, Howe began to squirm in his chair. "Ma'am," he finally said, "if there is something delaying the refreshments, perhaps we should be on our way."

Mary leaped to her feet and raised a hand in mock surprise. "Oh! This is so interesting—time just got away from me. Let me go see what's happening in the kitchen."

Five minutes later she returned from the kitchen, carrying a large engraved silver tray loaded with cinnamon muffins. Sooni followed with two large crystal pitchers of iced tea, crystal cups and saucers, and folded linen napkins. The women set the trays on the huge oak table that dominated the center of the parlor and Mary stood back.

"Please, gentlemen, help yourselves."

The officers rose and approached the table, with Susannah and Beulah pouring the tea and helping place the muffins on the crystal saucers.

The officers gallantly bowed to the two girls. "Ladies, would you care to be served first?"

Both girls smiled and blushed. "Oh, how kind. No. You are our guests. You should be served first."

The officers took their saucers and napkins and cups and returned to their seats, with Mary and the girls standing nearby. As the cups were drained and the saucers emptied, they exclaimed, "Oh, you must have more!"

On the third serving, Mary suddenly stopped and exclaimed, "I think it would be lovely to have just a little music!" She gestured to the polished harpsichord standing in one corner. "Susannah plays beautifully, and Beulah sings like an angel."

Beulah jerked her head to stare at her mother as though she had lost her mind, while Mary took Susannah's elbow to guide her to the bench in front of the harpsichord.

General Howe looked at the clock. "Missus Murray, you have been most kind, and it would be a welcome relief to hear music once again. However, we must be getting back to our command. I want to thank—"

Mary cut him off. "Oh, general, how thoughtless of me. But couldn't you take just a few more minutes while the girls play and sing?"

The six officers stood stone still, waiting for Howe's answer. He cleared his throat, glanced once more at the clock, and nodded.

"Just a few more minutes."

Susannah sat down while Beulah walked over to stand in front of the small instrument. After fidgeting and fussing to settle herself on the bench, Susannah struck the familiar strains of "Johnny Has Gone for a Soldier." On cue, Beulah launched into it, her voice strong, then soft, firm, then wavering, warbling off and on pitch at random as she rendered her absolutely unique interpretation of the sad message of the traditional folksong.

When she finished, the officers politely applauded, while General Howe started to rise. Mary faced him back down.

"You can't leave without hearing some of our dearest church hymns. Many of them are from England." Instantly Mary nodded to Susannah, who banged out the first few chords of a church hymn before Howe could respond.

Five hymns later, General Howe raised a hand and stood. "Ladies, you have been most gracious. You have our thanks for the warmth of your hospitality, your refreshments, and your entertainment. But we must go. We have an army outside waiting for us, and our orders require that we move along."

Mary looked at the clock and her eyes popped. "Whoever would have believed?" she exclaimed. "Oh, I hope you will forgive us if we have interfered in your day. We only meant to express our gratitude to you for leaving us and our home unharmed. Thank you. Oh, thank you!"

The three women hurried to return with the officer's hats, then led them to the front door and down the front walk, where they waited while the men untied their horses. General Howe gave his commands, his soldiers fell into marching order, and with General Howe and the six mounted officers leading, they continued north in pursuit of American general Israel Putnam and his tattered army.

The three women stood at the front gate to watch until the column was out of sight before they returned to the parlor, where Mary looked at the clock.

"We held them for just over two hours," she announced to her two daughters. "Do you think that was enough time for General Putnam to get away?"

The following day Mary Lindley Murray and her daughters learned they had succeeded. General Putnam escaped General Howe, to join forces with General Washington. The American army survived.

Today, a plaque in New York City on Park Avenue and 37th Street reads:

In honor of
MARY LINDLEY MURRAY
For services rendered her country
during the American Revolution, entertaining
at her home, on this site, Gen. Howe and his officers, until the
American Troops under Gen. Putnam escaped.
September 15, 1776/November 25, 1903
Erected by
Knickerbocker Chapter, New York
Daughters of the American Revolution

THE WOMAN
CANNONEER

NOVEMBER 16, 1776
FORT WASHINGTON, MANHATTAN ISLAND, NEW YORK

★ ★ ★

IN THE BRIGHT, CHILL MORNING SUN OF November 16, 1776,
Colonel Robert Magaw of the American Continental Army stood
on the ramparts of Fort Washington, built on the highest ground
on Manhattan Island. The west side of the fort was a nearly sheer
drop of over ninety feet to the Hudson River. The ground on the
north, east, and south sides was clear, sloping down to the lower
level of the island.

Magaw had his telescope extended as he peered over the thick
walls, estimating the number of red-coated British regulars and
the blue- and green-coated German Hessian soldiers taking
positions a half mile away on three sides of the fort.

"About eight thousand," he said quietly to himself. He turned and looked down at his own command, all within the walls of the fort. There were just over three thousand, the tattered survivors of the catastrophic battle on Long Island fought on August 27, 1776, in which General George Washington's Continental Army had been shattered and nearly annihilated. The American survivors had fled north on Manhattan Island, crossing to the mainland at King's Bridge and regrouping at White Plains. The British relentlessly tracked them down, and on October 28, 1776, for the second time in nine weeks, battered them bloody in a second battle at White Plains. The Americans then retreated back to Manhattan Island and took refuge inside the thick, heavy walls of Fort Washington, the one fort the Americans thought to be impregnable. General Washington had crossed the Hudson River to the New Jersey side and had taken temporary refuge in Fort Lee with most of what he had left of the army, leaving three thousand of his remaining soldiers under the command of Colonel Magaw in Fort Washington, where Washington thought they could stall the British without danger of the fort's being overrun.

Now, nineteen days after routing the Americans at White Plains, the determined British were encircling Magaw and his men and preparing for an all-out assault. The attack was to be under the command of German colonel Wilhelm von Knyphausen, leader of the feared Hessian mercenaries. Magaw was confident his force had enough cannon and muskets to hold the fort indefinitely, and just days earlier, when the British had sent their demand that he surrender to save his men, he had defiantly told them he would never surrender. He would fight to the last man.

What Magaw did not know was that one of his own officers, William Demont, had deserted on November 2, 1776, and had secretly gone to the British, to whom he had revealed every detail of the men, supplies, cannon, muskets, and inner structure of the fort. With that information, the British and Germans knew the strengths and the weaknesses of Fort Washington and had carefully planned their strike.

Suddenly Magaw's first officer pointed and exclaimed, "They're coming, sir!"

Quickly Magaw shouted his orders, and the soldiers with muskets swarmed to the ramparts, ready. Cannon crews ran to their guns and brought them to bear. Outside the north, east, and south walls of the fort, the Americans had dug cannon emplacements on the slanting ground, capable of shooting downhill into any enemy troops attempting to climb up to the fort. The commander of the gun crew on the north slope ran to Magaw, saluted, and exclaimed, "Sir, John Corbin is the sergeant in my gun crew assigned to swab and load the cannon. His wife, Margaret Corbin, has requested permission to go down to the gun emplacement with the crew, to be with her husband."

For a moment Magaw hesitated, then nodded. "Granted."

Within two minutes, John Corbin and the men assigned to the cannon on the north slope were hunched behind the breastworks of the emplacement, with Margaret Corbin among them. Tall, strongly built, she stood near her husband, watching his every move as they loaded the big gun and waited, each man judging the moment the Hessians were within range. Within seconds, the heavy British cannon below boomed, and the cannonballs came whistling overhead to smash into the walls of the fort. A moment later the Hessian infantry shouted their war cry and began their charge up the hill. Margaret held her hands over her ears as the American cannon blasted and the cannonballs tore into the oncoming blue-coated Germans.

Time became meaningless as the British and American cannon roared and the muskets fired. Smoke and flying dirt filled the air, amid the cries and moaning of injured and dying men. Margaret did not know how many times she watched her husband and his crew load and fire their gun; she only knew that she quickly understood what each man was assigned to do, and how he did it.

Suddenly a British cannonball struck the breastworks of her gun emplacement, and moments later a musket ball struck her husband full in the chest, and he fell backward without a sound. Instantly she was kneeling beside him, shaking him, talking to him, before she realized he was dead. She raised her head and saw that the others in the gun crew were also dead. She was alone.

She stood, grabbed the long pole with the wet sponge, rammed it down the smoking barrel of the cannon, followed it with a ladle full of gunpowder, then the dried grass, then the cannonball. She snatched up the burning linstock and slammed it down on the touch hole. The powder caught and the gun blasted. Without hesitating, she swabbed the gun again, reloaded it, and fired it again, and then again, and again, at the Hessians.

A Hessian musket ball struck her left shoulder and knocked her staggering backwards. She recovered, and struggled to reload the cannon and fire it one more time before two more musket balls ripped into her already wounded left shoulder. Her last clear recollection was of a horrendous blow and explosion as a cannonball nearly tore her left arm from her body. She went down unconscious as the Hessians stormed past the gun position and left her behind for dead, covered with dirt and debris.

The Hessians overran Fort Washington in less than half a day. They inflicted casualties of more than one hundred fifty on the Americans and took two thousand eight hundred and eighteen prisoners. Worse, they captured hundreds of cannon, thousands of muskets, and food supplies that were intended to feed the American army for months to come.

The second wave of Hessians came up the north slope, and as they passed Margaret Corbin's body, one of them thought he saw her still breathing. He called to a companion, and the two of them stopped to be certain she was dead. To their stunned amazement they saw she was a woman! Without a word they carefully picked her up and carried her back down the hill to the tent where British doctors were feverishly working with the wounded.

An astonished doctor stared. "Why, that's a woman," he declared.

"A very brave woman," the two soldiers exclaimed. "Save her if you can."

They saved her life, and her left arm, although it was nearly useless for the balance of her life. The wounded American prisoners were paroled to the American army, and Margaret was transported across the Hudson River to Fort Lee in New Jersey, where American doctors did all they could. Slowly she regained her health and finally was released to return to her home. When she could, she took any honorable work she could find to stay alive.

The story of her bravery and sacrifice became known. In 1779, the Continental Congress granted her a lifetime military disability pension, together with permanent employment at Fort West Point, doing work that she could perform despite her crippled arm, for the balance of her life, together with a new military uniform to be delivered to her once each year. She was the first woman in the United States to receive such honors.

In 1926, the Daughters of the American Revolution had her remains re-interred behind the Old Cadet Chapel at West Point and erected a monument honoring her. Today, at Fort Tryon Park in New York City, not far from the remains of old Fort Washington, a bronze plaque commemorates the remarkable bravery and heroism of the great woman patriot, Margaret Corbin.

THE WOMAN WHO
SHAMED THE MEN

MID-DECEMBER 1776
ELIZABETHTOWN, NEW JERSEY

★ ★ ★

HANNAH WHITE ARNETT, forty-three-year-old wife of Isaac
Arnett, cleared the supper dishes from the table in her modest
Elizabethtown, New Jersey, home and set them on the cupboard
beside the shallow wooden tub filled with steaming, soapy wash
water. While she washed them, she called to her husband in the
parlor, "When do you expect the men to arrive?"

"Half an hour," came his reply.

"It might snow," she said. "It's cold, even for mid-December."

"They'll come," he assured her. "The amnesty offered by the
British is far too important to let a snowstorm interfere."

She finished the dishes and emptied the wash and rinse water
out the back door, dried her hands, removed her apron, and made

herself presentable to receive guests. Minutes later a knock came at the front door, and her husband rose to welcome the first of the town fathers into his parlor. Hannah courteously bowed and extended her warm greeting before going into her kitchen to prepare hot tea for them.

Within ten minutes there were twelve men seated in the parlor, and Isaac called them to order. A sober silence settled in the room.

"As you know," Isaac began, "our purpose tonight is to consider the proposal recently received from the British. They have offered amnesty to any Americans who will sign a sworn oath of loyalty to England and the king within the next sixty days. It would be prudent to seriously consider the offer before making a decision."

In the kitchen, Hannah slowed in preparing the tea and turned her head to listen as the discussion, and the arguments, began tumbling out.

A deep voice came strong. "It has become clear that we have no real hope of winning a war against England. British general William Howe—one of their best—has an army in New York of some of the best-trained soldiers in the world. His force is many times larger than our Continental Army. His brother, Richard, is the best admiral in the British navy, and he's there with more than four hundred ships. We have no navy at all. We have no chance of winning a war with them!"

A voice responded. "Remember what happened at Long Island last August? A total disaster! George Washington led our army against General Howe, and in one day—just one day—the British nearly destroyed us altogether! We still don't know how many men we lost. We only know that we were beaten to pieces, scattered, disorganized, running to save anything we could."

A high, excited voice cut in. "Washington retreated in total defeat! Up Manhattan Island, across to the mainland, to White Plains to try to recover, and the British caught him again! They beat him soundly, and again Washington had to retreat just to save what he could."

Another voice answered. "Save what he could? He brought the army back to Fort Washington on Manhattan Island. We thought Fort Washington could not be taken. But when the British stormed the fort, we lost over two thousand men killed or captured in one day, and with them we lost over one hundred cannon with gunpowder and shot and food stores that would have lasted over a year!"

In the kitchen, Hannah placed the large silver teapot on a great tray with cups, sugar lumps, and thick cream, and carefully walked down the hall into the parlor. The discussion quieted as she placed it on the table in the center of the room and the men uttered their brief thanks for her thoughtfulness. She nodded to them and walked back into the hallway where she stopped to listen, concern growing in her heart.

In the parlor, a voice was raised in caution. "It's true that we have suffered some terrible defeats, but we must remember that we had much to learn, and there is much more that we must learn. Don't forget what happened at Lexington and Concord. We beat them badly. If we are careful, we can do it again. The real issue before us is, are we right in standing up for liberty and freedom? Is it worth the price we must pay?"

A voice responded, hot, intense. "History pays little attention to what is right or wrong. The single question that decides which way history goes is very simple. Who has the largest army and the most guns? We may be absolutely right in our quest for liberty, but without an army and navy and enough cannon to match the British, the only thing we can expect is our own destruction."

Another voice came in. "In this world, freedom and liberty have forever been bought at a high price. The sole issue before us tonight is do we value them enough to pay it?"

"You are wrong," came the heated reply. "The issue is, are we prepared to sacrifice ourselves, our wives, our children, and our homes, in a futile attempt to realize a dream that can never be?"

There was a pause before the deep voice responded. "Where is our army now? It is on the Pennsylvania side of the Delaware River at McKonkey's Ferry. Sick, starved, freezing, scattered. There isn't the slightest chance that army could face another British attack right now, and there is no reason to think it will even survive the winter. Come spring, we will have no army. Then what will we do to beat the British? That is the hard reality."

Isaac's voice came next. "Would it be wise to accept the British offer of amnesty, and then send a delegation to London to state our hopes to the king and parliament? Surely by now they realize how dearly we hold our liberty and freedom. Is there some way we could persuade them to grant them to us on a peaceful basis?"

The high voice cut in. "Utter nonsense! Do you really think the most powerful man on the face of this earth—King George III—would give up the least part of his control of the world just because we ask him to? Ridiculous! He has us by the throat, and he means to keep it that way."

Hannah felt deep resentment, and then anger, surging in her heart. Her breathing became rapid, and her face reddened.

The debate between the town fathers continued, hot and intense.

"History and common sense make it crystal clear that there isn't the barest hope of our ever winning a war with England! We should consider signing the amnesty agreement and settle for whatever we can get from the king and Parliament."

"No! No! Freedom and liberty—the right to decide our destiny—is worth whatever the price might be to obtain it!"

Slowly at first, then more rapidly, Hannah realized that those who favored giving up the American dream and signing the amnesty agreement with England were winning the heated debate in her parlor. The quest for liberty and freedom was slowly dying.

Then the voice of her husband, Isaac, reached her.

"Gentlemen, let us settle this. I propose that we make a public statement in which we declare our support for signing the amnesty, with the promise that we will do all we can to send a delegation to England to plead our cause to . . ."

Hannah could take no more. She straightened, squared her shoulders, and marched into the parlor to stop by the table with the tray and empty teapot. All twelve men looked up in startled surprise as she planted her feet and, with her hands on her hips, tore into them.

"I would never have believed that true Americans could do such a thing! Cowards! That's what you are! All cowards! And traitors! You should be arrested for treason! I have never witnessed anything as shameful as the twelve of you sitting here, willing to abandon the most precious gift God has given you, and go sniveling to King George, begging for his mercy! Men? You do not deserve to be called men! Don't you know that God is on our side? Don't you realize that every volley from our muskets is an echo of his voice?"

She turned to face Isaac. "If you and these men sign the amnesty, I am leaving this house, and I will never return. Do you understand that?"

Not one man moved, and none dared look her in the eye as she glared at each one of them in turn. Then she dropped her hands and marched from the room, down the hall to her bedroom, and slammed the door.

For a long time the twelve city fathers stared at the floor before one of them dared to look at another. Finally Isaac broke the strained silence.

"Gentlemen, I think we have our answer. This meeting is adjourned."

A few days later, on the night of December 25, 1776, the battered American army left the misery of its crude camp at McKonkey's Ferry, crossed the Delaware River to the New Jersey side in a raging blizzard, and hit Trenton the morning of December 26. They miraculously defeated the entire Hessian command, in what most historians agree was the first major turning point in the American Revolution. Eight days later, on January 3, 1777, they attacked the British at Princeton, twelve miles north of Trenton, and took down the entire command of red-coated soldiers in a fierce hand-to-hand battle.

Today there is a large bronze plaque marking the grave of Hannah White Arnett at the First Presbyterian Church burial grounds in Elizabeth, formerly Elizabethtown, New Jersey, inscribed with the following tribute:

HONORING THE PATRIOTIC DEAD
OF MANY WARS
LAID TO REST IN THIS HALLOWED GROUND
ESPECIALLY A NOBLE WOMAN
HANNAH WHITE ARNETT
PLACED HERE ON THE 45TH ANNIVERSARY OF
THE ORGANIZATION OF
BOUDINOT CHAPTER
DAUGHTERS OF THE AMERICAN REVOLUTION
SEPTEMBER 27, 1938

WASHINGTON'S SECRET SPY

DECEMBER 18, 1776
GRIGGSTOWN, NEW JERSEY

★ ★ ★

THE HIDDEN VOICE CAME SOFTLY. "Stand easy."

Over six feet tall, muscular and strong, John Honeyman hunched forward and searched the shadows in the dim, predawn gloom of the small milking shed on his Griggstown farm, six miles north of Princeton, New Jersey. He held the lantern high with one hand in the freezing December cold, with a bucket in the other hand, filled with rich, warm milk from the family Jersey cow.

"Who are you?" he demanded. "Come out where I can see you." The strong Scots-Irish flavor in his speech was unmistakable.

In the darkness, the figure of a man appeared from behind

stacked grain sacks in one corner, hands raised. "I have a message for John Honeyman."

"From who?"

"General George Washington, at McKonkey's Ferry, not far from Trenton."

Honeyman gasped. "Is he all right?"

"What's left of the Continental Army is there with him. They're starving, freezing, sick." The man paused for a moment, then went on. "Here's the message." The shadowy messenger reached into the folds of his heavy coat for a folded document bearing the wax seal of General Washington and thrust it forward. Instantly Honeyman set the milk bucket down, hung the lantern on a nearby peg, and read the document slowly in the yellow light while remembrances of his meetings with George Washington came bright and vivid in his mind.

Both Honeyman and Washington had served in the British army during the Seven Year War between England and France that ended with the surrender of France in 1762. Washington served as an officer, Honeyman as a private who had been unwillingly forced into military servitude by the British. Upon his discharge in 1763, following the war, Honeyman had two documents that were to prove invaluable. One was his honorable discharge from the British army, the other a letter from the famous British hero of the war, General James Wolfe, declaring the appointment of John Honeyman as his personal bodyguard, a result of Honeyman's unfailing bravery and courage as a soldier.

Eleven years later, in 1774, the Confederation Congress of the thirteen American colonies commissioned George Washington commander in chief of the infant Continental Army, to resist the increasing oppression of England. Honeyman, married and father of four children, yearned for independence from the tyranny of the British. A plan formed in his mind, and he acted.

Secretly he met with General Washington in Philadelphia and made a proposal. With his honorable discharge from the British army, and the letter appointing him personal bodyguard for the famed General James Wolfe, he was in a perfect position to lead the British to believe he was a loyalist—an ardent supporter of the monarchy and the British government. He would show the documents to anyone who would look at them and become loud and vociferous in condemning the thirteen colonies for their rebellion, while at the same time declaring his faithful allegiance to England and King George! He was a weaver by trade, but to the business of weaving he would add the profession of a cattleman, buying cattle to sell to the British army at bargain prices to feed the red-coated soldiers. Slowly he would work his way into the confidence of the British, to acquire all the information he could regarding their efforts to subdue the rebellious Americans, and by secret meetings, pass this information on to Washington.

No one, including Honeyman's faithful wife, Mary, was to know of this except Honeyman and General Washington. If his conduct angered the Americans and they came to harm him or his family or his farm, General Washington was to give a sealed letter to Mary, signed by Washington himself, ordering that neither she nor their four children were to be in any way harmed or molested. The reason was not stated in the letter, nor was there a word concerning the secret arrangement between Washington and Honeyman. Washington wrote the letter, signed it, and delivered it to Honeyman's wife, on her solemn oath that she would never disclose its contents except to save herself, the children, or the farm.

Honeyman moved his family to Griggstown and soon became

widely known as a radical loyalist, faithful to England and the king and a sworn enemy of the rebellious American army. He bought cattle and sold them to the British army at low prices, declaring his pride in supporting them and their cause. Twice, angry American mobs came to the farm to take him, and each time he fled, while Mary and the children and the farm were saved by the letter from General Washington.

Now, standing in the dim yellow light of his milking shed, Honeyman's mind came back to the document he was reading for the third time, studying each word and the signature. He raised his eyes to the messenger.

"You know what this says?"

"No. The general said it was for your eyes only. He said you're to memorize it and then burn it. I must leave before it gets too light. I can't be seen here."

Without another word the messenger was gone. Honeyman studied the message one more time, burned it, and ground the ashes into the dirt floor with his heel before he picked up the milk bucket and the lantern and walked to the house.

The message was simple. General Washington desperately needed all the information he could get regarding the fourteen hundred Hessian soldiers stationed in the small town of Trenton, about eighteen miles south of Griggstown, bordering the Delaware River. Could Honeyman help?

In thoughtful silence he ate his breakfast, then told Mary he would be gone for two days, return for one day, then be gone again for two more days. He did not tell her why, nor did she ask. Rather, she accepted it as one more of his unexplained absences that had become part of their life.

The bright, chill noonday sun found Honeyman two miles south of Princeton, mounted on his big bay plow horse, leading two Angus steers with ropes. In late afternoon he turned left onto Quaker Lane and passed an apple orchard and the remains of a cornfield bordering the town of Trenton. He went on to Second Street, north on Queen Street, then back south on King Street, loudly greeting each local citizen who he knew to be a loyalist, while his eyes never stopped searching, memorizing the homes that the Hessian soldiers had commandeered to use for barracks.

With the sun setting, Honeyman delivered the two Angus steers to the cattle pen beside the Old Barracks building. He took his receipt from the officer in charge, stabled his horse for the night, and walked rapidly to the huge, luxurious estate owned by Stacy Potts, an avowed loyalist who had invited the German officer in command, Colonel Johann Gottlieb Rall, to establish his headquarters. He handed the receipt for the two steers to the orderly, who knew Honeyman well from previous cattle purchases, and sat down to wait for the soldier to make the necessary entries in his books and count the coins from an iron safe kept in a corner.

Honeyman smiled at the man and leaned back in his chair, for all purposes appearing to be mildly interested in the whole bookkeeping procedure, while in fact he was memorizing the large map on the wall behind the orderly. The map was marked, showing the location of the soldiers, the officers, their stores of ammunition, cannon, gunpowder, saddles, muskets, food, and clothing.

Finally the orderly counted the coins for the cattle into Honeyman's hand, and Honeyman spoke to him. "I will come back in two days with three more cattle."

The German bobbed his head in understanding and Honeyman thanked him and walked out into the crisp late afternoon air. He went to the Old Barracks building, where he paid for his supper and lodging for the night, then climbed to the second floor and took a bed in one corner among the Hessians. For a time, he listened to the barracks talk of the German soldiers. After supper with them, he tugged on his heavy coat, walked out into the freezing street, and turned north to the Oak Tree Tavern. There he ordered a large pewter mug filled with hot spiced cider and took it to a table near a window to sit down. For more than two hours he sipped at the sweet cider while German soldiers came to drink their native dark beer and engage in talk and singing that became louder and more boisterous with each additional pint of their strong, dark brew. They were elated over the approach of Christmas day, less than a week away, when most of them would be given rum and a day off to celebrate. They were raucous in their expressions of disgust and hatred of the American rabble across the river that called itself an army.

The next morning Honeyman returned to his home, caught up three more Angus steers on ropes, and in the gray of dawn the following morning, once again saddled the big, plodding plow horse and made the journey to Trenton, leading the three steers. While yet a half mile from the small town, he turned into an open field and led the cattle to a thick stand of oak trees. For a time he watched to be certain no one had seen him, then he tied one of the steers to a tree, remounted his horse, and led the other two cattle back to the road. Forty minutes later he was again in Trenton, loudly greeting the loyalists in the streets while he counted soldiers and looked for cannon.

He delivered the two steers to the Hessian cattle pen, and while he was unbuckling the halters, he quickly counted the cattle—eighty-eight of them—then the cavalry horses in the adjoining corral. He waited for his receipt from the officer in charge of the livestock, thanked him, and then spoke to him.

"One steer got away, just north of town. I'll go get him. I will need a whip. I'll be back before supper."

The officer nodded his head. "Ja. Take a whip from the shed. Bring it back before night."

Twenty minutes later Honeyman was in the field north of Trenton, working his way to the lone steer tied in the stand of trees, whip and rope in hand. With his horse tied, he led the steer from the trees, west, deeper into the field, watching, waiting. Minutes passed before he saw what he had been waiting for—two oncoming riders. He stopped in his tracks, eyes narrowed as he studied them. They were still three hundred yards away when he recognized them as an American patrol.

Instantly he jerked the halter from the frightened steer and cracked the whip above its back. "Move, move," he exclaimed, and the animal trotted away from him, then stopped to look back, confused at being free, not knowing what to do. Honeyman charged him, cracking the whip, and the steer ran off with Honeyman following, shouting, "Stop, come back!" as the riders came in at a gallop.

They hauled their horses to a stop next to Honeyman, who pointed at the fleeing steer and exclaimed, "Go get him! I'll pay you! Get him!"

The nearest rider demanded, "Who are you? Your name."

Honeyman shook his head. "He's getting away!" he shouted and began to run after the steer.

Both riders dismounted and confronted him. "What is your name? Who are you?"

Honeyman seized the nearest man, and the three of them grappled, wrestling to the frozen ground. While one man sat on his chest, the other man quickly went through Honeyman's pockets, where he found the receipt from the Hessian officer for the two cattle just delivered.

"Honeyman," the man exclaimed. "You're John Honeyman! The loyalist traitor! We're American soldiers, and you're coming with us."

They tied Honeyman's hands behind his back and pushed him up onto one man's horse, behind the saddle, then looped a rope around his neck. Then both men mounted their horses, with the man behind holding the rope tied to Honeyman's neck to prevent any attempt to escape. They followed the frozen Delaware River west for eight miles, then crossed to the Pennsylvania side at McKonkey's Ferry, to the camp of the Continental Army. Honeyman was shocked at the desperate condition of the American army as they passed through the camp. The two soldiers stopped at the door of General Washington's headquarters and rapped loudly. An orderly led them to Washington's private office, where they faced Washington seated behind his desk.

"Sir, we have captured John Honeyman, the loyalist traitor!"

Instantly Washington rose to his feet, eyes flashing in anger. "Leave him here. I will interrogate him myself! Give me your names. I will write each of you a letter of commendation!"

One man paused. "Sir, are you certain you do not want one of us to stay?"

"I am certain. Leave his hands tied. I've waited months to have this man alone."

The two soldiers walked out into the shadows of dusk before Washington quickly untied Honeyman's hands and spoke in hushed tones.

"John! Are you all right? Did they harm you?"

Honeyman grinned. "No harm. I got your message. There are some things you need to know."

Quickly the two men moved to the business before them.

"I've spent three days in Trenton," Honeyman said. "Do you have a map of the town?"

In a moment Washington had a large map spread on his desk, and Honeyman began systematically relating the facts he had gleaned, moving his finger from place to place as he spoke.

The homes where the soldiers were housed—the Old Barracks—the places the gunpowder was stored—the muskets—the food—Rall's headquarters at the Potts's estate—the cattle—the horses—the church—the streets—the roads leading in and out—the open fields and orchards around the town, and the fields and orchards that were impassable.

Washington watched in silence, memorizing, missing nothing while Honeyman continued.

The contempt of both Colonel Rall and the German soldiers for the Continental Army—their certainty that the Americans could never cross the river—the low morale of the German soldiers who were thinking only about the approach of Christmas day when they would have a day off duty to drink and carouse freely.

"Has Rall built fortifications at either end of town?"

"None," Honeyman replied. "No trenches, no gun emplacements, no breastworks, nothing."

Washington was astounded. "Why has he failed to fortify?"

"He believes the Continental Army is defeated. He fears nothing from you."

There was a pause before Washington asked the vital question: "Is he gathering boats?"

Honeyman shook his head. "No. None. He has no plans to cross the river. He believes that by spring your army will either be dead or deserted. Either way, you will be gone."

Relief flooded through Washington. He continued.

"Where are his cannon?"

"I saw only two, guarding the Old Barracks."

Washington straightened in amazement. "Only two cannon? Where are the others?"

"Stored in barns or sheds. Only the two in front of his headquarters are battle ready."

For a time Washington studied the map in silence, then reached into a desk drawer to pick up a large key and hand it to Honeyman.

"Hide this in your coat. I am going to tie your hands again, but leave the ropes loose enough for you to work your hands free. Two guards will lock you in a small guardhouse at the west end of camp. That key will open the lock. Shortly before dawn a fire is going to break out in a straw stack at the east end of camp, near the powder shed. Everyone will go to put out the fire, including the men left to guard you. When they're gone, free your hands and use the key to open the door. From there, I can do nothing more to help you while you make your escape. If you're seen by pickets or guards, they'll try to shoot you, and I can't stop it."

Washington paused and watched Honeyman accept the circumstance before he went on.

"Run to the river and cross it. Then let a Hessian patrol find you and take you to Colonel Rall in Trenton. He will question you. Tell him the truth about what you have seen here—our deplorable condition. He knows most of it anyway."

Washington drew and released a great breath. "Is there anything else?"

Honeyman shook his head. "No, sir. I understand."

"All right. Let me tie your hands."

Two minutes later Washington strode to the door, threw it open, and called the guards.

"Lock this main in the guardhouse to the west!" he said sternly. "Watch him closely. He will be tried for treason and likely hung or shot."

The guards seized Honeyman and marched him through the black of night to the small hut with thick log walls, sat him down, wrapped a blanket around his shoulders, and locked him inside in the freezing darkness. Honeyman sat huddled, listening in the blackness to the scratching of rats on the floor. In time he dozed off to exhausted sleep, only to jerk awake at the frantic shout from the other end of camp, "Fire! Fire! Near the powder shed!" Without hesitation, every man in camp sprinted to stop the fire before it could ignite the gunpowder and blow half the camp into oblivion. The two guards at the door of the guardhouse looked at each other for a moment then left at a run to join them.

Quickly, Honeyman slipped the ropes from his hands, drew the key from his coat, and unlocked the door. He opened it half way, paused to listen, then started north toward the river as fast as he could in the darkness and snow and ice. He was halfway there when a shout came from behind, "Stop! Or we shoot!" He ducked and continued to dodge and run. He felt the impact and the sting of a musket ball on his right hip at the same instant that he heard the shot, and then a second musket ball sang past his ear as he reached the riverbank. He hunched low and ran east on the river ice, slipping, falling, until he could no longer hear the shouts of the pursuing Americans. Then he crept into the willows on the riverbank, sat down, and gathered his knees to his chest to save what little warmth he could, while he waited for enough light to see the river. As he grew colder, the throbbing in his hip gradually diminished. He dared not look at the wound, but given his continued ability to move, assumed the bone had not been broken.

In the gray of early dawn, the Delaware became visible, four hundred yards wide. Ice extended from both banks, but there was a channel of open water perhaps thirty yards wide running in the center. Honeyman stood to stamp his feet and flail his arms until the freezing numbness was gone, wondering how he could reach the far riverbank. At that moment, the sounds of American soldiers coming from the west reached him, and in the distance he saw them searching the willows along the riverbank.

He could wait no longer. He sprinted out onto the ice toward the far bank until he heard the loud popping as it began cracking beneath his feet, and he dropped feet first, sliding toward the open channel of black water. The ice thinned and crumbled, and he plunged into the freezing water. He battled back to the surface and swam for the far bank until the ice became thick enough to support him. He crawled to the New Jersey bank of the river where he rolled onto his back, numb from the cold, with ice forming in his beard and hair. His clothing stiffened as it froze, and for a time he lay still, gasping for breath. He could hear the American soldiers on the Pennsylvania side, shouting, cursing at him, but they dared not try to cross the river.

When he could, he stood and fumbled in his coat for the key Washington had given him and threw it skittering across the ice into the river. Then he turned and began the nine-mile walk back to Trenton. His clothing, hair, and beard were frozen stiff, and exhaustion was setting in when a six-man patrol of Hessian cavalry surrounded him.

"Who are you and what are you doing here?" their leader demanded.

"John Honeyman," he answered through chattering teeth.

"Captured by the Americans. Escaped. I've been shot." He showed them the bullet hole in his coat and trousers.

The Hessians recognized him. They lifted him onto a horse with a soldier mounted behind to hold him on and rode back to Trenton to the Old Barracks building. There they stripped his wet clothing, dressed the wound on his hip, which proved to be little more than a deep scratch, and wrapped him in blankets. While his clothing was drying before the large fireplace, a large mug of hot gruel warmed him further as the Hessians listened with rapt attention to his story.

Dressed once more in his own dry clothing, they escorted him to Rall's headquarters.

Rall, average height, sharp faced, knew Honeyman from the many previous times Honeyman had delivered cattle.

"You were captured by the Americans?" Ralls asked. "When?"

"Yesterday."

Rall nodded. "Yesterday we found a large workhorse tied in a cedar grove not far north of town. Would you know about that?"

"That is my horse. I was delivering three more cattle to you yesterday. One got away from me north of town. I went back to find it and bring it in."

"The Americans captured you and took you to their camp?"

"Yes, at McKonkey's Ferry. I was there until just before dawn this morning."

"You saw their camp?"

"I did."

Rall leaned forward, eyes narrowed in suspicion. "And you escaped? How?"

"A fire broke out in camp. Most of them went to put it out. I broke through the door and ran for the river. I crossed early this morning. Your men found me."

Rall looked incredible. "You crossed the Delaware River this morning? In a boat?"

"No, sir. Swam."

The captain who had brought Honeyman to Rall's headquarters interrupted.

"Sir," he said, "we found him on the river road this morning just before sunrise. His clothing was frozen. He had ice in his hair and beard. I do not believe he would have made it back to Trenton. There is a hole made by a musket ball in his coat and his trousers. There is a mark on his leg where the ball passed."

Rall settled back in his chair. "I see. Tell me, Mister Honeyman. In what condition is the American camp?"

George Washington's words rang in Honeyman's mind like a chant—*Tell Rall the truth!*

Honeyman cleared his throat. "I have never seen anything like it. Sick—freezing—starving—little ammunition—summer clothing—no shoes—hopeless."

Rall leaned back in his chair, drew and released a great breath, and smiled. "Thank you, Mister Honeyman. Is there anything you need before you return to your home?"

★　★　★

On Christmas day, 1776, a raging snowstorm swept down the Delaware River. At four o'clock in the afternoon, in the howling wind, negotiating the frozen ground and falling snow, General Washington led the first company of the ragged remains of his Continental Army to the banks of the Delaware River, where they loaded into Durham freight boats, thrity-two feet long, eight feet wide. The last boatloads finished the crossing at midnight, and they turned east to march nine miles to Trenton. Most of the soldiers did not have shoes, and the entire army could be tracked by the bloody tracks their frozen and battered feet left in the snow and ice.

At eight o'clock the following morning, December 26, 1776, the ragtag American army hit Trenton at both ends, catching the Hessian soldiers recovering from a day and a night of drinking. The fierce fighting raged hand to hand, face to face in the streets of the small town, and when the Hessians retreated to an orchard east of town, the Americans surrounded them and took nine hundred captives. The battle was over in just less than ninety minutes. When the casualty count was given to General Washington later that morning, he stared in stunned disbelief. The Hessians had lost about three hundred soldiers, with nine hundred more captured. A few had deserted by running down the Delaware River to escape. The entire German garrison was either dead, captured, or had deserted, including Colonel Rall, who was shot from his horse and taken to the Methodist church in town, where he later died. The Americans had suffered two officers wounded, and two enlisted men wounded. There were no American dead.

The brilliant victory of the Americans at Trenton electrified American patriots throughout the colonies. Their faith in their quest for freedom blossomed as never before. If their sick and starving army could cross the Delaware at night in a snowstorm, walk nine miles barefooted, and defeat an entire Hessian command in ninety minutes, they could do whatever was required to win their independence and freedom!

More than six years later, shortly after the war ended, the Americans the victors, Mary Honeyman was startled one day when three American officers rode to her door in Griggstown. She was stunned when the tall one removed his hat and requested an audience with her in her parlor.

It was General Washington. With her husband and family

gathered around, he quietly told her of the unbelievable heroism of her husband. He was generous in his praise of her and her children, who for more than ten years had endured the insults and attacks of American patriots who believed John Honeyman to be a British loyalist.

Within days the story spread throughout the countryside, and for the first time, John, Mary, and their four children were greeted in the streets by their neighbors with the reverence, warmth, and respect reserved for the true heroes of the American Revolution.

Three Who
Stepped Forward

December 30, 1776
Trenton, New Jersey

★ ★ ★

THEY STOOD AT ATTENTION IN SIX INCHES of frozen, crusted
snow on the New Jersey bank of the Delaware River, some barefooted, some with their feet wrapped in scraps of tarp and rags,
ice in their beards, dirty, starved, sick, hair long and matted, vapor
rising in clouds from their breath, shivering as they pulled their
summer tunics tight in the bitter, frozen midday sun. They were
the Delaware Regiment of the American Continental Army,
assembled in rank and file by order of their commander in chief,
General George Washington, muskets over their right shoulders,
one mile east of the small village of Trenton, New Jersey. Just west
of them was the Massachusetts Regiment, assembled in rank and
file, along with other survivors of their shattered army.

Too well did they remember the wild, horrifying chaos of the battle of Long Island, New York, August 27, 1776, in which the British had trapped the inexperienced Americans to scatter them in a disorganized, panic-driven horde running in every direction. Only the heroic action of John Glover and his thousand Massachusetts fishermen saved what was left of them when, under cover of darkness, they commandeered every boat they could find on the East River and ferried what was left of the Continental Army to Manhattan Island. Washington fled north, onto the mainland, to White Plains, hoping to salvage what he could of his beaten army, only to be attacked again by the British and driven back to Fort Washington on Manhattan Island, beaten again, and driven across the Hudson River to New Jersey, where he gave orders to run. Just run. Save what you can, but run. He led his small remnant of the army southwest across New Jersey, crossed the Delaware, and stopped at McKonkey's Ferry on the Pennsylvania side to try to save what he could of his desperate, demoralized troops.

It was there that General Washington came to himself. In pain and humiliation he realized that he had never previously had command of an entire army and that his lack of experience and mistakes in judgment had all but lost the entire revolution in the first major battle. He had failed his men and, worse, his country. He had nearly destroyed the American Revolution in its infancy. He rose above his grief and sorrow, admitted his failure, and resolved in his heart that he would never again commit such errors.

Then, on December 23, 1776, Thomas Paine, in the misery of the American camp at McKonkey's Ferry, with snow falling, sat before a fire with a drum between his knees and thoughtfully wrote "The American Crisis." The document reached General Washington, who read the essay over and over again.

"These are the times that try men's souls. The summer soldier and the sunshine patriot will, in this crisis, shrink from the service of their country; but he that stands it now deserves the love and thanks of man and woman. . . ."

Washington had the document printed and circulated among his men, then made a decision that stunned his staff. He was taking the troops back across the Delaware River the night of December 25, 1776, to attack the Hessian command at Trenton, nine miles downriver, on the New Jersey side. His staff rose in shock. These men? Sick, starving, freezing in summer clothing, no shoes, low on ammunition? Attack the Hessians—some of the best soldiers in the world?

"We're going," Washington replied.

At four o'clock in the afternoon, December 25, 1776, a violent wind-driven snowstorm swept down the Delaware River as John Glover and his Marblehead fishermen began loading the big Durham freight boats for the crossing. It was past midnight when they finished. They had not lost a man or a cannon or a horse. Washington gave orders, and the ragtag army marched east, down the Delaware. One could track them by the blood from the cuts made by the ice in their feet.

At eight o'clock on the morning of December 26, 1776, the Americans hit Trenton from both ends and caught the Hessians unprepared, most of them still asleep from their Christmas celebration the previous night, just as Washington had hoped. The battle lasted about ninety minutes. Four hundred Hessians were killed in the heavy, face-to-face, hand-to-hand street fight. Nearly nine hundred were taken prisoner in a wheat field and peach orchard on the east side of town, where they had fled. The Americans had two wounded officers and two wounded enlisted men; none dead. Washington, and most of the others, recognized the miracle.

When British general William Howe, commander of all British forces in America, received word in New York of the disastrous defeat of his troops at Trenton, he was nearly apoplectic with rage. Instantly he ordered one of his best commanders, General Charles Cornwallis, to take eight thousand British regulars, march them to Trenton, retake the town, and deliver Washington back to him in New York, dead or alive. Within twenty-four hours, General Cornwallis marched his eight thousand men out of New York, southwest across lower New Jersey, toward Trenton.

Washington's scouts brought word of their approach and estimated the British would arrive January 2 or 3, 1777. Washington sought his tent to quietly consider his course of action.

The single overriding factor was the condition of his own Continental Army. Almost every man had signed an enlistment that expired at midnight, December 31, 1776! The morning of January 1, 1777, Washington would have no army! Worse, when their enlistments expired, Washington would have no money to pay them their mustering-out pay, long overdue. How was he going to continue the revolution with no army and no money to hire one? Worst of all, he must have the answers within three days!

Washington issued his orders. "Send a runner to find Robert Morris immediately. He is the wealthiest man in America and a patriot. Tell him I need money to pay the Continental Army." He stopped for a moment to gather his thoughts. "Then assemble the troops a mile east of Trenton. I want to address them."

Thus it was that on the frozen midday of December 30, 1776, the Delaware Regiment, flanked by the Massachusetts Regiment and other survivors of the war, found themselves standing at attention on the banks of the Delaware River—hollow-cheeked, sunken-eyed, teeth chattering, wondering why General Washington had assembled them. The eyes of most men turned northwest at the sound of oncoming horses, and they watched as General Washington and his staff loped their horses toward them. The general passed the Massachusetts Regiment and stopped five yards short of the Delaware troops. Those nearest heard Washington address his staff of officers.

"Remain here. I'm going to speak to them."

His officers remained on their horses while Washington rode twenty yards farther and stopped his tall bay gelding before the first ranks. Vapor was rising from the horse's hide and a cloud rose from its muzzle. Washington was tall in the saddle, dark in his winter cape, and for a few moments he studied the emaciated faces of his troops. Then he began to speak.

"My countrymen, it is my great privilege to pay to you that praise and tribute which you have so abundantly earned, both from myself as your commanding officer, and from your country. The service you rendered four days ago in the battle at Trenton was a great tribute to your courage and your dedication to your country. News of your victory is reaching out to cities and people both here and abroad. Those who would rob us of our liberty will know that your dedication is undimmed. Your fellow countrymen will rise to new heights of support to the cause."

He paused and for a moment stared at the ground as though searching for words.

"I frankly confess my inability to speak with the power of Thomas Paine, but I do know that you are the soldiers of whom he wrote. You are not the summer soldiers who shrink at the trials of winter. You have so nobly suffered unbearable hardships and deprivations in silence, and finally have risen in impossible conditions to defeat a powerful enemy. For these things I, and your countrymen, are indebted to you forever.

"Were it in my power, I would send you home when your

enlistments expire tomorrow with my greatest blessings for your-selves and your families. But I cannot. Our victory at Trenton will surely bring the wrath of the British Empire down upon us, and unless we meet them and somehow turn them, we will have lost all we have gained at such a terrible price. I put the question to you: can we allow that to happen? We cannot. For that purpose I am here before you today to beseech you to consider the oppor-tunity that fate has now delivered into your hands. You can deliver to your country a service that may never again be within your power. As a reward, I am offering every man of you who will remain with the army for another few weeks, a bounty of ten dol-lars. It is little enough for what you have done and what you will yet do for your country."

Washington stopped, and for a few seconds he sat silent, try-ing to judge if he had said enough. Then he reined his horse around and returned to his staff of officers. Four of them spurred their horses forward and rode to face the Delaware Regiment, where one of them spoke.

"You have heard General Washington. You know what you have done and you know what you can yet do for your country. You have heard the bounty offered for those who will remain with the Continental Army for a few weeks past your enlistments."

He paused with his breath raising a vapor cloud, then concluded.

"Each man who will remain with the army after your enlist-ment has expired tomorrow, step forward."

Not one man moved in the awful silence. Instantly the tension in the frigid air was overpowering. Ten seconds passed. Twenty. Thirty. No one moved.

The officer stood in his stirrups, then reined his horse to trot back to Washington's side, unable to say a word to his commanding officer.

Washington straightened in his saddle and squared his shoulders. He raised his face, and his jaw was set like granite. The pale blue-gray eyes were points of light as he spurred his horse back to face the Delaware Regiment one more time.

Then the expression on Washington's face softened. A tenderness crept into his eyes that no one had seen before. The hard lines around his mouth disappeared, and his brows peaked as in one moved by seeing the deep suffering of another. He looked down into the faces of his men with a sense of compassion that none had supposed Washington possessed. Then he spoke, in a quiet, subdued, yet penetrating voice that reached every man in the regiment.

"My brave fellows, you have done all I asked you to do, and more than could be reasonably expected; but your country is at stake, your wives, your houses, and all that you hold dear. You have worn yourselves out with fatigues and hardships, but we know not how to spare you. If you will consent to stay only one month longer, you will render that service to the cause of liberty, and to your country, which you probably never can do under any other circumstances. The present is emphatically the crisis which is to decide our destiny."

He stopped, then raised a hand as though to speak further, but the expression on his face told his men that he could think of nothing more than he had already said. He slowly lowered his hand and reined his horse back around to his officers. The second in command licked dry lips, then spurred his horse forward, out before the Delaware troops. His voice was strained, too high, as he spoke.

"All those who will remain after their enlistments expire, step forward."

He stopped. There was nothing more to say. He returned to Washington's side.

It was only a few seconds, but it seemed an eternity before the silence was broken.

From the second rank, an old, bearded, hollow-eyed veteran, dressed in rags, ice in his hair and beard, with blanket strips tied to his feet, shuffled forward and faced the officers. His voice was high, scratchy.

"I can't go home if my country needs me."

From the first rank, another old, stooped soldier stepped forward, beard icy, clothes tattered, barefooted. "Neither can I."

Then, from the first rank, a fourteen-year-old boy, smooth-cheeked, small, thin, who had been with them from the beginning, stepped forward to take his place beside the two old soldiers. He came to attention, but did not say a word as he stood there, head high, musket over his shoulder.

Another stepped forward, and from the rear, men broke ranks to walk forward and take their place. And then, the entire regiment stepped forward. To the west, in the Massachusetts Regiment, men started stepping forward, one, then two, then many, then all, except those who could no longer walk.

January 1, 1777, the runner returned from the office of Robert Morris with a pouch containing 410 Spanish-milled dollars, two English crowns, 72 French crowns, 1,072 English shillings, and enough American coins to pay the army part of what was owed them.

January 3, 1777, Washington and his army hit Princeton, twelve miles north of Trenton, scattering British colonel Charles Mawhood and his entire command into a wild retreat that left the town, with all the British stores of food and ammunition, to the Americans.

WHEN SIX HUNDRED
STOPPED FIVE THOUSAND

JANUARY 2, 1777
TRENTON, NEW JERSEY

★　★　★

Edward Hand, clad in buckskins and moccasins, hawk-nosed, bearded, long hair tied back with a leather cord, stood beside the morning cook fire near the tent of General George Washington on the banks of the Delaware River just east of Trenton, New Jersey. Standing over six feet tall, soft-spoken, deliberate by nature, Hand carried the stamp of authority that made him a natural leader, respected and beloved by his men. A lieutenant colonel in the Lancaster County Pennsylvania militia, he commanded a regiment of riflemen who he had trained and who were reputed to be one of the finest fighting units in the Continental Army, deadly with their beloved long Pennsylvania rifles.

In the hour before dawn of January 2, 1777, Hand had been ordered to the headquarters tent of General Washington, to a conference between Washington and General Roche de Fermoy, who had recently arrived from his native France to volunteer his services to the Continental Army in their desperate struggle against the British. With the sun turning the light skiff of eastern clouds into an unbelievable kaleidoscope of reds and yellows, Hand stood leaning on his rifle, listening intently to the exchange between the two generals. A rare, warm wind had settled in the previous day, and a light rain had fallen in the night to turn the frozen world and the dirt roads into a morass of mud with dirty water forming into great bogs in the low places.

Washington's voice was crisp, concise. "You are aware that a British survivor of the battle at Trenton seven days ago reached New York and reported the loss of the entire Hessian command to General William Howe?"

"Yes, sir," de Fermoy answered in English, flavored with a strong French accent. "I am aware."

"General Howe was incensed. He ordered General Charles Cornwallis to immediately assemble eight thousand Hessian and British regulars and lead them in a forced march from New York to Trenton, with orders to utterly destroy every man in this camp."

De Fermoy blanched. "I did not know that, sir."

Hand's eyes narrowed in surprise, but he said nothing.

Washington continued. "I sent scouts north to locate them and report back to me. The scouts came in before dawn this morning. General Cornwallis and his army are at Princeton, moving toward us in rapid-march time on Princeton Road. Infantry, cavalry, and sixty cannon."

Instantly Hand straightened, tense, waiting for de Fermoy's response. Seconds passed while de Fermoy recoiled, stunned with the realization that within twenty-four hours a British and Hessian army large enough to overrun the ragtag American Continentals would in minutes be upon them. De Fermoy licked dry lips and began to speak, but his voice cracked. He swallowed hard and tried once more, his voice too high, too strained. "Eight thousand? With cannon?"

"And cavalry," Washington replied. "I am ordering you to take six hundred men and move north on Princeton Road to intercept them and delay them. I need one more day to prepare defenses to meet their attack. You are to slow them down and give me that extra day."

Washington fell silent while de Fermoy struggled to understand how six hundred starved, sick, freezing, emaciated men could bring eight thousand of the best fighting men in the world, angry and determined, to a standstill.

Washington gestured toward Hand. "I am including Lieutenant Colonel Edward Hand and his Pennsylvania regiment of two hundred riflemen in your command. These men are familiar with the country and understand the tactics that will be required. Are there any questions?"

General de Fermoy pulled his fragmented thoughts together. "When do we leave, sir?"

"As soon as possible. Every minute is critical. You are dismissed to assemble your men and go."

Within minutes de Fermoy had sent out two scouts with orders to find the British column and report back to him as he moved north. In less than one hour he mounted his horse to lead his column north on the Princeton Road that wound through the bare, leafless, wintry New Jersey forest, connecting Trenton with Princeton, twelve miles distant. The soldiers in the column sank ankle-deep in the muck and mud with every step in the ruts that had been cut by wagon wheels.

It was approaching nine o'clock when de Fermoy called a halt at the bridge spanning Five Mile Creek to wait for his scouts to come with their report. Twenty minutes later they were there, sweat running, muddy to the knees, breathing hard from their run. Edward Hand came trotting to hear their report.

"Are the British on the Princeton Road?" de Fermoy demanded.

"Yes, sir, just about one mile from here."

De Fermoy licked at lips that were suddenly dry. "How many?"

In the moment of intense silence that followed the question, Hand glanced at de Fermoy's face. It was white.

"About five thousand."

"Do they have cannon?"

"Twenty-eight cannon."

De Fermoy's eyes narrowed in doubt, and his voice was too loud, accusatory. "I was told they had eight thousand, not five. Are you now telling me that you have seen them? Only five thousand?"

The scout nodded vigorously, and Hand saw the flash of anger in his eyes as he answered. "I'm telling you straight out, there are eight thousand, but they left fifteen hundred at Maidenhead and over a thousand at the south side of Princeton. There's just over five thousand of 'em within a mile of here, marching hard, and they got cannon. We better do somethin' fast. That's the truth of it!"

De Fermoy suddenly straightened, turned on his heel, and walked away from the tiny gathering, staring downward into the mud. He stopped at his horse while those behind stared at each other blankly, startled that their commanding officer had failed to give a single order to prepare for the head-on collision that was descending upon them within half an hour. Hand drew a deep breath and silently signaled the men to give de Fermoy time to make his plan. Minutes passed before a rifleman trotted up to Hand.

"Sir, General de Fermoy is gone."

Hand's head jerked forward. "De Fermoy is *what?*"

"Gone, sir. Just mounted his horse and rode out. South, back toward Trenton."

"What did he say?" Hand asked.

"Nothing, sir. But I got to tell you. He drank some rum. I watched him."

"Rum! How much?"

The rifleman could not avoid an embarrassed grin. "I'd guess about a gallon, sir."

It took Edward Hand two seconds to recover and give his orders. He called the names of two captains from his Pennsylvania Rifle Company, and they came running.

"De Fermoy's gone," Hand exclaimed. "We got five thousand British due to arrive here within about fifteen minutes. This is what we're going to do. Divide our six hundred in two halves, and be sure we get half our riflemen in each group. Each half take one cannon. Bartlett, you take your half to the east side of the road, and Ungrich, you take your half to the west side. Wait until the British are on the Five Mile Creek bridge, and whichever side has the clearest shot, take it, then fall back into the woods to reload while those on the other side of the road fire a volley and fall back. They don't have a musket or a rifle that can reach us, and it'll take at least five minutes to bring up their cannon. When they get their cannon to the front, we fall back and disappear and wait for them at the next natural point of ambush. Any questions?"

There were none.

"Let's move."

A mile north of them, General Charles Cornwallis spurred his horse ahead and came quartering in beside Major Donlevy Furman, commander of the leading fifteen hundred infantry soldiers in the column.

"Major," Cornwallis, ordered, "move your command ahead and form an advance line immediately."

"Yes, sir."

Within minutes Furman's infantry was trotting ahead of the main column, cursing the mud as it splashed to cover their boots and white breeches. Behind Furman's advance line, Cornwallis and his officers rode horses caked with mud to their bellies, leading the main column as it sloshed on through the ruts and muck, struggling to keep the heavy munitions and commissary wagons and the cannon moving. Twenty minutes later Furman's infantry rounded a bend where the road angled southwest and came into view of the Five Mile Creek bridge. Furman signaled a halt, and every eye in his command squinted in the bright sun, searching for anything that moved. All was still. Beside Furman rode a proud Hessian officer, his green coat speckled with mud, his long, waxed mustache stiff, his tall hat sparkling in the morning sun. He glanced at Furman, impatient with the delay, the mud, and an American army that they could not find.

The bridge was clear, and nothing appeared in the leafless trees beyond. Furman signaled his men forward, muskets at the ready, bayonets gleaming. They came onto the bridge four abreast, boots clomping on the heavy timbers. The leaders were ten yards beyond the bridge when suddenly the Hessian officer beside

Furman threw both hands high as he pitched headlong from his horse, dead before he hit the mud in the road.

Major Furman jerked his horse to a stop to stare down at the body, unable to understand what had happened. A split second later the flat crack of a Pennsylvania rifle rolled past Furman, and by reflex he threw himself to one side of his saddle as a second .60-caliber bullet whistled past his ear, followed by the cracking report of a second distant, invisible rifle. He wheeled his horse around and drove his spurs home as he shouted orders that were drowned out by the first complete volley of three hundred American muskets and rifles, and the musket balls and rifle bullets came ripping into his infantry. Within ten seconds, fourteen pounds of grape shot came tearing into the column, followed by the blast of a single cannon.

"Return fire!" screamed the British officers, and watched as those still standing in the leading ranks raised their muskets and looked for a target. But they could see only a faint showing of white gun smoke in the trees on the west side of the road, three hundred yards ahead. Then, from the east side of the road came a second volley, and a second cannon blast, knocking officers from their horses, and sending men all up and down the line slumping to the ground. Bewildered, frightened by an enemy they could not see, the British fired their muskets blindly and heard the heavy .75-caliber Brown Bess musket balls smack harmlessly into the trees. Then the leading ranks broke and ran back across the bridge toward the main column.

When Cornwallis heard the shooting erupt ahead of the main column, he spurred his horse forward, desperately hoping he had finally encountered the full American army. He was met by Major Furman on a lathered, mud-splattered horse.

"Sir," Furman panted, "there is an American force at Five Mile

Bridge. They fired at a distance too great for our weapons to match."

"Casualties?" Cornwallis asked.

Furman shook his head. "I would estimate between fifty and one hundred."

"Reform and cross the bridge," Cornwallis ordered. "I'll order two cannon to support you. If we've found Washington's army, we must bring them to a stand!"

Five minutes later Furman's command stormed across the bridge while behind them, two officers supervised the loading of two British cannon, aimed at the trees beyond. With Furman leading, the infantry charged the trees to the west, shouting, bayonets thrust forward. They reached the trees without a shot being fired, and they stopped, waiting. Nothing moved. The only sound was a few brave crows in the trees, cawing at them, scolding them.

Furman raised his sword high above his head and shouted, "They've fled to the far side of the trees! Follow me!"

At the far side of the trees, he charged into a clearing four hundred yards wide with his men following, and drew rein on his horse. There was no American in sight. He plunged on, waving his sword, shouting, "Charge!" to his men. He was halfway across the open ground when he saw the first movement in the brush and trees on the far side and realized it was men raising their dreaded Pennsylvania long rifles to their shoulders. He opened his mouth to shout, "Halt!" when white smoke billowed in the trees and in the next instant he felt a tremendous blow where the two white belts crossed on his chest as the rifle bullet punched deep. He tipped backwards off his horse, landing on his shoulders in the sticky red-brown mud. His last clear impression was one of wonderment as he turned onto his side and did not move again. He never heard the cracking blast of the American volley that killed him and also thirty-three of his men.

The British captain behind him gaped at his fallen commander for a moment before he could rally his shattered thoughts enough to shout, "Halt! First rank, kneel and prepare to fire!" The soldiers in the first rank went to one knee and brought their heavy muskets up as the captain opened his mouth to shout, "Fire!" when the second American volley erupted from the trees. The captain was the first British soldier to drop, and behind him twenty-one of the kneeling regulars grunted as the rifle bullets knocked them over backwards.

The young lieutenant next in command sat his horse, white-faced, brain numb as he stared at the major, the captain, and fifty-four men from the first rank, all dead in the first minute of the fight. He raised his hand and was shouting his first command when the third volley rolled from invisible men in the trees. The young lieutenant and sixteen regulars behind him went down. Those still standing spun on their heels, and in an instant the remainder of the fifteen hundred advance command was in a full, panic-driven rout, plunging back across the clearing, through the woods, heedless of the tree limbs tearing at their faces and tunics in their wild run to reach Princeton Road and the main body of the British column.

East of them, on the far side of Princeton Road, the second group of hidden Americans held their position, watching, waiting, listening. To the north, Cornwallis stopped the main column, waiting for a report on the shooting ahead. One minute later he saw the first flash of crimson moving in the trees as the advance British infantry came plowing through. Most had lost their hats in their blind stampede but did not care as they ran on toward Princeton Road, sweating, mud flying.

Eighty yards east of the road, Edward Hand calmly watched as the British across the bridge with Cornwallis wheeled two cannon into place, loaded them with grapeshot, and stood with smoking linstocks, ready to fire on command. Across Princeton Road, the British regulars in their wild retreat were running directly toward Hand, thirty yards from the road. To his right were two of his most trusted officers and twenty-two of his select riflemen. Hidden twenty yards south of them was the balance of his command, with Captain Tom Forrest in charge of one cannon. Hand raised his left arm far enough for his men to see, and in ten seconds had silently given hand signals telling them what to do. Without a sound, his men raised their long rifles and picked their targets.

Hand waited until the retreating British were five yards from the road before he took aim with his own rifle on the British cannoneer, who was awaiting orders from Cornwallis to fire, and squeezed off his shot. The British gunner buckled and went down as the twenty-two men with Hand fired, and every man in the two British cannon crews crumpled and dropped.

The running British regulars just reaching the roadbed stopped so abruptly that half of them slipped to one knee in the mud. Stunned, they watched as six Americans a scant eight yards east of the roadbed appeared from nowhere, calmly drawing their ramrods to reload. The British regulars fumbled to bring their muskets to bear and in that instant nearly one hundred Pennsylvania rifles thundered and the leading ranks of the regulars staggered and went down. Those behind would take no more. They broke for the bridge in a wild melee and had not gone five yards when the remainder of Hand's group cut loose from twenty yards south. More than thirty of the fleeing redcoats dropped into the mud just as Forrest touched off his cannon and its load of canister grape shot came ripping. The survivors of the first British regiment did not look back as they ran headlong to be free of the deadly fire that came from nowhere to cut their ranks to pieces.

Incensed, General Cornwallis ordered his men to bring up five more cannon and men to operate them. With the guns in place, he ordered them to commence firing at the trees where the Americans had been seen, and for ten minutes the British cannon blasted, shredding the trees and brush.

"Cease fire!" Cornwallis bellowed. "Major Alexander, take a company of men into those trees and count their dead."

Twenty minutes later a wide-eyed Major Alexander galloped his horse back from the trees to face General Cornwallis. "Sir," he stammered, "there is not one American in those trees, dead or alive. They're all gone. We found only their tracks."

For long moments Cornwallis stared in disbelief. "Could you estimate how many there are?"

"About six hundred, sir. Some barefooted, some with moccasins."

"Forward with all speed," Cornwallis ordered. "We must catch them."

It was midafternoon when the British came in view of Shabbakonk Creek. The leading officers extended their telescopes and studied the road, searching for the bridge that had to be there. Astonished, one exclaimed, "The bridge is gone! They've pulled the bridge down." He rode back to tell Cornwallis.

The general did not hesitate. "Ford the creek!"

Dreading every moment, the leading ranks held their muskets high and waded into the frigid water up to their chests, struggled across, and were at the crest of the south bank when the American rifles hidden in the forest once again roared, and the British fell back. Again Cornwallis ordered his cannon forward, and again they blasted the trees to pieces. The British sent a party to ford the creek; the party reported that once more the Americans had silently disappeared. It took the British column more than an hour to ford Shabbakonk Creek, emerging on the south side dripping, cursing, expecting the invisible Americans to attack from all sides.

South of the British, Edward Hand paused to study the sun for a moment before he called his officers to him.

"Just about three more hours of daylight. General Washington wants us to hold them until dark." He pointed south. "About half a mile this side of Trenton is Stockton Hollow. That's our best chance. You know the plan. Let's move."

The sun was reaching for the western rim when the British soldiers came marching toward Stockton Hollow, with Trenton visible in the distance. They were at the north rim of the hollow when they stopped. The leading ranks marched off the roadbed, and suddenly twenty-eight British cannon appeared, spread five feet apart, all aimed at point-blank range across the hollow where the Americans were hidden.

Instantly Edward Hand understood. *Cornwallis intends to rake this rim with cannon, then send his infantry through the hollow with the big guns giving them cover!*

He did not hesitate. "Get the cannon crews first!" he shouted.

The distance from the American rifles to the line of British cannon was just over two hundred yards. The moment Hand shouted his order, the American riflemen steadied their weapons and fired their first volley. Of the eighty-one British cannoneers, seventy-three buckled and went down in the mud. At the same instant, the two American cannon roared, and grapeshot tore into the British soldiers moving up to the British cannon. In the forty seconds it took the Americans to load their rifles and cannon, British soldiers ran up to their own cannon and grasped the smoking linstocks to touch them off. The air above Stockton Hollow was suddenly filled with whistling lead that threw mud and snow and bits of trees and brush thirty feet in the air all around the Americans.

The American rifles and cannon answered, and the front ranks of the British lines sagged. Then the infantry came charging from behind, past the cannon crews, onto the low ground, charging straight at the Americans who held the high ground on the south of the hollow.

The sun was just disappearing behind the western rim, throwing long shadows eastward.

Edward Hand shouted, "Fall back, fall back." He led his men back one hundred fifty yards, where they stopped. Quickly they reloaded their two cannon and covered them with brush while the riflemen became invisible in the brush and trees. The British surged across the hollow, up the shallow south slope to the rim, and came charging straight at the hidden Americans. In early dusk Edward Hand gauged the distance, eighty yards—sixty—forty—thirty—and shouted, "Fire!"

At nearly point-blank range, the American rifles blasted, and not one rifle ball missed. British officers collapsed, and the three leading ranks went down. Those behind recoiled, then surged forward once more, stepping over and around their fallen comrades. Once again the American rifles fired, and the British slowed.

In deepening dusk Edward Hand glanced south, to where the junction of Princeton Road and King and Queen Streets of the town of Trenton joined.

One more hour. We've got to hold for one more hour.

"Fall back, fall back," he shouted, "two hundred yards. We've got to hold them!"

Once again the Americans faded before the oncoming British

cannon and stopped at two hundred yards. They took cover wherever they could find it, reloaded, and waited, knowing this was where they had to make their last stand.

The British came on steadily, their cannon in the lead, and once again the Americans raised their rifles and took aim. They had fired their next volley when suddenly Hand heard the unmistakable whine of a heavy cannonball passing directly over his head, coming from behind him. It was instantly followed by the blast of a cannon at the far end of Trenton, near the Delaware River. Instantly Hand swung his head around, and in the purple shadows of deep dusk saw the flare of four more cannon blasts and heard the cannonballs pass overhead, to explode in the leading British lines.

"Washington!" Hand exclaimed. "General Washington is firing his big guns to give us support!"

With darkness fast upon them, Hand and his men held their positions, loading, firing, with British cannonballs coming from the north, and American cannonballs whistling over from the south. Then two mounted horsemen came stampeding from behind, right up to the Americans, and Hand recognized General Henry Knox and General Nathaniel Greene, riding like wild men, shouting, "Hold fast! hold fast!" and behind them came the roar of five hundred shouting voices as Americans came surging up through the streets of Trenton to join Hand.

In full darkness they held the British for a time, and then their officers ordered a slow, steady withdrawal through the small town. They reached the Queen Street Bridge that crossed the Assunpink Creek at the south end of Trenton, and they crossed it with General Washington sitting his big gray horse on the south end of the bridge, with British cannonballs blasting mud and ice thirty feet in the air on all sides of him. The British followed the

Americans through the town, and three times tried to storm the bridge, only to be cut down, until British soldiers lay four deep on the bridge. It was only then the British withdrew and retreated to the north end of town.

General Cornwallis had lost. Not knowing the strength of Washington's army, he dared not attack in the dark of night. He camped his beaten army on the north end of the town to wait for the dawn.

In the night, Washington ordered his army to wrap the wheels of their cannon with burlap and tarp to silence them as he led his army southeast nearly four miles, then turned north and in near total silence crept past Cornwallis' army to take the Old Quaker Road twelve miles north. On the morning of January 3, 1777, Washington attacked the town of Princeton and defeated the British forces there, under the command of British colonel Mawhood.

The American victories at Trenton on December 26, 1776, followed by the victory at Princeton on January 3, 1777, changed the course of the revolution in favor of the Americans.

Colonel Edward Hand became a legend in his own time.

WHEN KING GEORGE II
LOST HIS HEAD

JANUARY 3, 1777

PRINCETON, NEW JERSEY

★ ★ ★

THE EXCITED YOUNG LIEUTENANT FACED Captain Joseph
Moulder in the freezing air, vapors rising from his face as he
pointed and spoke. "Sir, there's a lot of British soldiers inside.
We'll need cannon to get them out."

They were standing on the campus of the College of New Jersey
in Princeton, and the lieutenant was pointing at Nassau Hall, a
great, two-story structure with stone walls two feet thick and
reputed to be the largest building in America on that frigid morning
of January 3, 1777. The Continental Army had hit the town that
morning, met by British Colonel Charles Mawhood and his command of red-coated regulars. With General George Washington
leading, the Americans had plowed into the British lines like a tidal

wave to scatter the king's soldiers in all directions in a panic-driven retreat. Within two hours the Americans were in control of the city of Princeton, save for more than a hundred British troops who had frantically sought the protection of the thick stone walls of Nassau Hall. They had slammed the great doors, jammed the immense crossbar into place to lock them, knocked out the windows of the great assembly hall and chapel on the first floor, and were maintaining a steady stream of musket fire from the broken windows to keep the swarming Americans at a distance. It quickly became obvious that the only way the Americans were going to get the British out of Nassau Hall was with cannon.

For a moment Captain Moulder peered at the building through narrowed eyes, then turned to the young lieutenant. "Find Lieutenant Alexander Hamilton. He and I brought two cannon from Trenton. Get those guns here. Now."

Ten minutes later, a half dozen American soldiers, ragged, bearded, gaunt, some barefooted, others with their feet wrapped in rags, rolled the two cannon up behind Captain Moulder.

"You wanted these guns?" one of them asked.

Moulder wasted no time. "Get them loaded with grapeshot."

Experienced cannoneers stepped forward to ram ladles of gunpowder down the barrels, followed by dried grass, then a load of one-inch lead balls, followed by more dried grass to hold it all in place.

"Loaded, sir."

Moulder bobbed his head. "We need volunteers to roll those guns within twenty yards of the big doors and fire them at the windows on both sides," he explained. "We've got to stop the British who are shooting muskets from those windows."

Four men leaped forward and, using the cannon as shields against the steady stream of British musket fire, rolled the guns forward, side by side, then aimed them point-blank at the two huge windows on each side of the tall oak front doors.

"Fire!" shouted Moulder, and the men laid smoking linstocks on the touch holes. The powder caught, and the cannon bucked and roared. Twenty pounds of lead balls ripped into the windows, splintering the frames and knocking the British soldiers back inside the massive, high-ceilinged assembly hall. Inside, caught by surprise, the British soldiers hunched down among the benches, the heavy draperies, the beautiful mural paintings on all the walls, and the great painting of their monarch George II, father of their King George III, that dominated the back wall, directly opposite the doors. The painting of King George II, dressed in his royal finery, smiling benignly down on his subjects, was a masterpiece in which all the British soldiers took great pride.

Outside in the ice and snow, the American gunners quickly reloaded, and on Moulder's command, fired their second load of grapeshot. Window frames disintegrated altogether, rock chips flew from the stone casings, and the British soldiers inside flattened themselves on the floor.

Moulder shouted, "This time load with solid shot and try for those big doors. See if you can break the crossbar on the inside."

Once more the powder ladles were driven home, the grass to hold the gunpowder in place was rammed in, then the heavy cannonballs, followed by more grass to lock them in. The gunners seized the trails on the carriages and swung them slightly to bring them to bear directly on the seam where the two thick oak doors met, at the place where the cross-bar should be on the inside. The two men with the linstocks glanced at each other, nodded, and simultaneously ignited the powder at the touch holes. Both guns erupted in the same instant, and the cannonballs smashed through the seam where the doors met. One cannonball hit the crossbar and shattered it, and the doors began to slowly swing open. The other cannonball ripped through the doors, flew the length of the big assembly hall, and unbeknownst to the Americans, punched into the painting of King George II. It wasn't that it hit the painting so much as it was *where* it hit the painting. It caught the head of George II dead center! One moment he was benignly smiling down on his soldiers, and the next instant he was headless!

One white-faced British soldier glanced at the monarch and gasped. Others heard it and turned to stare. A strange, unexpected feeling began to creep through the soldiers as they peered at their great monarch, everything perfect, except that he had no head! Was it some sort of evil omen?

Outside, the Americans came charging at the doors, a shouting horde with bayonets and swords in hand, ready for the hand-to-hand fight that waited them inside the huge hall. They had nearly reached the doors when the first white flag appeared at a window, tied to a British musket. The Americans slowed, then stopped in utter amazement. The British were surrendering?

Another white flag appeared, and then the first of the British soldiers walked through the shattered doorway, out onto the frozen ground and into the frigid air, where he laid down his musket and raised his hands. Another came behind him, and another. Within minutes the entire contingent of British soldiers who had made their stand inside Nassau Hall had surrendered.

The American victory at Princeton on that wintry day was complete, in part due to the contribution of King George II, when he lost his head.

THE RIFLE SHOT THAT
TURNED THE WAR

FEBRUARY 25, 1777
WHITEHALL, LONDON, ENGLAND

★ ★ ★

Bᴿɪᴛɪꜱʜ ɢᴇɴᴇʀᴀʟ Jᴏʜɴ Bᴜʀɢᴏʏɴᴇ—the handsome, dashing darling of the London political and social whirls—leaned forward in the cab of the hack to peer out the window into the fog that had rolled up the Thames River in the wintry night of February 24, 1777, to lock London in a thick, bone-chilling morass that drenched all it touched with tiny, icy droplets. Sunrise had changed the freezing dead blackness to freezing dead gray.

Anxious, impatient, he thrust his head forward and narrowed his eyes, trying to penetrate the blanket that hid the familiar buildings on Duke Street, Cleveland Row, and Whitehall, where the highest and most powerful men on the face of the earth kept their offices, just steps away from Downing Street and the great palace where King George III now resided. After a time, the cab slowed and stopped, and the driver called down, "Whitehall, sir."

Whitehall! The office of Lord George Germain, secretary of state for the American Colonies and Burgoyne's longtime friend and ally in the treacherous game of world politics. With his reputation established as a fearless, competent leader of his famous Light Horse Brigade, the ambitious Burgoyne had yearned for the glory of being the British general who put down the rebellion now festering in the American colonies. He had adroitly requested his old friend to wrangle a parliamentary commission authorizing Burgoyne to take an army across the Atlantic to crush the rebellious Americans.

The day before, Burgoyne had received an electrifying message from Germain: "Be at my office tomorrow morning at ten o'clock."

Burgoyne stepped down from the cab onto the slick cobblestones, paid the driver, and trotted as fast as the fog and the icy cobblestones would allow to the huge double doors of the Whitehall building. He barged in, hat in hand, fumbling with the latch of his cape.

Two minutes later an orderly rapped on a door, opened it, and announced, "Mister Secretary, your ten o'clock appointment is here." Burgoyne stepped into the large, immaculate office. The two old friends shook hands warmly, spent little time on small talk, and Germain came directly to it.

"Yesterday, Parliament authorized your appointment to take an army to North America to bring George Washington and his army to heel. Lord North and King George have agreed."

Burgoyne was ecstatic. As long as history survived, John Burgoyne would be revered as the general who brought America back into the British Empire.

Germain continued. "Your commission authorizes you to proceed to Hudson Bay in Canada, then take an army south on the waterways: the Richelieu River, Lake Champlain, Lake George, then to the Hudson River. A force will join you at the mouth of the Mohawk River. You are to continue south to take Fort Ticonderoga and then Albany. General William Howe will meet you there. Your combined forces will then cut off New England from the middle and southern colonies, and subdue them in order. Do you understand?"

Burgoyne nodded emphatically, and Germain went on. "At the very earliest time possible, give me a written statement of what you will need."

"I'll have it in your hands within three days."

★　★　★

On February 28, Germain pored over Burgoyne's immaculately hand-written statement of what he would need, complete to the last detail: eight thousand regulars; one thousand Indians to be employed as scouts; two thousand Canadians, most of them with axes to cut timber, clear roadways, build bridges, and protect the critical supply line; one hundred thirty-eight cannon; and enough ships, barges, longboats, muskets, medicine, blankets, wagons, and horses to outfit the expedition.

Germain was startled at the last paragraph of Burgoyne's requisition. He had named the commanders he wanted: Major General Baron von Riedesel, an outstanding German officer to lead the mercenary German Hessians; and British brigadier general Simon Fraser, one of England's most competent and beloved military figures, to command a critical regiment.

By late May 1777, Burgoyne's huge armada had crossed the stormy Atlantic and was anchored in Hudson Bay, Canada. By

June 20, they had reached Lake Champlain, and Burgoyne was struggling with the realization that his worst enemies were the terrain through which they needed to pass and the hostile environment: dense forests of trees, their canopies so thick the blue sky disappeared; poisonous snakes; swarms of pesky, black flies; millions of malaria-bearing mosquitoes; thunder that shook the ground and cloudbursts that turned unnamed rivers and streams into raging torrents that could carry away a wagonload of flour in an instant.

He accepted it and pressed on, with troops beginning to show fatigue.

He pushed to the headwaters of the Hudson and continued south to Fort Ticonderoga. In a stroke of military genius, he had cannon hauled to the top of Sugar Loaf Mountain, a position from which he could with impunity blast the fort and all the Americans in it to rubble in two days. Recognizing the deadly peril represented by the big guns, American general Schuyler, in command at Fort Ticonderoga, abandoned the fort during the first week in July 1777, without firing a shot. When news of this astonishing victory reached London, the king frightened the queen out of her wits by bursting into her bedroom, shouting, "I have beaten them! I have beaten the Americans!"

Elated, on July 11, Burgoyne pressed on toward Albany. July 30, 1777, his army reached Fort Edward, where they were forced to pause for thirty days, waiting for supplies and mounts. When scouts reported that horses were available from the colonists at Bennington, not far to the southeast, Burgoyne sent German colonel Baum with six hundred Hessian troops to get them. On August 16, 1777, this German column was shattered and destroyed by an American force commanded by General John Stark, aided by some of General Schuyler's men from Fort

Ticonderoga. When Burgoyne sent four hundred more Hessians to rescue them, they were also lost—nine hundred men in one day!

Burgoyne began to realize the critical danger of his situation. Low on supplies, lacking horses to pull his five hundred wagons, men fatigued by the unending labor of cutting a road through the forest in the sweltering heat of summer, he knew he was vulnerable. Then he received a blow that sobered him even further. The force that was to join him at the mouth of the Mohawk River did not appear, and he learned that General Howe was not coming to join him in Albany. Worse, the Americans had sent General Horatio Gates and a huge command to stop him. Among them was General Dan Morgan, who commanded three hundred of the finest riflemen in the Continental Army, and Brigadier General Benedict Arnold, who was to be Gates's second in command. The Americans were gathering at a place called Saratoga, some thirty miles north of Albany, near the Hudson River.

Burgoyne faced the harsh reality. Fall was upon them, with winter coming. His fighting force had been reduced by battle losses, exhaustion, and sickness to three thousand two hundred regulars. His supplies and stores of ammunition were dangerously low. He still had time to retreat back to Fort Ticonderoga and admit he had failed; or, he could rapidly push on, hoping to cut through the Americans and take Albany. He could not bear the thought of failure.

September 19, 1777, dawned cold and foggy, with rain falling at Saratoga. Burgoyne launched his attack that centered on a place called Freeman's Farm. The battle raged until midmorning, when the fog lifted and American Dan Morgan led his riflemen into the heart of the British lines. By midafternoon the sun had turned the battlefield into a sweltering inferno, with Burgoyne's exhausted soldiers beginning to falter. At day's end, neither side could claim victory.

For the next sixteen days, the two opposing forces regrouped, sniping at each other, preparing for the next major engagement. By October 6, 1777, Burgoyne knew that with no help coming from either General Howe or General Clinton, he had to break out of the box he was in, or surrender.

On October 7, in a desperate attempt to escape, Burgoyne gave the order to attack, at a place called Bemis Heights, not far from Freeman's Farm. The Americans counterattacked, and the advantage shifted back and forth. By early afternoon, it was clear the British were slowly pushing the Americans back. Twice, General Benedict Arnold rode to the sound of the guns and returned to tell General Horatio Gates that he must order more men to take the huge cannon emplacement called the "Breymann Redoubt" that formed the center anchor of the British lines, or lose the battle. If the Americans could overrun the Breymann Redoubt, they would have clear passage behind the British lines and could force Burgoyne to surrender. But Gates failed to give the order, and refused to leave the safety of his headquarters three miles from the fight to see for himself.

Infuriated by Gates's refusal to take the fight to the British, and without permission from Gates, General Benedict Arnold led the Continentals forward again and again, cutting into the British lines, driving them back. Enraged by Arnold's unauthorized actions and recognizing that Arnold was rapidly becoming the shining star of the battle, Gates stripped Arnold of his command and ordered him to his tent for the duration. Trembling with outrage, Arnold reluctantly complied, and Burgoyne continued to push the Americans back.

By midafternoon Arnold could take no more. He strode out

of his tent, looked Gates in the eye, mounted his big black horse, Warren, and galloped to the sound of the guns with Gates shouting at him to stop. Arnold did not even look back. He gathered the scattered Americans as he rode, finally leading them in a head-on assault on the big Breymann Redoubt. His horse was shot out from under him, and still he charged, sword in hand, shouting, "Follow me, boys, follow me!" A musket ball smashed the bone in his upper left leg, and he went down. He refused help, ordering the men to leave him and storm the redoubt. They obeyed.

Six hundred yards to the east, British General Simon Fraser with his regiment of British regulars saw the Americans surge forward, saw them at the walls of the redoubt, saw the German defenses beginning to collapse, and realized the entire battle hinged on holding the big cannon emplacement. Instantly he started down a slight incline toward the Breymann Redoubt, shouting, "Follow me, my good men! To the redoubt! To the redoubt!"

Within ten feet of the front wall of the big redoubt, American General Dan Morgan glanced east and saw Fraser making his charge, and Morgan realized that the fate of the battle would be decided within the next three minutes. If Fraser's regulars flanked the Americans and broke their charge, the British would hold the redoubt and the battle would be lost. Fraser had to be stopped.

Instantly Morgan turned toward the west and shouted, "Tim!"

Timothy Murphy, a young Irishman, heard the voice of his beloved commander above the roar of the guns, and within two seconds located him next to the redoubt. He waved.

Morgan waved back and shouted again. "That man!" He pointed to Fraser. "He has to go!"

Through norrowed eyes, Tim studied the oncoming British charge until he located Fraser, and suddenly understood. The entire battle of Saratoga came down to one thing: stop Fraser, or it was lost.

Tim nodded his understanding to General Morgan, and within seconds was fifteen feet up a tall tree with his Pennsylvania long rifle.

Tim Murphy was perhaps the best rifle shot in the entire Continental Army. Born on the frontier, he had learned early in life the mode of forest warfare from the Indians. Of necessity, he became the master of his Pennsylvania long rifle. Of all the weapons in the American arsenal, the British feared those rifles most of all. The range and the accuracy of a Pennsylvania long rifle in the hands of one who understood it, was legendary.

With narrowed eyes, Tim studied Fraser, mounted, moving. He judged the distance at a long 450 yards—so far distant few men would believe a rifleman could make such a shot. He studied the drift of the smoke of the battle—a slight wind, north to south, following the flow of the river. He laid the barrel of the rifle over a tree branch, eared back the hammer, lined the sights, elevated the muzzle for distance, adjusted it slightly for the wind, and squeezed off his first shot.

The bullet cut hair from the mane of Fraser's horse, and Tim saw Fraser's aides swarm to his side, begging him to dismount and take cover. Fraser refused. Tim quickly reloaded, once again brought the rifle to bear, and fired his second shot.

With the instincts of a born rifleman, he knew the second shot was going to hit Fraser. He watched and sucked air through clenched teeth as the bullet struck Fraser full in the chest. Fraser buckled in the saddle, and his aides caught him as he fell, mortally wounded. Before he passed into unconsciousness, Fraser ordered his men to leave him and save the redoubt, but they refused. They would not leave their stricken commander. Fraser's charge slowed, then stalled, and then his regiment began a slow withdrawal in a vain attempt to save their beloved leader.

Lacking Fraser's reinforcements, the Germans were routed from the redoubt, with General Breymann and his staff among the casualties. When the redoubt fell, the Americans punched through to take up positions behind the British lines. With his battle positions now surrounded by Americans, Burgoyne made one last, futile, desperate attempt to retreat, but found himself trapped, with General Stark and his wild New Hampshire regiment behind him, Morgan and his riflemen in front, and Americans under General Schuyler, from Fort Ticonderoga, swarming all around.

October 17, 1777, after hasty negotiations, Burgoyne surrendered his entire force to General Gates.

The battle at Saratoga was over.

Pursuant to standard practice, Horatio Gates wrote a full report of the battle at Saratoga to the United States Confederation Congress. The report glowed with statements and claims leading Congress to believe it was the bravery, courage, and genius of Gates, not Benedict Arnold, which carried the day. The name Benedict Arnold did not appear in the report. Nor was the name Timothy Murphy mentioned.

Upon receipt of the report, Congress realized what they had. Quickly they sent the message across the Atlantic to Benjamin Franklin, currently the American ambassador to France, with access to the court of King Louis XVI, in Paris.

It took Franklin less than one minute to recognize what had to be done. The message was delivered to Comte de Vergennes, the political genius who presided in the French government and on whom King Louis depended for all major decisions. Vergennes was both stunned and ecstatic. Was it possible the ragtag

American rebels had beaten the world-renowned John Burgoyne? If so, was there reason to believe that the colonies might win their war with England? If that were possible, could France avenge her defeat by the British in 1762 by joining the Americans now and assisting them in beating the hated British?

Vergennes paced the floor for a time, caught in the dilemma of finding a way to keep the political balance between Spain, England, and France, while creating a way to covertly become the ally of the rebellious Americans. Vergennes succeeded. The secret alliance between France and the United States was signed February 6, 1778, and made public in the courts of France on March 20, 1778.

True to their commitment, the French sent seven thousand of their best infantry across the Atlantic, led by General Rochambeau, perhaps the finest officer in the French army, with orders they were to serve under the command of General George Washington. Then France ordered French admiral De Grasse, with thirty-eight of its best battleships, to also report to Washington.

August 1781, in a brilliant tactical maneuver and forced march from New York, Washington arrived at the small tobacco trading village of Yorktown, Virginia, at the mouth of the York River, where it flowed into Chesapeake Bay. With him were most of the Continental Army and the French infantry—all together about seventeen thousand seasoned troops. In Yorktown, attempting to refurbish his exhausted army of more than six thousand British regulars, was British general Charles Cornwallis. The British troops were protected by more than thirty British battleships under command of British admiral Graves, anchored in Chesapeake Bay. The British were stunned when the thirty-eight French battleships arrived to challenge them.

The sea battle between the opposing navies raged for several days, with the French finally driving the British out of Chesapeake Bay into the Atlantic Ocean, then down the coast to South Carolina. Back in Yorktown, Cornwallis was suddenly landlocked without the protection of the guns of the British navy. Then Washington, with the assistance of the French infantry, placed the British troops under an incessant cannon siege, day and night, and sealed the fate of Cornwallis's army when the Americans and the French stormed and took the last two cannon positions held by the British—redoubts numbers nine and ten. On October 19, 1781, General Cornwallis formally surrendered.

This marked the virtual end of the Revolutionary War. The humiliated British signed the final peace treaty on September 3, 1783.

Today, on the Saratoga battleground, is a large plaque honoring Timothy Murphy, the Irish rifleman who fired the shot that took down British general Simon Fraser and turned the battle for the Americans, brought the French into the war on the side of the patriots, and resulted in the ultimate victory of the United States. ·

BENNINGTON

★ ★ ★

THEY'RE COMING! THEY'RE COMING!"

In the sweltering New England heat of August 1777, the cry swept through the states of Vermont and New Hampshire like wildfire.

"British general John Burgoyne, with an army of Germans and Mohawks and Canadians and who knows who else, are coming right down Lake Champlain, and they're headed for the Hudson River! They mean to burn our towns and steal all our horses and cattle and everything we have and make us prisoners and then take Albany and then right on down to New York and get Gen'l Washington!"

Terrified Americans clamored, "How do we stop Burgoyne? What do we do?"

A frightened John Langdon, speaker of the General Court in New Hampshire, rose to his feet in session and declared, "I have three thousand dollars in hard money, and I will pledge my plate for three thousand more. I have seventy hogsheads of Tobago rum which shall be sold for the most it will bring, and all the money shall be delivered to the service of the state. If we succeed in defending our homes, I may be remunerated. If we do not, the property will be of no value to me. Our old friend John Stark, who so nobly sustained the honor of our state at Bunker's Hill, may be safely entrusted with the conduct of the enterprise, and we will check the progress of Burgoyne!"

Instantly others pledged what they could to the cause of defending their homes and small villages from the juggernaut British army that was marching steadily south from Canada, first on the Richlieu River, then Lake Champlain, then Lake George, and on to the headwaters of the mighty Hudson River, the great water highway of New England. Within two days, a breathless messenger banged on the door of New Hampshire militia general John Stark at his home and was invited to confront the general in his library.

"Sir, I've been sent to tell you. Gen'l John Burgoyne is coming from Canada. He has a big army. He intends burning all our homes and towns and taking Albany, and then on to New York to trap Gen'l Washington. John Langdon sent me to tell you."

"WHAT!" American general John Stark of the New Hampshire militia reared back in his library chair in utter shock. Tall, well-built, with a nose that was too long and dominated his long, narrow face, and with blue-grey eyes made of tempered steel that could stare a hole through a rock, John Stark was without doubt one of the toughest, smartest, most fearless leaders in the American military. His heroic leadership had distinguished him at

Bunker Hill and other battles, and there was scarcely a man in New Hampshire or Vermont who would not follow him into war—any war—without asking a single question. He was married to Molly Stark, one of the most beautiful women in New Hampshire.

Stark jerked to his feet and leaned forward, arms stiff, palms flat on his desk. "British general John Burgoyne and his British redcoats are *where?*"

"Well, sir, they're over on the Hudson River right now, coming south."

"With who?"

The messenger shook his head. "I never seen such a collection, sir. British red-coated regulars, some soldiers dressed in blue with great big boots—German I think—some Canadians, dressed in moccasins and buckskins, some Mohawk Indians, and a fair sprinkling of Americans who favor England. Strangest lookin' army I ever seen."

"Doing what?"

"Right now they're trying to cut their way through the forest a little northwest of Bennington. There's about eight or ten thousand of 'em, and they brung about five hundred wagons filled with everything you can imagine, and they got about fifty cannon, and women, and some children along. We got men over there pluggin' up the roads with cut-down trees and makin' it miserable for 'em, but Burgoyne's Burgoyne, and it looks like he means to keep on comin'."

Stark strode around his desk to a large map of New Hampshire and Vermont, mounted on one wall. "Well, we'll see about Mr. Burgoyne! You go back and tell John Langdon I'll have an army on the way within one week." He paused to study the map for a few moments, then smacked his finger down on the tiny village of Bennington, in Vermont. "Bennington! Our people have horses and cattle there, and Burgoyne's going to need both. He's bound to arrive at Bennington sooner or later, and I intend being there to meet him. Tell John Langdon!"

The messenger swallowed hard. "Uh . . . sir . . . it's most likely Gen'l Schuyler will want you at Stillwater. That's where he figgers to have the Continental Army."

Anger surged in Stark, and he shook his head violently. "I have no patience with the United States Congress and how they handle their Continental Army. I am bringing a New Hampshire militia army. I take my orders from the New Hampshire General Court, and no one else! We'll be at Bennington. Tell John Langdon. And on your way, stop and tell Colonel Seth Warner and his Green Mountain Boys to meet me there, at Bennington. Understand?"

The messenger stared at those blue-gray eyes that could transfix people. He licked his dry mouth and nodded. "Yes, sir. I'll tell Langdon and Colonel Warner."

To the west, on the Hudson River watershed, General John Burgoyne sat in his tent, lamenting the fact he had suddenly realized his army was in deep, deep trouble. He was commanding an assembly of men the like of which he had never seen before. There were thirty-seven hundred of his beloved British regulars, three thousand German Hessians who could not speak English, four hundred Mohawk Indians who loved British rum and the flamboyant uniform of the German cavalrymen, and about two hundred fifty Canadians and assorted nonmilitary civilians who still remained faithful to England. He also had brought fifty-two cannon on carriages that had to be drawn by horses. Because of his abiding love for luxury, he had also brought about four hundred wagons filled with necessary supplies for his men, but also dozens of cases of champagne, choice food delicacies, and a wardrobe of dashing, colorful uniforms for himself.

To move all of this, he had brought in excess of one thousand horses, only to learn that moving this number of men, with a few women and children, and the wagons, and the cannon, and the cavalry through the New England countryside was nigh onto impossible. At one time, with every man sweating to cut a road through forests so thick his men couldn't see twenty feet, and to build bridges across streams and swamps, he had been able to move a scant twenty miles in twenty days. One mile a day! In the process, he had lost more than a hundred horses, while his army had eaten most of its rations.

With his army stalled, he had cast about for an answer to the single most critical problem of finding sufficient horses for his wagons and his German cavalry. The Brunswick Dragoons—the German cavalrymen—were all but dead from exhaustion. Their uniforms included great cocked hats with a plume, leather coats, leather breeches, and the biggest boots in the history of military warfare. Those boots extended a foot above their knees, with thick, hob-nailed soles, and weighed twelve pounds per pair. Their huge spurs jingled. The swords they carried were monstrous! Mounted on horses, these cavalrymen were beautiful. On foot, walking like infantry, they were ridiculous! Those great boots and their uniforms had them sweating and their swords dragging behind them in the dirt.

Without the necessary horses, Burgoyne realized he may have to return to Canada and face the consequences of a court-martial for his unforgivable failure.

Not him! Not the great John Burgoyne! Desperately, he cast about for an answer to the single question, where could he find horses and food for his faltering army? He pored over his maps and listened intently to the reports of his patrols.

Bennington! Less than thirty miles to the east. Horses, cattle, wheat, dried fruits and vegetables—it was all there. And best of all, hadn't Colonel Skene assured him that the citizenry in the village was friendly to the British cause? They would be more than willing to supply the needy British army.

Quickly Burgoyne summoned Baron General von Riedesel and Colonel Friedrich Baum to his tent, both German officers in command of the German Hessians in Burgoyne's army. Baron von Riedesel spoke broken English. Colonel Baum spoke none.

Burgoyne issued his orders. Colonel Baum was to take command of a column that was to proceed to Bennington. The citizens in the settlement were friendly, loyal to England, and would be willing to sell him horses and supplies. He was to pick his column and leave as soon as possible. In any event, he was to preserve his column, since it was crucial that Burgoyne maintain full strength in his army. Baum was to proceed with all caution and stealth, "in secrecy."

Baum selected his men: 50 British marksmen, 100 German grenadiers, 300 Tories, Canadians, and Indians faithful to the crown, 170 dismounted Brunswick cavalrymen without their horses, 50 Brunswick infantry, and 90 local residents who all swore they were loyal to England. And, for reasons never explained by anyone, Baum brought along his German band. A German band? Moving through the forest in secrecy? That brought the total in his command to eight hundred. In mid-August, Colonel Friedrich Baum marched his nearly comical column of British, Germans, Mohawk, and Canadians west toward Bennington.

At that same time, General John Stark was marching his army

of fifteen hundred of his New Hampshire militiamen combined with five hundred more militiamen from Massachusetts and Vermont for a total of just over two thousand men, east toward Bennington.

Baum continued in fine style with his band blasting out German music,which could be heard for three miles. On the farms, local citizens stared at each other in utter confusion at what they were hearing. Flutes and bugles and drums? Had Judgment Day arrived? The citizens left their fields and came streaming to the road to stand in amazement at the sight of this strange army marching toward their town. Soon there were hundreds of citizens, gawking in disbelief, staring at Baum and his eclectic procession.

Within minutes Baum became uneasy, then alarmed. These citizens were supposed to welcome him, not stand in the trees near the road staring! Concerned, he ordered an officer to pick a few men and return to General Burgoyne with all possible speed, requesting that reinforcements be sent at once. Something was wrong.

When Burgoyne received the message, he instantly ordered Lieutenant Colonel von Breymann with six hundred fifty men and two cannon to hurry to the rescue of Colonel Baum. Breymann, for reasons never explained, chose to use parade-ground formations for his march to catch Baum, and his speed was cut to about one mile per hour.

On August 15, 1777, a chill, rainy day, Baum's force moving east nearly collided with Stark's force moving west along Walloomac Creek, not far from Bennington. Shaken to his foundations, Baum immediately took a position on the high ground of a low hill near the road and dug his men in against an attack.

That night Stark formed his plan. His men were dressed in the clothing of farmers and ordinary citizens, not soldiers. He instructed them to mount a white piece of paper in the hatband of their hats—the sign that they were faithful to England—to trick the Germans into thinking they were friendly. Then they were to quietly surround the hill in groups, not in military formations, and wait for his signal to attack the next morning.

At daybreak the following morning, August 16, 1777, Baum studied the clusters of men at the bottom of the hill, with the white paper patch clearly visible in their hatbands. General Burgoyne had assured him that men with white paper patches in their hatbands were to be considered friendly. Baum turned to Colonel Skene and asked him if his understanding was correct. Skene assured him that they were friendly. On this advice, Baum held his fire and waited for them to come up the hill to support him.

Then Stark rose from among his men, pointed his sword up the hill, and shouted the words that have made his name famous in the annals of American history:

"There, my boys, is the enemy! We will beat them, or Molly Stark sleeps a widow tonight!"

The Americans all fired their first volley at the same instant, and the blast rocked Baum and his men at the top of the hill. Instantly the Mohawk Indians and the civilians in Baum's command broke and ran pell-mell. The Brunswick cavalrymen fired their muskets in return, and the furious battle raged on into the morning. With their ammunition exhausted, the surviving German Brunswickers drew their huge swords and tried to cut their way through the Americans. The Americans, their blood hot, and led by John Stark, closed their lines and refused to let them through. They herded them back onto the top of the hill, and by noon had overrun them completely. Baum took a fatal wound and went down. The Germans remaining on their feet threw down their swords and raised their hands in surrender.

By noon it was over. Baum's entire command of eight hundred was dead or captured. Stark slid his sword back into its sheath and was giving orders to his men when one of his officers suddenly pointed.

"Sir, there's more of them coming!"

Breymann and his reinforcements from Burgoyne had arrived! All six hundred fifty men came swarming toward Stark's command.

At that same moment, Seth Warner and his small command arrived to reinforce Stark's men, and without a word they came charging into the side of Breymann's column like a swarm of angry bees. Stark whipped out his sword and led his men charging down the hill into the face of Breymann's column and set them back on their haunches. Between Stark's command and that of Seth Warner, they ripped Breymann's column into shreds. By dark, Breymann had lost two-thirds of his men and both his cannon, and his remaining men were in a full-out sprint back toward Burgoyne in a desperate attempt to escape the determined Americans.

By morning of August 17, 1777, General Burgoyne was struggling to grasp what had happened to his army.

They were nearly out of food and supplies. They were in the midst of a nearly impenetrable American forest. They were critically crippled by the loss of horses to pull their wagons and cannon and for their cavalry. And in one day, he had lost almost one thousand men, more than half of them his British regulars.

Burgoyne had no choice but to press on. He had been advised that he would be met by a British army led by General William Howe, at or near Albany. General Howe failed to appear.

At a place called Saratoga, not far north of Albany, the Americans met General Burgoyne in open battle. Crippled by lack of supplies and the loss of nine hundred men at Bennington and other failures, General Burgoyne was forced to surrender the remains of his army to the Americans on October 17, 1777.

The surrender was reported to Benjamin Franklin, America's ambassador to France. Franklin reported it to King Louis XVI, who was unable to believe the Americans had beaten the vaunted British general John Burgoyne. When the American victory at Saratoga was confirmed to him, King Louis committed and delivered to America about seven thousand French infantry under the command of French general Rochambeau and a sizeable portion of the French Navy under command of French admiral de Grasse. It was the French ships and infantry that made the final American victory possible at Yorktown on October 19, 1781, ending the war.

THE WEAK-MINDED
ENEMY HERO

★ ★ ★

HAN YOST SCHUYLER, BEARDED, DIRTY, disheveled, clad in old, worn clothing and battered shoes, sat silent at the plain, scarred table in the square, sparse room of the old stone building near Fort Dayton on the Mohawk River, not far from the place it emptied into the Hudson River to the east. Standing on either side of him were two guards of the American Continental Army, armed, ready, watching his every move, while the spectators in the crowded room murmured and gestured. Han Yost's dull eyes were shifting from the door to the table on the raised podium facing him, where the three-man panel of American officers appointed as judges, led by Colonel Marinus Willett, had just concluded his trial. He had been charged with being a Tory, loyal to England

118

and the king, and for repeated acts of treason against the thirteen American colonies. Only minutes earlier, the three officers had gone into another room to reach a verdict. It had not been three days since a board of American officers had conducted the trial of Lieutenant Walter N. Butler on the same charges, found him guilty, and sentenced him to death.

The door opened, and the three officers returned to their places on the podium while the guards prodded Han Yost to his feet. The murmuring stopped, and the room fell into charged silence.

Colonel Willett drew a deep breath before he spoke. "Han Yost Schuyler, it is the judgment of this court that you are guilty of high treason. We hereby sentence you to death by hanging."

People gasped and exclaimed, but Han Yost hardly changed expression. He glanced at his guards, searching their faces for some explanation of the sentence pronounced by Colonel Willett, trying with his feeble mind to understand what was happening. Han Yost was a coarse, ignorant, unschooled man, widely known to be mentally slow, considered by most to be insane.

The guards seized him roughly and pushed through the crowd to lock him in the small jail to await his hanging.

Within hours, American general Benedict Arnold, together with a small attachment of American officers and soldiers, marched into Dayton to present themselves to Colonel Willett at his headquarters.

"To what do I owe the welcome surprise of your arrival?" Willett asked.

General Arnold handed him a document. "I have been sent by General George Washington to do what I can in relief of Colonel Peter Gansevoort and his command of soldiers, who are under attack and cannon siege at Fort Stanwix, west of here, on the Mohawk River, near Lake Ontario. As you know, British colonel Barrimore M. St. Leger sent messengers to Gansevoort, demanding he surrender his command and the fort, or suffer destruction by a cannon siege."

"I am aware," Willett said. "Gansevoort sent back a message to St. Leger. He said he would fight to the last man. Surrender was out of the question."

Arnold nodded. "A very brave man." He paused, then went on. "I am told the British, together with a large gathering of Mohawk Indians led by Chief Joseph Brant, have the fort under siege. They intend overrunning Gansevoort, then sweeping this way down the Mohawk Valley to join General John Burgoyne on the Hudson River and help him capture Fort Ticonderoga, then Albany, and on to New York to attack General Washington. My orders are to save Colonel Gansevoort and our men at Fort Stanwix and to stop the British and the Mohawk Indians, if I can."

Colonel Willett shook his head. "If you hope to raise a fighting force here, I'm sorry to disappoint you. We have very few men available. We had scarcely enough to conduct a few trials in which we convicted some men of treason and sentenced them to hang."

Caught by surprise, Arnold asked, "Who? What are their names?"

"Lieutenant Walter N. Butler, for one, and a feeble-minded man named Han Yost Schuyler, for another."

"Han Yost?" Arnold exclaimed. "Isn't his mother the sister of our General Herkimer?"

"The same," Willett replied. "Do you know Han Yost?"

"I do," Arnold answered. "Where is he now?"

"In our jail. He's to be executed within two days."

Talk between the two officers continued until a short time later, when a knock came at the door and Willett's aide stepped inside. "Sir, a rather . . . coarse . . . woman is here, with a man.

Claims to be the mother of Han Yost Schuyler. They demand to speak with General Arnold."

Willett looked at Arnold, who nodded, and Willett said, "Show them in."

The woman's clothing was ragged and filthy, her face haggard and dirty, her hair snarled and matted, her language coarse and profane. The man with her was her son Nicholas. She wrung her hands while she pleaded and harangued with Arnold, begging for the life of her demented son, Han Yost. Arnold listened intently, then raised a hand and she stopped.

What she, and Willett, did not know was that Arnold had previously dealt extensively with the Iroquois Indians, among them, the Mohawk tribe. He had been fair with them and had earned their respect by his honesty and bravery. In their high regard for him, they had given him the name "Dark Eagle." In learning of their ways, Arnold had become aware of a peculiar superstition of the Iroquois. The Indians believed persons who were mentally retarded to be "special" and treated them with near reverence.

"I have a proposal," Arnold said sternly. "Bring Han Yost here."

Within minutes two guards brought the demented, disheveled man to the room, hands tied, grinning like a fool, staring blankly, first at his mother, then at General Arnold. Arnold took a deep breath and spoke.

"I will spare Han Yost's life on the following conditions: he must go to the British camp and tell them that I have arrived here with an army of three thousand. He must persuade them that I am marching on them immediately and will destroy them all. Their only hope is to retreat at once, cease their attack on Fort Stanwix, and abandon the Mohawk Valley. If they do not, they are doomed."

Willett peered at Arnold in amazement. Did he expect Han

Yost, a near-idiot, to make the British and the Mohawk believe such a wild, ridiculous story?

Arnold went on. "We will send Han Yost along with one of our half-breed Indians, Thomas Spencer, who will report the same story to the Mohawk Chief—Thayendanegea—Joseph Brant, and to the British commander St. Leger. We will also send two or three more of our Indians to arrive at their camp shortly after Han Yost and Thomas Spencer arrive, to tell the same story."

Arnold paused to gather his thoughts. "We'll keep Nicholas here, to be certain Han Yost does what he is told. If Han Yost fails, we will execute Nicholas in his place."

The woman gasped and clapped her hand over her mouth for a moment.

"Do you understand?" Arnold asked.

She nodded without speaking.

"Is it agreed?" Arnold pressed.

"It is agreed," the mother affirmed.

Arnold continued, "Han Yost will leave today. Before he goes, we will shoot holes in his coat and hat, and he can claim he made a desperate escape with us shooting at him. That should help persuade them that his story is true."

With General Arnold directing, the surprised guards hung the old, ragged coat on the branches of a nearby tree and shot a half dozen .60-caliber musket ball holes in it, as well as two in the nondescript hat worn by Han Yost. Then they watched as Han Yost and the half-breed Thomas Spencer disappeared into the forest, moving west up the Mohawk Valley at a trot, toward the Indian camp bordering that of the British. Minutes later, two other Indians, well-coached by Arnold, followed.

As Han Yost and Thomas Spencer came into sight of the sprawling Indian camp, they stooped and crept closer, stopping often to peer into the thick forest and listen for any sounds of Indian scouts, but there were none. Thomas tapped Han Yost on the shoulder, then pointed to the north. Han Yost nodded in agreement. He would come into camp from the north, while Thomas circled in from the south.

Half an hour later, Han Yost suddenly stood and trotted into the Iroquois camp, stumbling, breathing hard, mumbling to himself. Instantly he was surrounded by Iroquois warriors who recognized him and took him directly to Chief Joseph Brant.

Brant, who had spent a year in London as a welcome guest of King George III, and who spoke seven languages, confronted Han Yost, his face stern and impassive.

"What is your purpose in being here?" he demanded.

Han Yost appeared to take control of himself. He straightened and looked Brant directly in the eyes.

"The Americans were going to hang me because I helped the British. I escaped. They shot at me." He pointed at the bullet holes in his coat and hat, and loud murmuring erupted among the Iroquois as they reached to touch the holes made by the heavy musket balls. They rolled their eyes at each other, and nodded their heads knowingly.

Han Yost fell quiet, and Brant watched the slow-witted man search his brain for what he should say next. After a moment, Han Yost went on.

"Dark Eagle is at Fort Dayton. He is coming here. He will kill us all."

For a moment Brant gaped in disbelief. "You mean American general Benedict Arnold? How do you know this?"

"I was there. I saw him. I saw his army. He is coming."

Silence settled on the gathered Iroquois as Brant asked the critical question. "How many soldiers does Dark Eagle have?"

Han Yost licked dry lips, and it appeared he tried to think of the number, but his mind could not conceive it. Then he peered up into the trees of the surrounding forest and raised one hand to make a sweeping arc. "As many as the leaves in the trees."

Instantly, bedlam seized the Indian camp. Dark Eagle—Benedict Arnold—was coming with thousands of soldiers? As many as the leaves in the trees? They would overrun the entire Iroquois camp as well as the British command under Colonel St. Leger. There would be nothing left!

Joseph Brant raised both hands and shouted them back under control. "Bring this man. He must tell his story to the British colonel St. Leger."

Brant led his Indians to a council with Colonel St. Leger, who stood in utter shock as Han Yost once again blurted out his message. At that moment, Iroquois scouts interrupted to bring in Thomas Spencer, the half-breed. He was sweating, breathing heavily, as though from dodging and running through the forest.

St. Leger turned to him. "For what reason have you come?"

"I have been in Fort Dayton. Dark Eagle is there. He is on his way here to destroy this entire camp. I escaped and came to warn you."

St. Leger's mouth dropped open. "How many soldiers?"

"Above three thousand. Maybe close to four thousand. They are only hours away."

St. Leger's mind went numb, and he stood mute while the Iroquois burst into shouts of fear and anger. Han Yost had told the truth! They must run! Retreat! The British had promised them the scalps of the Americans at Fort Stanwix and many muskets and much plunder—lies—all lies! If they stayed another minute, they would all be massacred! Their only chance was to flee!

"Stop," bellowed St. Leger. "We have only the word of these

two men, and nothing more. We have not heard from our scouts. We do not know that these men have told us the truth. If you will stay, I will give you all the rum you want."

The Indians quieted at the promise of rum, and at that moment the last two Indians coached and sent by Benedict Arnold came trotting into camp, winded, appearing frightened.

"They're coming," they exclaimed. "Dark Eagle and his army. We don't know how many—close to four thousand. Just hours away."

Now there was no controlling the terrified Iroquois. They broke and ran, stopping in the British camp long enough to steal all the liquor they could find and most of the British supplies and to attack the red-coated soldiers who tried to prevent them. In minutes, the entire fighting force of Iroquois warriors was gone, together with several British soldiers, fleeing northwest to Lake Ontario.

Colonel St. Leger stood rooted while he struggled to accept what had just happened. He had lost the Iroquois warriors, a major portion of his fighting force. The few hundred remaining red-coated regulars would have no chance against three thousand American soldiers under the leadership of Benedict Arnold, coming in from the east, combined with the force of Colonel Gansevoort in Fort Stanwix in the west. If Arnold was only hours away, he did not have one minute to spare.

He gave the fateful orders.

"Retreat! Leave everything but your muskets and gunpowder and what food supplies you can gather in your knapsacks. Fall into company formation immediately. We leave in fifteen minutes on a forced march to Oswego."

On August 23, 1777, General Benedict Arnold left Fort Dayton with a handful of soldiers, moving west up the Mohawk

River, to do what he could in relief of the Americans at Fort Stanwix. He had been gone less than half a day when his advance scouts brought in a messenger from Colonel Gansevoort, who commanded the fort.

"Sir," the messenger said, "the British ended their siege on Fort Stanwix and suddenly disappeared, along with all their Iroquois warriors. Colonel Gansevoort does not know why. He only knows that he and his command, and the fort, are presently safe."

Dark Eagle smiled. "Carry a message back to your commander. Give him my congratulations on duty well done. Tell him the reason the British and Mohawk disappeared is a story he will find hard to believe. "

When the Iroquois Indians deserted British colonel St. Leger and St. Leger and his command of soldiers were forced to abandon any attempt to meet General Burgoyne coming down the Hudson River, it left General Burgoyne without a significant part of the fighting force that was intended to take Albany and then go on down the Hudson River to New York. Without his full fighting force, General Burgoyne's army was weakened. Determined Americans met him at the place called Saratoga, just above Albany, where Burgoyne was defeated and surrendered his entire army. It was a major turning point in the Revolutionary War.

The best historians have pondered what would have happened at the battle of Saratoga if Burgoyne had had the full force of the missing British regulars and the Iroquois warriors from the Mohawk Valley, all of whom abandoned Burgoyne because of the actions of the weak-minded Han Yost Schuyler, one of the enemy.

The Quaker Lady Who
Saved Washington

December 2, 1777
Second Street, Philadelphia, Pennsylvania

★ ★ ★

LYDIA DARRAGH PARTED THE LACE drapes covering the front windows of her modest home on Second Street in the city of Philadelphia, and in the shadows of approaching dusk, peered across the street to the home of her longtime friend and neighbor, John Cadwalader. Middle-aged, five feet tall, just under one hundred pounds, dressed in the austere style of Quakers, Lydia noted that her hand trembled as she stood transfixed, intently watching the front door of her neighbor's home.

Too well did she remember the morning of September 26, 1777, when British general Howe marched into Philadelphia with his army and at bayonet-point forced hundreds of Americans to vacate their homes because he needed housing for his British soldiers. He had forced John Cadwalader out into the streets and declared that home to be his headquarters. Minutes later he sent his adjutant general, Major Jean Andre, to tell Lydia that she and her Quaker husband would also have to surrender their home, since General Howe would need it for private conferences with his officers. It was only after Lydia tearfully pled with her second cousin, a British officer named Barrington who by pure chance was on the staff of General Howe, that she received permission to remain in her home, provided she would reserve her library for private meetings whenever Howe required it. She had agreed and sent her two young children away to stay with relatives until the day the British would leave Philadelphia.

Each day she had watched the Cadwalader home, nervous, frightened, not knowing when to expect the British to come marching across the street to bang on her door and demand use of her library. Today, in the frost and cold of a wintry December, she had watched several British officers with large tricorns and spirals of gold braid decorating their capes arrive at the Cadwalader home in the afternoon. The sun had set, and deep dusk had now darkened the streets, and they were still inside.

They have been there too long, she thought as she peered out into the gloom of approaching darkness. *They're discussing something fearful. Something important.*

Then, through the parted curtains, she saw the front door across the street open, and in the shaft of light she watched Major Andre hunch his shoulders against the cold and trot across the street to rap loudly on her front door. For a moment she froze in dread, then hurried to open the door a scant six inches.

"Yes?" Her voice was trembling.

"Madam," Andre announced, "General Howe will require use of your library this evening for a private conference."

Twenty minutes later, General Howe and seven of his officers were gathered around her library table with the door to the room closed and bolted. Frightened, but obsessed with her need to know their intentions, Lydia silently positioned herself in a linen closet adjoining the library and closed her eyes to listen through the wall. Minutes became an hour, then two hours, as she stood transfixed, catching snatches of words and half-sentences. It was past nine o'clock when she suddenly realized what they were planning.

In two days, General Washington is going to move the Continental Army from Whitemarsh to a new location. The British intend taking five thousand troops and cannon to trap him when he is defenseless on the road and destroy him! Her eyes widened in fear. *My son! Charles! He is with Washington at Whitemarsh! They mean to do harm to my Charles! They must be stopped!* She clapped her hands over her mouth to stifle an outcry.

When the sounds of chairs being pushed back from the library table reached her, she quickly left the linen closet and fled to her bedroom, where she hurriedly pulled her nightcap over her head and slipped into her bed with her back to the door. When Major Andre came to tell her the British officers were leaving, she lay perfectly still, eyes closed, breathing deeply and slowly. He closed the door and left the house, convinced she was sound asleep.

Through the night she paced the floor in the dark of her bedroom, afraid to light a lantern. *What can I do? A lone Quaker woman against the British army?*

Slowly, a plan formed in her mind. With the morning sun shining cold and chill in the east, she dressed in her warmest winter coat and bonnet and hurried out the door into the freezing December air. In her hand she carried an empty flour sack. She crossed the street to the headquarters of General Howe, entered through the great double doors, and stopped at the desk of the orderly in charge.

"Sir," she said timidly, holding up the empty flour sack, "I am Lydia Darragh. My home is across the street. I am out of flour. I need your permit to leave the city to get more at the Frankford Mill, north of town."

Five minutes later she smiled and thanked the officer for the permit, which she had to have before the British sentries would allow her to leave the city and return.

An hour later she laid her permit and the empty flour sack on the table at the Frankford Mill, and ten minutes later she folded the permit into her pocket, took the filled sack onto her back, and struggled out the door. She did not turn south, back toward Philadelphia, but rather north, toward Whitemarsh. She hid the sack of flour in a clump of cedars and hurried on in the crusted snow and ice that remained from the last snowstorm. She had traveled nearly two miles before she saw a log building with a sign, "Rising Sun Tavern." She was within a hundred yards of the tavern when sounds of an oncoming horseman reached her from behind and she turned.

The rider was Thomas Craig, a soldier in the Pennsylvania Militia and a beloved childhood friend of her son Charles!

She raised both her hands, and Craig reined his bay mare to a stop, startled to see Lydia Darragh so far from the city, and alone.

"Thomas," she exclaimed. "The Almighty has sent you."

Craig dismounted, and in stunned amazement listened as the story poured out of Lydia in a torrent of words and gestures.

She stopped speaking, and Thomas spoke slowly to ask, "Let me be clear, Mother Darragh, General Howe intends trapping General Washington and the Continental Army on the road as he leaves Whitemarsh tomorrow? And Charles is among them?"

"Yes! Yes! You have to warn them!"

Craig swung back onto his mare. "Mother Darragh, General Washington will know this before noon."

She watched the young man wheel his horse and set his spurs, and soon Craig had disappeared at a gallop.

With a silent prayer in her heart, Lydia turned back south. She retrieved her sack of flour from the cedar grove, and with it on her back, trudged back to her home.

It was four days before the news reached Philadelphia.

General Howe and his five thousand troops had quietly, carefully formed their ambush on the road leading away from Whitemarsh and had waited for General Washington and his army to march squarely into the trap. He did not come. They waited for two days before they realized that somehow, someone had reached Washington to tell him of the ambush, and the Old Fox had escaped once again.

Though he tried, the furious General Howe never did discover who it was that had saved the Americans and left the proud British redcoats frustrated.

It was his adjutant general, Jean Andre, who had the last word. "One thing is certain. The enemy had notice of our coming, were prepared for us, and we marched back like a parcel of fools. The walls must have ears."

VON STEUBEN—
PROFANITY AND SALVATION

FEBRUARY 1778
VALLEY FORGE

★ ★ ★

HEAVY, CRUSTED SNOW COVERED THE frozen ground, and
there was thick frost on the window panes of the two-story stone
residence that had become the headquarters of General George
Washington in the winter camp of the Continental Army on the
banks of the Schuylkill River. It was February in the bleak, harsh
winter of 1778, at the place called Valley Forge, Pennsylvania,
about twenty-six miles from Philadelphia, where Washington had
brought the ragged, tattered remains of his army to maintain sur-
veillance of British general William Howe and his red-coated
army, which had occupied Philadelphia for the winter. There was
a nearly humorous irony in the name "Valley Forge," since the
area had no valley and no forge. The land had some slight rises

here and there, but no real valley, and the British had burned the forge, owned by the Isaac Potts family, the preceding September.

General Washington was seated at the desk in his private office, poring over the endless reports and paperwork that are required to maintain an army, when the knock came at his door.

"Enter."

His adjutant stepped into the room and closed the door, and instantly Washington saw the baffled, puzzled expression on his face.

"What is it?"

"Sir," the adjutant began, "there is an officer here wearing a uniform I've never seen before, with an interpreter. Says he's from Prussia or Germany, I don't know which. He says he has a letter from Benjamin Franklin that he must deliver to you personally. His name is Von Steuben. Friedrich Wilhelm Von Steuben. I've never heard of him."

Washington sat forward in his chair. "Benjamin Franklin sent him?"

"That's what he says."

"Is he or his interpreter armed?"

"No, sir. Both in uniform, but no arms I can see."

Washington reflected for a moment. "Bring them in, and remain here until we know what this is about."

"Yes, sir." The adjutant turned on his heel, and two minutes later ushered the two visitors into Washington's office. The two men faced Washington's desk at full attention, heels together, chests thrust forward, chins drawn in tight. Washington stood and also came to attention. They saluted, he returned the salute, and gestured to the two hard-backed chairs facing his desk.

"Please be seated, gentlemen."

They understood the gesture, and each settled stiffly onto the nearest chair while Washington sat down and for a brief moment studied both men. The officer, rather short, stout, with a noticeable air of no-nonsense surrounding him like a cloak, had his chin up, staring back at Washington. The interpreter, taller, wiry, with the look of a man who worried too much, sat waiting for the conversation to begin.

"To what do I owe the pleasure of this visit?" Washington inquired.

The interpreter spoke to his superior, listened, and interpreted from German to English.

"I am Friedrich Wilhelm Von Steuben. I am a Prussian officer, trained in the army of Frederick the Great. I have come to offer my services to the American Continental Army. I am here on the advice of Benjamin Franklin, who is the American ambassador to France. I visited with him in Paris, where he gave me a letter and recommended I deliver it to you personally."

The man drew a sealed letter from inside his tunic and offered it to Washington, who took it, broke the seal, and for more than one minute read it in silence. He studied the signature carefully, then read the brief letter again. Then he raised his eyes to Von Steuben.

"Ambassador Franklin recommends you to me as an officer who may be of assistance to the Continental Army. Do I understand this correctly?"

"Yes. I would be honored."

"This letter from Ambassador Franklin states you were a German general. Is that true?"

"No, sir. I was a captain, not a general."

Washington smiled at what he instantly recognized as a classic Ben Franklin exaggeration.

"What service do you feel you might render?"

"I can train this army, sir."

Washington leaned forward, eyes narrowed as he studied the blank face and the unflinching eyes.

"Train the army?"

"Yes, sir. Train the army."

Washington drew a deep breath. *Franklin must have seen something in this man or he wouldn't have sent him. What can be lost by giving him his chance?*

"Captain Von Steuben," Washington said, "may I invite you to take quarters in this building for a few days. I will authorize you to inspect this camp in any way you wish, for as long as you find it necessary. The camp extends eleven miles on the banks of the river. When you are finished, report back to me with a plan that you think will improve this army. I will make a decision after I have considered your plan. Is that agreeable?"

"Ja!"

Washington took quill and parchment to draft written orders, stood, and handed the folded paper to Von Steuben. They exchanged salutes, and Von Steuben marched out of the room, followed by his interpreter. Washington's adjutant closed the door and turned back to Washington, shaking his head.

"I never saw anything like that in my life, sir."

Washington smiled. "Nor have I."

For two days Von Steuben rode in a carriage, up and down the camp, one end to the other, stopping incessantly to study everything in sight and silently listen to the men while he watched their faces. The morning of the third day he was in Washington's office, again facing the general with his interpreter. He held a document of several pages in his hands as he spoke.

The interpreter read from Von Steuben's written report: "I have never seen an army in the conditions I see here. Your men are starving. No food. Sick. No medicine. Freezing. Removing their own frozen toes with pocket knives. Most with no shoes. On picket duty at midnight barefooted, standing on a felt hat to keep their feet from freezing to the ground. Dressed in summer clothing. Living in quarters that allow the wind and snow to come through the walls. Muskets out of repair and no way to make them serviceable. Almost no ammunition, no gunpowder. No military bearing. A wagon passes through camp every morning picking up those who have died of starvation and freezing and sickness during the night—six hundred of them every month. I have seen less than twenty men who understand the meaning of the term *soldier*. There is not an army in Europe that would remain in service under such condition. They would simply pack their knapsacks, pick up their muskets, and go home. I do not—cannot—understand what is holding these men here."

He handed the document back to Von Steuben, who laid it on Washington's desk and said in broken English: "There is my written report in which you will find the detail on all I have said."

Washington leaned back in his chair. The expression on his face had not changed.

"What do you propose you can do to assist us in our problems?"

Von Steuben leaned forward, eyes alive, voice firm. "I can train them, sir. I can make soldiers of them. I cannot provide food, or medicine, or weapons, but I can make them into an army."

It was in that moment Washington saw what Benjamin Franklin had seen in this rather small man. He reflected for a moment, then asked, "What compensation will you expect for your services?"

136

"Nothing, until you approve of what I have done. Then we will agree on the compensation."

For one split second Washington stared in disbelief. Then he leaned forward. "I will draft your commission today. You will begin at once. As for what is holding these men here, may I suggest it is the fact they have had a taste of freedom, and they cannot let go of it."

The following morning, bearing his commission, with his own interpreter and an American interpreter on either side of him, Von Steuben called a council of the officers in command of all twelve regiments of the American army.

"Each of you will select ten men from your regiment to report to me every morning at eight o'clock on the drill field. I will train them, and then they will train each of your units."

The following morning, one hundred twenty men assembled on the drill field, some arriving as late as twenty minutes past eight o'clock. They stood in groups, muskets in hand, waiting while Von Steuben paced, waiting for the late ones.

"You are late," Von Steuben announced in loud, clipped words. "You will be on time, or you will be punished. Now fall into rank and file."

Their lines were crooked, and the men held their muskets in any way they wished.

"Your lives will depend on your muskets! You will treat them with respect. They belong on your right shoulder. Your lines are crooked. They will be straight. You will be one arm's length apart—exactly twenty-eight inches. Or you will be punished."

The Americans stared in defiance while Von Steuben marched up and down the lines, pushing one soldier backward, another forward, positioning them at the exact intervals he dictated, straightening their muskets on their shoulders, thrusting his nose within six inches of theirs as he barked his orders in German with the American interpreter giving an instant translation, white-faced, horrified at the mutiny he expected at any moment.

On the fourth day, the Americans were still showing their utter contempt for what they took as the sheer idiocy of intervals and heels together, toes pointed outward, chests out, chins in, lines perfectly formed. They were in this army to fight the British! That meant their real value lay in how well they could shoot and use the bayonet in battle. Intervals? Straight lines? On the battle-field? Who was this officious little German who strutted about, purveying such nonsense?

None of the Americans knew that every morning Von Steuben was out of his bed at exactly three o'clock. He first dressed, drank a cup of scalding, strong black coffee, then sat at his desk, steadily writing a manual of arms, first in German, then with painstaking accuracy translating it into English to be passed out to every officer in the Continental Army.

On the fourth morning, when he saw the stubborn faces and eyes of the one hundred twenty men on the frozen drill field, Von Steuben exploded. He ripped into them with a voice that stopped soldiers and officers two hundred yards distant, cursing them with profanity that shook both interpreters to the core. For minutes he blasted away, shaking his fist, pacing back and forth in front of them, while they stared at him, stunned into shocked silence. When Von Steuben finished he turned to his own interpreter.

"Tell them!" he exclaimed.

For a moment the interpreter stood in silence, then asked in a voice that croaked, "Uh . . . sir . . . you want me to repeat every-thing you just said?"

"Ja! Ja! Every word. Exactly as I said it."

The American interpreter peered pleadingly at the German interpreter.

"Yes, sir," the German interpreter said and launched into a full translation of every word Von Steuben had said.

For the first ten seconds the Americans stood without moving a muscle, unable to believe the river of profanity that was flowing from the interpreter. After half a minute, one American ducked his head and grinned. After one full minute, three or four others were grinning. After three minutes, one of them chuckled out loud. Before the interpreter finished, most Americans were grinning and chuckling. In their lives, they had never heard such a torrent of profanity.

At the midpoint of the interpreter's tirade, Von Steuben was studying the demeanor of the Americans, puzzled at their grins and chuckles. Didn't they understand? Did they not realize they were being insulted in the strongest language he could deliver? When the interpreter concluded, Von Steuben ordered them into their rank and file lines, drilled them until noon, and returned to his quarters, deep in thought. It was after evening mess, while he was sitting in his chambers, still struggling to understand the American soldiers' response, when the words of General Washington came to his mind.

"As for what is holding these men here, may I suggest it is the fact they have had a taste of freedom, and they cannot let go of it."

It struck him with a force he had never felt before. *Of course! Of course! The Americans have learned to think for themselves! Not like the Europeans! The Americans are their own men! How could I have missed it? How could I have missed it?*

He sat at his desk in the yellow light of the lamp, searching for the words that would make the lesson simple, and slowly they came.

In Europe, you tell a soldier to do a thing, and he will do it. In America, you tell a soldier to do a thing, and then you tell him why! And when he understands why, THEN he will do it!

He slept soundly that night and arose at 3:00 A.M. as usual. Dressed, he sipped at his steaming coffee and began correcting the manual of arms he had been working on each morning. At 8 o'clock he was on the drill field, waiting for the Americans to fall into rank and file. By ten minutes past the hour, they were there. He stood before them and spoke loudly.

"In battle, habit and discipline alone will save your lives. Habit and discipline are what you do without thinking—what you do because you have trained yourself to do it. When General Washington orders you to begin an attack at 8:00 A.M., he is depending on you to begin the attack at 8:00 A.M. for good reason. It could be that he has ordered his artillery to begin firing at precisely 8:00 A.M. to give you support, or it could be that he has ordered another regiment to begin a flanking maneuver on the enemy at exactly 8:00 A.M. You may not know the reason, but that is not your concern. Your concern is to attack at exactly 8:00 A.M., as ordered."

Von Steuben paused and for long moments peered into the faces of the men nearest him. For the first time he saw the question in their eyes, and could see their minds working, waiting. He continued.

"My orders are to prepare you for the battlefield. Prepare you to attack at exactly 8:00 A.M. if that is what your officers require. To teach you habits and discipline that will save your lives and the lives of the men next to you in battle. For that reason, I hope to teach you the habit of being where you are ordered to be, on time. Your orders are to be in rank and file on this drill field at 8:00 A.M. daily. Am I asking too much?"

For the first time, Von Steuben saw the dawn of understanding come into the eyes and faces of the Americans.

Von Steuben went on. "I have ordered you to be in rank and file, lines straight, at twenty-eight-inch intervals. The reason is this. As you move into battle, each of you must have sufficient room to move and turn, according to need. If you are crowded together, you can not do that. Some day, straight lines and correct intervals will save you or the man next to you."

Again Von Steuben paused, then went on.

"May I now give you orders. Fall into rank and file at the proper interval."

They moved slowly, but when they finished, the one hundred twenty poorly clothed and disheveled men were in lines that were straight, at perfect intervals, heels together, muskets on their shoulders, chests out, chins in, eyes straight ahead. Wordlessly, Von Steuben walked up and down the lines, face aglow in the freezing morning air. For the first time, morning drill was very nearly flawless. Thoughtful men responded to orders without question.

At noon, after they were dismissed, the soldiers gathered into groups to return to their regiments. One of them chuckled and said to the others, "You know that string of profanity we got from him yesterday?" The others nodded their heads, grinning, and he continued. "The longer I think about it, the more I admire it. Why, that profanity was so beautiful it ought to be in the Bible."

Throughout the winter months and into the spring, Von Steuben spent endless hours drilling the men, disciplining them, teaching them battle tactics and use of weapons. The bond between him and the Continental Army became legendary. By the month of May, Von Steuben had picked up enough English to personally conduct the military drills. While the men were drilling, he marched with them, calling, "Left , right, left, right, vun, doo, dree, foh." The day came when the entire command echoed him, "Left, right, left, right, vun, doo, dree, foh," and uncontained laughter rang over the drill field.

So proud was Von Steuben of the discipline he had injected into the new Continental Army that he ordered one day in June to put on a huge demonstration of their flawless skill in all the maneuvers he had taught them, to be followed by a great banquet for the officers.

He was surprised at the response. "Sir, we can't attend a banquet. Most of us don't have pants that are fit to wear at such a gathering."

Von Steuben didn't hesitate. He sent out new invitations to every officer to attend his banquet, "sans culots." The entire command burst into laughter when they understood the translation. The officers were to attend "without pants."

And they did! In the history of the United States army, no banquet has ever equaled the raucous, uproarious good time those officers had when they appeared at the banquet, wearing nothing from the waist down except their underwear!

It was the army trained by Von Steuben that engaged a British force near a small town in New Jersey, at a place called Monmouth, on June 28, 1778, for their first test in battle. With Von Steuben and the other general officers mounted, shouting the orders, the Americans attacked the British column commanded by British general Clinton. The stunned British were unable to believe their eyes as the Americans maneuvered efficiently, responding instantly to every order they received. Von Steuben was seen nearby, mounted and standing tall in the stirrups, shouting orders, and repeating to himself again and again, "Mein kinder, mein kinder." My children, my children! Shortly before midnight the British withdrew, conceding the battlefield to the victorious Americans. Von Steuben's army had won! They had met the best England had to offer in open battle, and they had won!

Von Steuben remained with the Continental Army through the balance of the Revolutionary War, rising to the rank of major general. In the final great battle at Yorktown in October 1781, he was in command of one of the main divisions of Washington's army. The book of orders and regulations he had worked on so faithfully during the dark days at Valley Forge was published in a blue cover under the title *Regulations for the Order and Discipline of Troops of the United States.* It became the official "Blue Book" of orders and regulations for use by the United States military and remained in use until World War II. It is still available at West Point, Annapolis, and the Air Force Academy.

Von Steuben never returned to his native Prussia. He applied for American citizenship in 1784, and in March of that year, by an act of the Pennsylvania legislature, became an American citizen. He died November 28, 1794, and at his request, is buried in America.

It has been said that no man did more for the Continental Army than Friedrich Wilhelm Von Steuben, save and except George Washington.

LADY WASHINGTON

FEBRUARY 10, 1778
VALLEY FORGE, PENNSYLVANIA

★ ★ ★

IN THE FREEZING MORNING AIR OF FEBRUARY 10, 1778, Martha Custis Washington, plump, scarcely five feet tall, face plain and round, blue eyed, quiet, industrious, sat bundled in her coach as it lurched over the frozen, rock-hard ruts and the ice and snow of Gulph Road that wound through the Pennsylvania forest to the camp of the Continental Army at Valley Forge on the Schuylkill River. The vehicle jolted past the divisions commanded by General Poor on the left and General Glover on the right, and by the old schoolhouse at the junction of Gulph Road and Baptist Road. On her orders, the coach's curtains had been thrown open so she could see the country and the soldiers as she passed. With a blanket drawn about her legs and feet, she sat wide-eyed, appalled at the sight of the hollow-cheeked, scarecrow soldiers with sunken eyes. Those who recognized the coach came to attention, paying silent respect as it lurched on.

Frozen, half-decayed carcasses of dead horses were scattered about the camp. A wagon rolled by, traveling in the opposite direction, and Martha gasped when she beheld arms and legs above the sideboard, fingers and toes black, frozen solid. She turned to peer into the wagon bed after it had passed, and saw the bodies of fourteen men who had frozen to death the previous night.

The coach crossed Inner Line Drive, passed the intersection with Port Kennedy Road, and rumbled on to the junction with Valley Road, where it turned right. The driver hauled the horses to a stop in front of the Potts home, where General George Washington, her husband, had established his headquarters. The driver climbed to the frozen ground and helped Mrs. Washington step from the coach as her husband came rapidly down the cobblestone walk from the two-story home, vapor trailing his bare head. There was a light in his eyes as the general embraced his beloved Martha, kissed her on the cheek, and took her arm to lead her back inside the home, to a large chair before the fireplace in the library. By his orders, they were to be given time to talk undisturbed.

It was one o'clock when they sat down in the plain, austere dining room to their midday meal of roasted mutton and potatoes. They bowed their heads in silent thanks before Washington carved the mutton and they began to eat. Martha glowed at the sight of him, relishing her simple meal, as though he had never tasted such cooking before.

With the meal finished, Martha spoke of the heartrending

conditions she had observed in the camp. "I've never seen men in such terrible living conditions," she said.

Washington met her with his direct gaze. "The worst I have ever seen. We lack everything on which an army depends. Food, blankets, clothing, shoes, money, wagons—everything."

She leaned forward and placed her hand on his forearm. "Is there something I can do?"

He remained silent, thoughtful for a time. "Yes. Go out among the soldiers as you always do. You can do tremendous good."

"May I visit the hospital this afternoon?"

"I will have Colonel Alexander Hamilton escort you," he answered.

It was just past two o'clock when Alexander Hamilton assisted Martha into her coach, took his seat opposite her, and pointed down to a shallow iron box with many small holes on the lid, sitting on the floorboards.

"Madam, the foot warmer is filled with hot bricks. Your feet will remain warm."

Martha smiled her thanks, placed both feet on the warmer, and wrapped a blanket about her legs as the driver reined the four horses onto Gulph Road. They turned onto Port Kennedy Road where General McIntosh's division was camped, passed a rifle pit where inexperienced soldiers were being taught the use of the musket, and soon stopped before an old wooden structure. The horses blew and stamped their impatience as Hamilton helped Lady Washington from the coach and walked her inside the huge, cold, dimly lit building. The sole source of heat was a stove in one end.

"This was once a barn," Hamilton explained. "The stalls and stanchions have been removed to make room for the beds. It is not our general hospital. We use it because the larger hospital is already filled to capacity."

The stench of filthy bodies and decaying human flesh and the sounds of human beings in agony flooded over them. For several seconds neither of them could breathe, and both covered their noses and mouths with a hand while they waited for their eyes to adjust to the twilight inside the long room.

Makeshift cots of wood and canvas were placed everywhere one would fit on the bare dirt floor. Blankets lay beneath the cots, and emaciated, sunken-eyed men lay on the blankets, some with raging fever, others with fingers or toes or feet or hands missing. Most had open sores on their bodies and in their beards. Six women in the uniform of nurses, harried and exhausted, walked among the beds, doing what little they could to relieve the pain and suffering of the men. A weary doctor came forward to meet Hamilton and Martha.

Appalled, Martha asked him, "Have these men enough food?"

The doctor shook his head. "Scarcely enough to keep them alive. Half of them would recover within days if we could feed them properly."

Hamilton led Martha back out into the freezing air and assisted her into the coach. It lurched forward, jostling, wrenching over ruts and ridges frozen hard as stone, to the larger general hospital. The driver hauled the horses to a stop, and Hamilton assisted Martha out, down onto the frozen ground, where all three of them stopped, staring at a wagon backed up to the big doors. The tailgate was down, and while they watched, two soldiers came through the door, each carrying one end of a stretcher on which the shriveled remains of a dead soldier lay. They heaved the body into the wagon on top of twelve other bodies, fastened the tailgate, and the driver gigged the horses to a walk. Martha watched, her face set, eyes filling with tears as it rumbled away.

Inside the massive room of the hospital, the odors of putrid flesh and the sounds of men in agony were beyond belief. A haggard nurse quickly confronted Martha and Hamilton.

"You must leave! We have typhus and diphtheria in this room. Perhaps smallpox. You cannot stay!"

"I'm so sorry," Martha exclaimed. "I did not mean to interfere. I am Martha Washington."

"Oh," gasped the nurse. "I didn't know."

Martha peered at her. "Child," she said, "you're shaking. Is something wrong?"

"No. It's just that . . . it's so hard to see these men in all this suffering."

For a moment Martha lowered her eyes in understanding. Looking up, she asked, "Is there anything I can do to help?"

"Could you pray for us?"

"I do that every day," Martha replied. "Perhaps I could bring back some food?"

"Oh!" exclaimed the nurse. "You don't know what that would do for these men."

Back in the coach, Hamilton sat in respectful silence as Martha stared out the window in deep thought. They stopped at the Potts home, where Hamilton escorted her to the door and she entered, to go directly to the headquarters of her husband.

"Could I have your authority to request some items of food brought to this house?" she asked.

His answer was immediate. "You have it."

At noon the following day, soldiers carried six huge black kettles, all with lids tightly fastened, out of Martha's kitchen to a waiting wagon and hoisted them inside the bed. Twenty minutes later they stopped at the smaller hospital and unloaded two of them to men who wept when the lids were lifted and the rich, steaming stew of venison, potatoes, carrots, and turnips was portioned out to them in bowls.

The wagon clattered on to the larger hospital, where the remaining four kettles were carried inside. Tears streamed down faces into beards as the sick and emaciated men ate in silence, raising their eyes only to gaze at Martha in worshipful reverence. "Lady Washington," they murmured over and over again as she walked among them, helping a trembling hand work with a spoon or refilling an empty bowl. They reached just to touch her arm or her hand or her long, gray dress as she passed.

It was midafternoon, while Martha was helping the nurses gather the empty bowls, when one of them came to her.

"Lady Washington, could I ask a very special favor?"

"Of course. What is it?"

There was a catch in her voice as the nurse explained. "Yesterday we sent a young sergeant home. He's dying of wounds and fever. We can do nothing for him. He wanted to be with his wife in his last days."

The nurse stopped for a moment, and Martha waited for her to go on.

"I've held back a jar of your stew. Would you consider taking it to him and his wife? They live in a little cabin nearby. It will not take much time."

"Of course, my dear."

Bundled in her heavy coat, Martha took the jar of stew and was soon knocking on the door of a small log cabin with a column of smoke rising from its chimney straight up into the blue sky. The door was answered by a young woman scarcely seventeen years of age.

"Yes?" she said.

"I'm Martha Washington. A nurse told me your husband is here. She said he's special. I thought I could come meet him."

"Martha Washington?" The young woman gaped. "Why . . . why . . . do come in!"

There was a fireplace at one end of the single room and a table in the center, on a cold dirt floor. Straw was piled two feet deep against one wall, and a young man lay on it, beneath a blanket. He was sweating and shaking, and his teeth were chattering as he opened his eyes and tried to focus in the light of the single lantern on the table.

"Polly, did someone come?" he asked.

"Yes," his wife exclaimed. "Martha Washington! Wife of your commanding officer."

"Lady Washington? Lady Washington is here?"

"Yes, Enoch. She is."

Martha drew a chair up beside him and placed a cool hand on his forehead. She felt the sweat running.

"Sergeant, a nurse told me you're special. I wanted to meet you."

By force of will the man controlled his shaking. "I am honored. Deeply honored."

Martha smiled. "How long have you been serving with the general?"

"From the beginning, ma'am. The battle of Long Island. Marched through all of it with him."

Martha took his hand and he clutched hers.

"I'll tell the general. He'll be proud. Is this your wife?"

"Yes. Polly. Been married a little over a year. So proud of her."

"You should be," Martha said. She drew the jar of stew from

the depths of her coat. "I've brought you something. Venison stew."

The young man gaped. "Venison stew? Can't remember the last time we had good food. I don't know how to thank you."

Martha turned to Polly, who stood in disbelief at the sight and aroma of the stew. "Do you have a bowl? Could he eat a little of it now?"

For fifteen minutes Martha patiently spooned small amounts of warm stew from a wooden bowl and held it to Enoch's lips while he chewed and swallowed. When he finished, she set the bowl on the table.

"That's enough for now. I'll leave the rest for later. Polly, you can help him. I have to go now, but I'll return when I can. I'll tell the general about you, sergeant."

He reached to take hold of her arm. "If I . . . if things go . . . wrong, take care of Polly for me. Will you do that?"

She looked directly into his eyes. "I promise."

He relaxed, and a look of peace stole across his face. "Thank you."

For a moment Martha stood silent, and then suddenly she knelt beside him and took his hand in hers. She bowed her head and spoke. "Almighty Father, humbly we thank Thee for our blessings . . ."

In firm, pleading tones, Martha invoked the blessings of the Almighty on the young, dying soldier and his wife, and she heard their reverent "Amen" when she finished and rose to her feet.

"Thank you. Thank you," Enoch said.

"God bless you, Enoch," she answered.

She heard a quiet sob from behind and turned to Polly, reaching for the girl and drawing her close and holding her while Polly buried her face on her shoulder and wept. When Polly stopped shaking, Martha held her at arm's length, looked into her eyes, and smiled.

"You'll be fine. I must go now."

Polly followed her to the door, and Martha spoke quietly.

"When God calls Enoch home, I'll take care of you and see to it you are taken back home to your people. You must promise you will come to me."

Polly threw her arms about the plump little woman. "I promise. Thank you, Lady Washington. Thank you. God bless you."

Within days, Enoch died. As promised, Polly sought out Martha, who took her in as her own through the winter and in the spring provided an armed escort of soldiers to take her home to her people.

THE UNKNOWN
SAILOR

★　★　★

THE LAST RAYS OF A SUN ALREADY SET were reaching high to set
the low skiff of western clouds on fire. There was little wind, and
the dark blue waters off the English coast were glassy calm. Dusk
came stealing, silent and serene, to encircle the four American
men-of-war battleships that were far from home, prowling English
waters for British warships. Captain John Paul Jones commanded
the largest of the American ships, the *Bon Homme Richard,* an
ancient French merchant ship that had been converted to a slow,
awkward gunboat of forty-two cannon. With Jones were the
thirty-two-gun frigates, *Pallas* and *Alliance,* followed by a twelve-
gun brigantine, *Vengeance.*

Jones, short, wiry, decisive, firm, and totally fearless, stood against the rail of his quarterdeck, telescope extended, searching in the fading light for sails on the horizon, when the excited shout boomed down from the bearded, barefoot sailor in the crow's nest, seventy feet up the mainmast.

"Sails ho, nor'east. Convoy. Merchantmen. Two battleships for escort."

Instantly Jones pivoted with his telescope and brought the oncoming ships into focus, with his mind leaping ahead. *They've got to be British—only a British convoy would be in these waters.* They were less than six hundred yards away before Jones could read the names on the two gunboats in the fast-fading light.

"The *Serapis,*" Jones announced. "She's new. Mounts fifty guns on three decks. The other battleship is the *Countess of Scarborough*! Twenty guns."

Jones did not hesitate. He bawled orders, and his men ran the signal flags up the mainmast, ordering his three American ships to fall into battle line at once and attack the *Countess of Scarborough*. Jones, with his old *Bon Homme Richard* outgunned and outclassed, would attack the *Serapis* alone.

In the gloom of late dusk, the *Richard* bore down on the larger British ship, with the British captain, Richard Pearson, watching in stunned surprise. "She intends to ram us!" he shouted. Five seconds later the bow of the *Bon Homme Richard* plowed into the *Serapis* near her stern. Railings and timbers on colliding vessels crunched and splintered, and for a moment no one on either ship moved, waiting to see if the hull or the keel of either had been broken, while the two vessels swung sideways in the water and smashed into each other broadside, pointed in opposite directions. The railings of the ships were virtually jammed against each other.

Instantly Jones shouted, "Tie them to us!"

Before the shocked British could react, American seamen had

looped hawsers around the railings of the two ships and bound them together. In full darkness, the two men-of-war lay in calm water, tied together. High on the masts, the yardarms of each ship were interlaced with those of the other, with the ropes and riggings hopelessly entangled.

The cannon crews of both ships shook their heads and shrugged off the shock, and the deadly cannon duel began at point-blank range. The first broadside from the three decks of guns on the *Serapis* blasted holes in the hull of the ancient *Richard* and blew more than half of her cannon out of commission. The answering broadside from the *Richard* was a near total disaster! Two of the three heaviest cannon blew up, knocking the gun crews out of the fight. The crew of the third heavy cannon backed away from their gun, fearful that it too would explode and cripple or kill them.

The battle quickly became a frantic, disorganized mix of cannon flashes lighting up the night sky, while desperate men grabbed up muskets and pistols and swords and fought face to face. Some threw small, hand-held bombs onto the deck of the other ship. Fires broke out. A few seamen leaped to the rope ladders and scrambled into the rigging to fire muskets down into the sailors of the other ship, only to be hit by opposing musket fire. With their superiority of heavy cannon, the British were methodically blowing holes in the waterline of the *Richard,* and Jones soon understood his ship was sinking. He had four feet of water in his hold, and the pumps were failing. It was clear the *Richard* was going down.

An American seaman seized three of the small, hand-held bombs, stuffed them inside his shirt, and scrambled up the mainmast of the *Richard* to the second yardarm, forty feet above the wild melee raging on the decks below. He quickly walked the ropes to the interlocked yardarm of the *Serapis*. A British sharp-shooter on the deck saw the vague, shadowy figure high above, aimed his musket, and fired. The musket ball came singing past the overhead seaman as he crossed to the yardarm of the British ship and quickly cat-walked to the mast.

Below, the commanding officer of one of the three cannon still operating on the *Richard* saw the last of his crew crumple and fall and could take no more. He shouted to Captain Pearson on the British ship, "Quarter! We ask quarter!"

Shocked, Jones glared at his gun commander as Captain Pearson called, "Did you ask for quarter? Are you surrendering?"

Incensed, Jones took two steps and struck his own gun commander unconscious with his pistol. The man dropped, and Jones defiantly shouted back to Pearson the words that would enshrine his name so long as the American navy survived.

"I have not yet begun to fight."

At that moment, overhead, the lone American seaman in the British rigging lighted and dropped his first small bomb onto the deck of the *Serapis* and watched the flash when it exploded. As quickly as possible, he lighted the second bomb, watched the fuse burn for a moment, and threw it downward, where it disappeared into the blackness below.

The tiny bomb hit the deck, bounced once, and dropped through an open hatch into the second deck, where sweating cannon crews were loading and firing their cannon as fast as they could. In the darkness of the second deck, the bomb fell unnoticed into an open barrel of gunpowder, called a "budge barrel," next to a cannon crew, and exploded. The barrel of gunpowder exploded with it, and for an instant the entire second deck was filled with a deafening roar and blinding flash as flame leaped outward. In the next instant, twelve more budge barrels in the second deck exploded with a roar and a flash that could be heard and seen for miles.

The entire ship shuddered. Cannon were blown clear through the sides of the ship, into the sea. The main deck rose six inches, and flame leaped through the cracks. The mainmast of the huge ship shivered. Captain Pearson, on the quarterdeck, grabbed the railing to hold his balance, while every seaman on the huge British gunboat came to a standstill, terrified in the certainty that their ship was sinking.

Pearson could see no other choice. He shouted to Jones, "I surrender!"

Jones accepted the surrender and, as fast as possible, transferred his crew, with their dead and wounded and everything of value, from the *Richard* to the *Serapis.* He cut the old ship loose, and within hours, the *Richard* sank. Jones sailed the *Serapis* back to his beloved United States, victorious, with his place in history secured by his battle cry, "I have not yet begun to fight."

The name John Paul Jones will live as long as the United States navy exists, because of his victory over the superior *Serapis,* while no one knows the name of the American sailor who won the battle.

THE CROSS-EYED
WOMAN PATRIOT

FALL 1780

WILKES COUNTY, GEORGIA

★ ★ ★

Mother, some men in red coats are coming through the back gate."

Fear showed in the eyes of young Samantha Hart as she stood in the kitchen, peering up into the face of her mother, Nancy Hart, who continued stirring the vinegar mix for pickling the cucumbers just gathered from her kitchen garden.

Nancy was close to six feet in height, solidly built, beautiful, auburn-haired, her face slightly scarred from the effects of smallpox, with but one physical defect. She was badly cross-eyed. She paused to glance out the window at the five British soldiers as they approached the house, their muskets slung over their shoulders and their crimson tunics and crossed white belts shining in the bright September afternoon sunshine. She was wiping her hands on her apron when the soldiers banged on the kitchen door.

She lifted the latch and faced them. "What do you want?"

"Supper," they replied. "You are going to prepare supper for us."

She shook her head. "I have nothing to prepare for you."

Contemptuous, arrogant, as the red-coated regulars were prone to be with the rebellious Americans, one said, "Yes, you do." He took three steps back into the yard and seized a young turkey. Quickly he wrenched the head off and handed the bird to her.

"Prepare that!" he demanded.

Without a word, Nancy took the bird and turned back into the kitchen with the five soldiers following. They leaned their huge Brown Bess muskets against the wall in a line and sat down on chairs to watch her work, waiting for their supper.

While Nancy was plucking the turkey, she quietly whispered to her young daughter, "Go get the men from the field." Within minutes the child had quietly slipped out of the kitchen and through the house and was running for the nearby field where her father and two neighbors were shocking wheat.

Nancy finished preparing the turkey for cooking, laid it on the table, and walked to the cupboard for a roasting pan, when she passed the muskets. Without a word she seized the first one, cocked it as she turned, and from hip level, brought it to bear on the astonished soldiers.

For an instant the five redcoats stared in stunned surprise. A cross-eyed woman? Threatening us with our own muskets?

What the British soldiers did not know was that despite being cross-eyed, Nancy Hart was one of the finest musket shots within one hundred miles. She was a distant relative of Daniel Boone and a cousin of American general Daniel Morgan. When driven to it, she was famous for her willingness and her ability to fight with anything available, including muskets, tomahawks, knives, or even her fists. The Cherokee Indians had long since sorrowfully learned to call her "Wahatchee" in their language, which means "War Woman" in English.

The nearest British soldier made a lunge for her, and without a change of expression she pulled the trigger. The blast shook the kitchen as the musket ball hit home and the British soldier went down, critically wounded.

A second soldier leaped from his chair to seize her, but before he took his first step she snatched up the second musket and shot him. He went down, dead.

She dropped that musket and seized the third one, cocked it, and stood loose and easy with the muzzle moving back and forth, covering the three remaining soldiers.

Within seconds the door burst open, and her husband plunged into the room with the two neighbor men right behind. The haze and the smell of gun smoke still clung in the air, and her husband stopped in his tracks at the sight of two British soldiers on the floor with two muskets beside them, and his wife standing with a third musket covering the three remaining soldiers.

It was the demeanor of the three soldiers that surprised him most of all. They were all on their feet, backed up against the wall, hands high in the air, white-faced and trembling, wide-eyed in terror. As cross-eyed as Nancy was, they could not tell which one of them she was looking at, and none of them dared move for fear of finding out the hard way.

Today, Georgia boast a county named Nancy Hart County, a highway named Nancy Hart Highway, and a high school named Nancy Hart High School, all to honor the memory of Nancy Hart, the cross-eyed patriot who won her battle against five British soldiers.

THE OVERMOUNTAIN BOYS

MID-SEPTEMBER 1780

NORTH CAROLINA

★ ★ ★

IN THE RARE SEPTEMBER BEAUTY of the woods of the North Carolina Blue Ridge Mountains, Moses Hollenbeck, bearded, dressed in buckskins and moccasins, long hair tied back with a leather thong, swung down from his long-legged bay mare and faced Colonel Isaac Shelby, American leader among the patriot militia who were fighting the British for their freedom and liberty. The lanky Moses shifted the quid of tobacco stuffed in his cheek, spat, wiped at his tobacco-stained beard, thrust a sealed document toward Shelby, and shook his head.

"I dunno what that message says, colonel. I only know it was give to me by a fella back at Gilbert. He was real serious and says I gotta git that delivered to you, so I done it. That's all I know."

Gingerly, Shelby took the paper and for a time studied the wax seal. The imprint of the Royal British Crown was pressed into it.

"Hmmm," Shelby said. "Looks like the British army's got somethin' to tell us." He took a deep breath, then said decisively, "Let's go git Jerusha to read what it says."

Five minutes later Shelby and Moses stood quietly in the kitchen of the small log hut where Jerusha Peebles lived with her husband and six children. Jerusha, plain, lean, hawk-faced, was one of the few women in the remote mountain community of Sapling Grove in Sullivan County, North Carolina (now Tennessee) who could read, and the two men waited while she broke the seal. They watched her face intently as she silently read the document and recoiled when she reared straight up, her face flushed with anger.

"What's it say?" Shelby asked anxiously.

"Why . . . why . . . ," she blustered, "this here's from a British colonel named Patrick Ferguson. He's camped over at Gilbert with more'n a thousand British troops. Says you boys been shootin' at their soldiers. Talks about them little scrapes you had lately at Wofford's Iron Works, and Musgrove's Mill, and that time you laid into their men at Thicketty Fort and Cedar Springs. That's all true enough, but that ain't what this is all about. "

She paused to bring herself under control.

"Then he says, right here—" she held the letter out and pointed, "that you boys got to stop fightin' against the British, and if you don't, this here Colonel Ferguson is goin' to march his army over the mountain an'—" she read aloud from the document— " . . . hang the leaders and lay the country waste with fire and sword."

Colonel Shelby's head jerked forward, his eyes popped wide,

and his mouth dropped open in stunned surprise. "He says *what?*" Shelby exclaimed.

Jerusha repeated it, her voice too high, too loud. "Stop fightin' the British or he's comin' here to hang the lot of you and burn the place down."

For long seconds Shelby stared at Jerusha, stunned at the audacity of a British officer who thought he could come over the mountain and hang the men and burn the few log huts of their small village.

When he recovered enough to speak, he stammered, "I reckon we better see what some of the other boys got to say about this." With Moses following, he walked back out into the clearing, squinting in the bright sunlight. "I'll go see John Sevier," Shelby said to Moses. "While I'm gone, spread the word and tell the boys to think on it. I'll be back soon as I can."

Two days later, Shelby reined in his gray horse at the cabin door of Colonel John Sevier in neighboring Washington County. Sevier met him at the door, and the two men sat down in the Sevier kitchen to pewter mugs of cider while Sevier read the letter.

In dead silence he laid the wrinkled parchment on the rough-cut plank table and stared at Shelby. "I didn't figger Patrick Ferguson to be so ignorant," he said quietly. "Why, that man has been a good officer for the British for years. Invented a new-fangled rifle that loads at the wrong end. Whatever ails him to think he can scare us into quittin' the war just by sendin' a letter like that?"

Shelby shook his head. "I got no explanation."

Sevier took a healthy swallow of cider and wiped his beard. "'Appears to me maybe we oughta go over the mountain and have a talk with Ferguson," he said.

"I agree. I'll get some of the others while you round up your

163

boys. See you at Sycamore Shoals over on the Watauga River on September 25."

Sevier swallowed the last of his cider. "We'll be there."

Dawn broke clear and warm on September 25 at Sycamore Shoals, with five separate bodies of Carolina militia moving through the dense forest from five separate directions to gather in a great clearing. Shelby arrived with his militia first in the late afternoon, followed by Sevier with his hundreds. Then Colonial William Campbell marched into the clearing with his militia, followed by Colonel Charles McDowell and Colonel Andrew Hampton with their men from Burke and Rutherford counties. With the evening cook fires burning, the five colonels gathered and surveyed their fighting force.

Just over one thousand strong, the men were bearded, dressed in buckskins and moccasins stained from years of use, with many wearing coonskin caps. Every man had his horse, a tomahawk and scalping knife in his belt, and one of a variety of firearms, with the muzzle-loading, long-barreled Deckhard rifle being the predominant weapon of choice. Few of them could read. None was in uniform. None knew the formalities of military discipline. But every man there had fought Indians in the thick forests of the Carolinas as far back as memory could reach. Each could be invisible in the forest at ten feet, move like a shadow, and hit with his rifle anything he could see. Not one of them was afraid of a fight.

With dusk falling, and the militiamen finishing their evening meal and spreading their blankets, the five colonels met near the huge fire in the clearing. Shelby opened their war council.

"That British General—Cornwallis—has been movin' north lately. Word is he figgers to put down anybody in these parts who disagrees with him, and then move on up to cross the Delaware and finish anybody up in the north states that won't surrender."

Sevier nodded. "He sent Ferguson over our way to take care of us so he wouldn't have to worry about anyone comin' at him from our side of the mountain. Cornwallis don't want any distractions when he takes on Gen'l Greene or Gen'l Washington."

Campbell spat a huge stream of tobacco juice hissing into the fire. "Reckon we ought to go visit Ferguson," he said.

McDowell and Hampton nodded their agreement, and the war council was over.

The following morning, the colonels rode out with their mounted fighting force strung out behind, following on the winding, narrow forest trail, moving east. For five days they continued, with Colonel Benjamin Cleveland and Colonel Joseph Winston and three hundred fifty more fighting men from Wilkes and Surry counties joining them, bringing their small combined army to almost fourteen hundred. Shelby paused and called the other officers together.

"We got a sizeable gather of men here," he said, "and we don't have no real authority to do what we're doin'. Maybe we ought to get a gen'l officer here, with the authority we need."

The war council agreed, and on October 4, 1780, sent Colonel McDowell to find General Horatio Gates and ask him to either get a general officer to come take command of their little army, or to give written authority for them to proceed on their own.

The following afternoon, October 5, one of their lead scouts, breathless, excited, came galloping his horse back to meet them.

"Ferguson heard we're comin', an' he's left Gilbert Town, headed for Charlotte. He figgers to get close enough to Cornwallis and the main British army that we won't dare attack him."

Shelby quickly called the officers together.

"What are we goin' to do? After what Ferguson said in that letter, are we gonna let him get away?"

The others scratched their beards thoughtfully. "Naw, that ain't what we come to do. If we push on, we can catch Ferguson before he gets to Cornwallis. That's what we ought to do."

Shelby hesitated. "We ain't got the authority from Gen'l Gates yet."

Again they scratched their beards. "We didn't have no authority to do what we done at Lexington or Concord or Charleston, neither. We just done it."

Stifled grins showed through the beards. "Let's get on with it."

Before dawn, the Overmountain fighting force was moving east through the crisp October air. At Gilbert, they learned that Ferguson had fled with all speed. Shelby paused long enough to gather the other colonels.

"He's trying to catch up with Cornwallis, for protection. Are we going to let him?"

"No! We got about nine hundred men with strong mounts. We can leave the foot soldiers and those with weak horses behind to catch up when they can, and go after him with those who got the horses strong enough to do it."

They told the foot soldiers and poorly mounted riders to follow as best they could, and those with the best and strongest mounts pushed on as fast as the narrow, winding forest road would allow.

At Cowpens they were joined by Colonel James Williams, Major Andrew Hambright, and Major William Chronicle, with additional mounted fighting men. It was Colonel Williams who gathered the officers together for a moment.

"Ferguson's got his army on top of King's Mountain." A wry

grin split his beard. "And he says that he's king of that mountain and that there ain't no power on earth that can drive him off."

The other officers smiled. "We'll see about that." They mounted their horses and turned them east at a trot.

On October 6, 1780, Ferguson's scouts reported to him: "The Overmountain men are past Gilbert and coming fast!"

Instantly, Ferguson wrote and sent a message to Cornwallis. "The Overmountain forces are fast approaching. We need reinforcements. Three or four hundred good soldiers would finish the business. Something must be done soon." Then he reached for the whistle he used to blast out commands to his men above the deafening roar of musket fire. No other officer on either side of the war used a whistle to give commands during battle, and the fact that Ferguson did, coupled with the checkered hunting shirt he wore over his uniform, made him highly visible.

At dusk, thick gray clouds rolled in, and in the late evening high winds brought heavy rains driving from the northeast to drench the Overmountain men. They did not stop to make camp, but pushed on through the mud in the pitch black, horses and men equally drenched. The rain held through the night. Dawn came dark with rain still falling, but by midmorning the downpour slackened and breaks appeared in the purple clouds. Just after noon, amid intermittent showers and bright sunlight, the Overmountain men reached the base of King's Mountain with steam rising from the dripping forest.

The mountain (a hill, really) rose sixty feet above the surrounding valley floor, with heavily forested, steep sides. The top of the mountain was flat and resembled the imprint of a giant shoe. The plateau was 600 yards in length, tapering from 70 feet wide at one end to 120 feet wide at the other. Clearly, Ferguson had the high ground, with every advantage against the

Overmountain men, who would have to scale the steep sides of King's Mountain under the muskets of Ferguson's troops.

Quietly, the Overmountain men scattered in the forest until they had completely surrounded the mountain. Then, just before three o'clock in the afternoon, with their officers still mounted, they started up the sides, moving silently in the cover of the trees and huge stone formations. Ferguson had correctly judged that the oncoming Overmountain men would have to expose themselves to the muskets of his soldiers if they intended reaching the top, but he had failed to realize that his soldiers would have to step out in the open to shoot at them. Too late, Ferguson recognized his fatal mistake. His men had been trained to shoot like soldiers, but the Overmountain men had been trained as hunters—to shoot quickly and hit moving targets as far as they could see.

Steadily, the leather-clad, bearded men from the backwoods moved upward, firing their deadly Deckhard rifles, disappearing to reload, then advancing to fire again. Ferguson blew the attack order on his whistle, and two divisions of his men jammed bayonets onto their muskets and charged. The upcoming patriots simply fell back and disappeared into the woods, leaving Ferguson's men standing wide-eyed, frustrated, with nothing to shoot at, while other regiments of the Americans pushed in around them to seize and hold a portion of the mountaintop. Some of the American riflemen climbed trees, affording them a broad field of fire, and began cutting down Ferguson's officers.

For just less than one hour the fighting was fierce, with Ferguson's men advancing, then retreating, but paying always a terrible toll in dead and wounded. The oncoming Americans eventually reached the summit in force, and slowly Ferguson's command was pushed back, surrounded, battered, disorganized, beaten.

Then, still mounted, Ferguson blasted the "charge" signal on his whistle, and one second later threw his hands in the air and pitched headlong from his horse, with one foot still locked in the stirrup. Eight American rifle bullets had pierced his body. He was dead before he hit the ground.

The battle of King's Mountain was over.

Ferguson's second in command raised a white flag, and the battered, beaten remains of Feguson's command surrendered. For long minutes the British survivors stood white-faced, filled with terror as they looked into the faces of the Overmountain men who closed in around them. Bearded, with tomahawks and scalping knives in their belts, the mountain men had revenge in their eyes as they remembered what the British officer Banastre Tarleton—"Bloody Tarleton"—had done at Waxhaw. It was at the battle of Waxhaw that hundreds of Americans had tried to surrender to Tarleton. Instead of accepting the Americans' capitulation, Tarleton had ordered all of them shot. Now, on top of King's Mountain, the tables were turned, and the survivors of Ferguson's command feared they were about to be slaughtered.

Slowly the Overmountain men rose above their need for revenge. They disarmed Ferguson's survivors and held them as prisoners of war while their officers gathered to decide what to do with them.

"If Cornwallis is coming," Shelby said, "we better leave. We'll assign men to march these prisoners to Hillsborough and deliver them to the military authorities there. The rest of us better get back home to defend our families if the British send an army to try to punish us."

The prisoners were marched to Hillsborough; however, on the way, the Americans held court. Thirty-six of Ferguson's men were found guilty of breaking into and burning homes and killing American citizens. Nine were hanged on the spot.

General Charles Cornwallis was shaken to his roots when the message reached him that the Overmountain men had caught Ferguson and his command at King's Mountain and engaged them in a battle wherein Ferguson and nearly half his command were casualties, with the remainder taken as prisoners of war. With Ferguson gone, Cornwallis had no one guarding the left flank of his army, and he had no choice except to change his plan for conquering the northern states. He was forced to retreat back to the south.

It was the beginning of the end of the Revolutionary War.

Today, on the southern slope of King's Mountain, among a great mound of granite stones, is a simple grave marker. Colonel Patrick Ferguson remains at the place from which he once declared no power on earth could drive him.

THE IMMIGRANT WHO SAVED THE AMERICAN REVOLUTION

1781

PHILADELPHIA

★ ★ ★

Haym Salomon, slight of build, energetic, seated behind the desk in his business office on Front Street near the Delaware River harbor in Philadelphia, raised his head from the financial document he was studying to answer the knock at his door.

"Yes, do come in," he called.

The door opened and his assistant stepped inside. The well-kept office was of moderate size with shelves on two walls, filled with books on the American Revolutionary War along with the financial statements and records of many banks and brokerage firms, both in Europe and the United States.

"Mr. Robert Morris is here to see you."

Salomon rose to his feet. Robert Morris was the financial

genius who had repeatedly answered the desperate call from both Congress and General George Washington to somehow find money to save the Revolution and the Continental Army. The Second Continental Congress had just recently appointed Robert Morris superintendent of finance for the infant United States government, in the fading hope that he could find a way to save the country from the financial chaos that was threatening total bankruptcy and disintegration of the union of the thirteen states. The Articles of Confederation that bound the foundling states together did not give them the power of taxation, leaving them without any way to pay the cost of government, with the result that the American government had to depend on contributions from the states to pay its bills. When the states failed to make the contributions, the American government could not pay its debts, and it had repeatedly turned to Robert Morris for salvation. Many, many times Morris had quietly sought out Haym Salomon for assistance.

Morris, large, portly, authoritative, walked into the office and faced Salomon with a slight bow. "It is good to see you again," Morris said.

"It is my pleasure," Salomon replied. "Do have a seat."

Morris lowered his bulk into a chair facing the desk, and while he waited for Salomon to take his seat opposite, the history of this slight, sharp-eyed little man flashed through his mind.

Born to Jewish parents in Lissa, Poland, in 1740, Salomon had early felt the bitter hatred and animosity that was prevalent in Europe against all Jews. In 1760, when mobs threatened his life, home, and property, he fled to Holland. Discrimination against the Jews was rampant in Holland as well, and to escape the persecution, for the next ten years Salomon moved from one country to another. He arrived back in Lissa, Poland, in late 1770, only to find the persecution had become worse. In 1772 he fled Europe to England, and from there crossed the Atlantic to New York in the American colonies. On the day he arrived in New York, he could speak eight languages, including English, and had earned an international reputation as an exceptionally skilled banker, merchant, and financial broker.

Salomon was overwhelmed by joy at the sense of freedom and liberty that was growing in the colonies and soon joined a group of Americans called the Sons of Liberty. Their goal was to free the colonies from the oppressive yoke of England. In 1776, Salomon was arrested with other Sons of Liberty, condemned as a spy, and sentenced by the British to prison. However, when the British learned of his ability to speak fluent German, they assigned him to work as translator for German general Philip von Heister, who was in command of the German Hessian soldiers hired by the British to assist in putting down the rebellious Americans. While Salomon served as von Heister's translator, he quietly used his influence to persuade many Hessian soldiers to desert the British and go over to the American army. After his release from custody, he married Rachel Franks, the daughter of a prominent New York merchant, and continued his efforts to sway the Hessian soldiers to change sides.

He was arrested a second time in 1778 on a charge that he was one of a group accused of planning to burn the British royal fleet in New York harbor, the penalty being death by hanging. However, he bribed the Hessian guards with gold coins he had hidden in his clothing, escaped, and secretly traveled to Philadelphia, where he offered his services to the Second Continental Congress and opened his office on Front Street as a financier and broker dealing in securities. His reputation for absolute honesty and integrity in all his dealings spread rapidly, and soon he was a prominent figure in the highest government and financial circles in Philadelphia.

In 1779, responding to a desperate request of George Washington, it was Salomon who brokered a $400,000 loan that provided money to pay the soldiers and save the Continental Army. Quietly, he also arranged for loans and grants to assist James Madison, James Monroe, and other rising stars in the quest for American independence.

Then, in 1780, with the colonial government staggering and bankrupt, the Confederation Congress appointed Robert Morris as its first superintendent of finance and gave him one mandate: *Save the Colonies!*

Morris knew that if he were to succeed, he would have to have the assistance of Haym Salomon, the little man with the skill, the genius, the impeccable reputation, and the connections with France, Holland, and other European sources. Now, sitting in Salomon's office, Morris spoke to Salomon in somber, foreboding tones.

"I have been advised that unless money is available immediately, the war is lost. The government has debts to foreign countries it cannot pay and soldiers who have not been paid for up to three years."

Salomon sat back in his chair for a moment in deep thought. "Do you have an estimate of how much money is needed?"

"Not in full. But it will be in the hundreds of thousands of dollars."

Salomon did not flinch. "You say 'immediately'? How soon?"

"Days. I will need your help."

Salomon nodded. "I'll start today."

Two days later Salomon appeared in the office of Robert Morris with a satchel in hand and drew out two documents.

"Will this help?" he asked.

Morris studied the papers, and relief flooded through his system. They were negotiable notes for more than ninety-two thousand dollars!

"You have no idea," Morris said. "The government must pay a debt of one hundred thousand dollars by noon tomorrow. How did you acquire these notes?"

Salomon shrugged. "I will be back soon with others."

Five days later Salomon again appeared in the office of Robert Morris, to lay more documents on his desk. Morris stared at them in amazement.

"Three hundred fifty-three thousand dollars! From what source?"

"Subsidies from France and Holland. They are much interested in our revolution. They would like to see us succeed."

Morris locked eyes with Salomon. "You have not had time to communicate with brokers in France and Holland. That takes weeks. How did you acquire these subsidies?"

"I know their representatives here in Philadelphia. They were gracious enough to accept my personal guarantees in these matters."

Morris shook his head in disbelief. "How much is your commission in these transactions?"

Salomon tossed a hand indifferently. "Nothing. No commission."

"You're giving your commission to the cause?"

"This is my country, my home. It is little enough that I do. I'll be back next week."

During the weeks and months that followed, Salomon returned regularly to the office of Robert Morris with more funds. In the three years from 1781 to 1784, Haym Salomon brokered more than seventy-five financial transactions that provided hundreds of thousands of dollars for food, blankets, ammunition, medicine, muskets, and cannon for the Continental Army, as well as pay for the soldiers and the government officials who were carrying the war on their shoulders. He did so willingly, asking nothing in return. He contributed his own personal fortune of hundreds of thousands of dollars to the cause. Selflessly he worked long, arduous hours, tirelessly traveling to New York, Boston, and other cities to meet with representatives of foreign banks and institutions to obtain the money so desperately needed to meet the unending financial crises that the new nation was experiencing.

Then, in the last weeks of 1784, his health began to fail. Doctors diagnosed tuberculosis and instructed him he must have complete bed rest or risk losing his life. Still he worked on, driven by his love for liberty and his new country.

It was too much. On January 6, 1785, at the age of 45, Haym Salomon died. Only George Washington and Robert Morris, with a small group of patriots who knew the source of the hundreds of thousands of dollars that had saved the United States, mourned the loss of the little Jewish patriot who had heroically given everything he owned, and finally his life, to save the new nation.

Haym Salomon was interred at Mikveh Israel Cemetery on Spruce Street in the city of Philadelphia.

In 1941, long overdue, author Howard Fast wrote his book titled *Haym Salomon, Son of Liberty*. That same year, the famous sculptor Lorado Taft, assisted by Leonard Crunelle, completed a huge monument in which George Washington is the central figure, with Haym Salomon on his right, and Robert Morris on his left—the three men who saved the American Revolution. The monument stands at the corner of Wacker Drive and Wabash Avenue in downtown Chicago. In 1975 the United States Postal

Service issued a commemorative stamp honoring Haym Salomon for his contribution to the cause of the American Revolution. The following tribute accompanied the publication of the stamp: "Financial hero, businessman, and broker Haym Salomon was responsible for raising most of the money needed to finance the American Revolution and later to save the new nation from collapse."

In World War II, the United States Navy christened the Liberty Ship SS *Haym Salomon* in honor of the little man who helped save the United States.

Susanna's Desperate Ride to Save General Lafayette

Summer 1781
Appomattox River, Central Virginia

★　★　★

Susanna Bolling, sixteen years of age, slight, dark hair, dark eyes, regular features, stood in the center of the parlor of her family home near the Appomattox River in central Virginia, staring at the British officers who had just opened the front door and were facing her father. Dusk was settling at the end of a hot summer day. The officer with the most gold braid on his crimson tunic said in a loud voice, "We are requiring the use of your home tonight to quarter our officers."

Her father stood his ground. "On whose authority?"

The officer's voice became threatening. "That of King George III of England and General Charles Cornwallis, who is here with us."

Susanna's eyes widened in shock. General Cornwallis! Here? He was supposed to be far away, pursuing Francis Marion, the Swamp Fox! No one had told the Bolling family that Marion had led Cornwallis on a chase across half the rivers and through most of the swamps in North Carolina, until the exhausted red-coated British soldiers were sick, starving, and in desperate need of finding refuge where they could recover. To save his command, Cornwallis was taking them to Yorktown, on the York River, at the place where it emptied into Chesapeake Bay. To reach Yorktown, Cornwallis would need to get past American general the Marquis de Lafayette and his small command.

There was nothing Susanna's father could do except allow the British officers to occupy his home for the night. Susanna and her mother quickly set food on the table for them. When the officers finished their supper, they entered the small library, closed the doors, and took their places around the table in the center of the room. Fascinated, Susanna stood near the closed door, listening intently to catch some of the words of the officers.

She heard a gruff voice say, "He's at Halfway House with his command of rebellious Americans."

A voice calmly inquired, "How many soldiers does he have?"

"Many fewer than we have here. We do not have the count."

"What is their condition?"

"Worse than ours, but those Americans seem to be able to survive on very little."

"We must reach Yorktown to meet our ships and Admiral Graves. Lafayette is directly in our path. We can attack and defeat him at his camp at Halfway House, and then continue on to Yorktown, where our navy is waiting with supplies."

"Agreed!"

Susanna clamped her hand over her mouth to stifle a gasp.

They intend attacking General Lafayette and destroying his entire command! Someone has to warn Lafayette! Silently, she slipped away from the library door and went to her room, where she paced the floor, frantically searching for some way to send word to the Americans at Halfway House that the British planned to attack them. Slowly an unbelievable plan formed in her mind.

It was close to midnight before every light in the house had been extinguished and silence had settled. Noiselessly, Susanna dressed, took her shoes in hand, and crept to the kitchen. She raised the edge of the large, braided oval rug in the center of the floor and felt in the dark for the iron ring attached to a trapdoor that opened to a tunnel beneath the kitchen floor. The trapdoor and the tunnel had been constructed when the home was built many years before, as a way to escape from the home in case of Indian attack. The tunnel was narrow and led nearly one hundred yards to the banks of the Appomattox River.

Susanna lowered herself into the tunnel, silently closed the trapdoor, dropped to her hands and knees, and in the blackness slowly crawled the hundred yards. She breathed in relief when she emerged at the river, where a small boat was tied. With the quarter moon overhead, she climbed into the boat, pointed it across the wide river, and heaved into the oars with all her strength. When the boat bumped on the far bank, she dragged it as far as she could, then turned and hurried to a narrow, rutted, winding road alongside the river, and followed it east. Minutes later she came to a farmhouse, with the windows dark and silent.

She banged on the door and soon a light glowed at the kitchen window. A man, still dressed in his nightshirt, opened the door a crack and held his lantern high.

"It is two o'clock in the morning," the man said. "Who are you?"

"Susanna Bolling. I rowed across the river. Oh, sir, I need help. I must reach Halfway House as fast as I can."

"Halfway House? There are soldiers at Halfway House. Why must you go there?"

"I must tell the soldiers something."

Susanna heard a woman's voice speak from behind the man. "What is it?"

"A young girl. Says she must reach Halfway House."

"Let me talk to her."

In the yellow lamplight, it took Susanna five minutes to persuade the woman of the house that she desperately needed to reach the soldiers. The woman turned to her husband.

"I believe her. We must help."

The husband dressed, led Susanna to the barn, and saddled his horse. "Follow this road east. Watch for British patrols. Return the horse when you can."

He helped her into the saddle and handed her the reins, and she left the farmyard at a gallop, moving rapidly eastward through the black forest on the winding dirt road. Twice she heard wolves close by and spurred the horse on. Once, a voice at the side of the road challenged her, but she paid no heed as she galloped past. The sun was rising in the east when she saw the American flag on a pole and the tents of an American army camp. She brought the tired, winded horse to a halt in front of the largest tent, where two soldiers stood at the entrance with muskets.

"I have a message," she blurted. "I must see an officer."

The two bearded men looked at her in puzzlement. "You? Why, you're just a child! What message could you have?"

"Please," she exclaimed. "Is there an officer nearby?"

From inside the tent came a voice. "Is someone there?"

One soldier pulled the tent flap open. "Yes, general. A young girl. Says she has a message."

"How curious. Show her in."

The soldier shrugged, held the flap wide open, and motioned Susanna inside. She stopped in front of a table, facing an officer seated on the far side. He was young, with rather sharp features and alert, intense, blue eyes. She suddenly realized she was facing the famous French general, the Marquis de Lafayette, and for a moment her mouth dropped open.

He nodded to her. "Please have a seat. Did you wish to speak with me?"

She dropped into the chair facing the desk, and her words came in a torrent. "Yes, sir. I was at my home yesterday when . . ."

Lafayette smiled and held up a hand to stop her. "Young lady, you're among friends. Collect your thoughts. Where do you live? What is your name?"

"I am Susanna Bolling. I live with my family near the Appomattox River west of here about forty miles. Yesterday afternoon, late, General Charles Cornwallis and some of his officers came to my home and demanded supper and rooms for the night. They met in our library and I heard them talking. They plan to come here and attack you and continue on to Yorktown."

Lafayette slowly eased back in his chair, mind racing. "How many?"

"They said they had many more men than you have here."

"How soon do they plan this attack?"

"As soon as they can make the march."

Lafayette leaned forward. "Can you describe General Cornwallis for me?"

"Older. Heavier. Jowls. Large paunch."

A slow smile crossed Lafayette's face. "That is our beloved

General Cornwallis." For a moment he tipped his head forward and stared at the top of the table. Then he raised his head and spoke to her.

"I will make preparations for such an attack. In the meantime, I will give orders that you are to have breakfast, then private quarters to sleep. My men will tend your horse. You are welcome to remain here as long as you wish, but I suggest you return home as soon as you feel strong enough, perhaps leave in the early morning."

He paused, then finished. "You have done a very brave thing, Miss Bolling. Perhaps someday you will understand what you have done for your country. God bless you."

The following morning Susanna Bolling returned safely to her home.

Four days later General Charles Cornwallis led his soldiers into the American campsite at Halfway House, only to find it absolutely deserted. There was not a tent nor a soldier in sight. Mystified, he continued his march to Yorktown, where he was met by thirty British warships, prepared to defend him with their cannon while he refurbished his tattered army. It was then that thirty-eight French warships engaged the British navy and drove them out into the Atlantic, while General Washington and the Continental Army, with the help of seven thousand French infantry, trapped Cornwallis and his British soldiers, who surrendered on October 19, 1781. Among the forces assisting Washington in the defeat of Cornwallis were those led by General Lafayette, who had been saved by the heroic deed of young Susanna Bolling.

HOW THE SWAMP FOX
GOT HIS NAME

SUMMER 1781

SOMEWHERE IN THE SWAMPS OF SOUTH CAROLINA

★ ★ ★

IN DEEP DUSK, GENERAL FRANCIS MARION of the American Continental Army hunkered down near the low cook fire of his small camp deep in the South Carolina swamps. Plate in his hand, continuing to fork beans into his mouth, he listened to an old, lanky, bearded scout who had just come in from the south and was squatted down facing him with a pewter plate of beans in one hand and a fork in the other.

"Gen'l," the old scout said, wolfing down a mouthful of the beans, "Banastre Tarleton's about a half a day behind us, and he's madder'n a stepped-on alligator. Cornwallis give him near fifteen hundred redcoat soldiers with orders to find us and kill us, and Tarleton figgers he aint gonna stop till he does."

Elijah glanced at his commander, who was small, slightly built, hatched-faced, known as a thoughtful, generous, quiet man. Born in 1732 in South Carolina, Francis Marion had been a frail, sickly child, prone to illness. Doctors expected him to die, and in response, the boy had disappeared into the swamps for months at a time, returning stronger after each absence. Slowly he gained his health, and with it, the reputation of being the master of the swamps. Some claimed he was able to talk to alligators and pet the deadly copperhead and cottonmouth snakes.

Marion glanced at his chief scout with hardly a change of expression. "Only fifteen hundred?" He stopped to consider for a moment. "We got near fifty men ourselves. What is that—thirty of them to one of us? Sounds about right. Shouldn't be too much trouble."

"You know Tarleton's reputation," the scout continued. "He's the one that burnt down every building and all the crops and slaughtered half the cattle and sheep on the farm of Gen'l Richardson, and left widow Richardson with nothin', just to get revenge for what Gen'l Richardson done to the British. And he done all that long after Gen'l Richardson was dead. Meanest man under the British flag. Tarleton don't take no prisoners. Just massacres 'em like he done at Waxhaw."

Marion nodded. "So I heard." He kept working at his beans.

The scout swallowed a mouthful and forked in another. "Anyway, I figgered you oughta know he's comin' and that he means to get the lot of us."

Marion finished his beans in thoughtful silence, then dropped the plate and fork in the steaming black kettle of wash water and spoke to his trusted scout.

"Elijah, you remember that little difference of opinion we had with that uppity British colonel over on the Santee River north of

Charleston? We led that bunch through about nine swamps and across three or four rivers—the Black, the Wateree, the Cooper—before their cannon carriages wore out. They loaded the cannon barrels in wagons and left the carriages behind. Remember that?"

Elijah grinned. "Yessir, I do. That British colonel had more'n five hundred men with him. Some of the things they was sayin' about us afterwards was purely un-Christian!"

Marion smiled back. "How far do you calculate those worn-out cannon carriages are from here?"

"You mean just the wheels and axles?"

"Yes."

Elijah scratched his scraggly beard. "Mebbe, say, one day's travel, if someone was in a hurry and knew about swamps. If you mean how long will it take Tarleton with all them soldiers and wagons they got, more likely three days. They ain't yet figgered out how to travel through swamps."

"That's what I think. Tomorrow we'll wait for them to find us, and then we'll move on toward the Santee River."

Elijah squinted one eye. "Colonel, you figgerin' what I think you're figgerin'?"

Marion smiled. "Most likely."

Marion's command of bearded volunteers, hair tied back with leather thongs, clad in leather hunting shirts and breeches and moccasins, each armed with a Deckhard rifle and tomahawk and each wise to the ways of the swamps in the southern colonies, finished their evening mess, put out the cook fires, and went to their blankets. They were up with the sun and had finished their morning meal when Marion called them together.

"Banastre Tarleton is about half a day south of us, coming this way. Half of you men assigned to morning scout go down there and find him. Report back here when he's one hour away. The other half of you scouts, head northeast towards the Santee River. We need to know if there are any British between us and the river. We'll be following you. Find us and report when you know. The rest of you get packed, ready to leave."

There was a murmur among the men, and one of them asked, "Is there somethin' special over on the Santee River?"

Marion answered, "That depends on what we find when we get there."

It was past noon when the scouts returned from the south. "Tarleton ought to be in sight in about one hour, gen'l."

"Good. Go back about a mile and wait until you see him, then come tell me. The rest of you, get ready to leave. We'll move on towards the Santee when he's seen us."

The sun was reaching for the western mountains when the scouts trotted into camp. "He ought to be in sight in about ten minutes, gen'l."

Fifteen minutes later Marion extended his telescope and for a time studied the movement among the trees along the edge of the swamp, about one thousand yards to the southwest.

"It's him. Move out in the open where he can see us."

Marion watched as the British soldiers hastily fell into marching formation. Banastre Tarleton, astride his high-headed bay gelding, clad in his green tunic and green hat with a huge green plume waving, started forward at a trot, leading his command around the swampy ground that separated him from Marion and his tiny band of volunteers.

"He's seen us," Marion said calmly, "and he's coming to attack. Let's go."

One minute later Marion's command had disappeared into a forest of cypress trees with the moss hanging thick from the lower branches. The men moved a half mile before Marion brought them to a stop and once again used his telescope to search their back trail. Nearly an hour had passed before he saw movement in the trees five hundred yards behind. He turned back to his men.

"Move around for a few minutes so he can see us, then follow me."

Throughout the day into deep dusk, Marion taunted Tarleton, moving on northeast, stopping frequently, staying just out of musket range, moving on to draw the British column deeper into the swamps and rivers. In full darkness Marion called a halt and told his men to make cold camp. No fires. Then he took Elijah and twelve scouts aside.

"Go on back to the British camp. Keep them awake through the night. If you can, scatter their horses. Be back here when the morning star begins to fade. Be careful."

The British pickets were at their posts with the moon high overhead and the fires burning at intervals throughout the camp when the first spine-tingling wail of a panther came echoing from the swamp. The nearest pickets jerked their muskets from their shoulders and cocked them, jittery, searching in the surrounding Cyprus trees and lily pads for the yellow eyes of the great cat, but there was nothing. Across the camp, an answering growl came drifting, and then another, and another from all around the camp until all the pickets were crouched, muskets on full cock, peering into the silvery blackness of the swamp, searching for the eyes of great black leopards that were not there. The five hundred horses, tied fifty each to ropes stretched between trees throughout the camp, reared and snorted, dancing, wide-eyed in terror, at the sounds of the deadly cats all around them. They finally broke free and stampeded through the camp, snorting, knocking tents askew, plowing through baggage and supply boxes. Frightened soldiers in nothing but their long underwear came pouring out of their tents with their muskets and began firing into the darkness until the entire British camp was a bedlam of snorting, bawling horses, soldiers running helter-skelter in their long underwear, and blasting muskets.

The moon was nearing the western rim and the morning star was fading before the British camp quieted. Half an hour later Elijah and his men were gathered around Francis Marion, grinning in the early dawn.

"I doubt they'll ever find all their horses," Elijah chuckled. "And I reckon they're still looking for those panthers that started the whole thing."

Marion grinned. "Good work. Get some rest. We move as soon as we can see them following."

Throughout the sweltering heat of a South Carolina summer day, Banastre Tarleton led his weary soldiers onward, catching sight of Francis Marion's tiny band of patriots just out of musket range a half-dozen times, pushing on through the muck and ooze of swampy soil, cypress trees, and swamp grass, watching intently for alligators and the deadly cottonmouth and copperhead snakes that were invisible until they moved. At day's end, Tarleton stopped his men on the only solid section of ground they had encountered that day, and in exhausted resignation made camp. The sun was down and the cook fires burning when the first rifle bullet came singing into camp to punch a .53-caliber hole in one of the huge, black cooking kettles hung from tripods. An instant later the crack of the rifle echoed through camp, but not one British soldier could tell the direction from which it came. Within minutes, eight more rifle bullets came whistling, and eight more cook kettles spurted steaming brown mutton broth. A hundred furious, exhausted British soldiers in muddy uniforms snatched up their muskets and fired blindly into the deep shadows of late dusk, hiting nothing but the hard trunks of the cypress trees.

It was just past two o'clock in the morning when the howling of wolves had the horses jerking at their tether ropes, threatening another chaotic stampede through the camp.

The following morning Marion's scouts returned from the Santee River and made their report.

"Gen'l, ain't no British between us and the Santee. We got a clear run."

Marion called for Elijah. "Take twenty men with some axes and saws and go on ahead to the place on the Santee River where the British abandoned those cannon carriages. Fix up as many as you can. Cut new spokes or new axles from the trees if you have to. Then cut some logs about a foot in diameter and six or seven feet long. Mount them on the cannon carriages to look like cannon. Cut some long poles that look like ramrods. Then get the cannon lined up in the trees, near that open place where the swamp is divided by that high ridge of dry ground. Understand?"

Elijah grinned through his heavy, graying beard. "Yessir, I remember the place." He chose his twenty men and disappeared in the heat of the swampy forest at a trot.

That day and the day following, Marion's men moved steadily toward the Santee River, stopping at intervals to allow Tarleton to see them, provoking him, tantalizing him with the hope that he would somehow catch them and shoot them all. The morning of the third day of the pursuit, Tarleton had reached the limits of his endurance. Fuming with rage, he issued orders to his men.

"First and second battalions, pack rations for three days and discard everything except your muskets, powder horns, and shot pouches. You will follow me within the hour. The remainder of you men will remain here with the wagons, cannon, and horses until we return. It is clear we will never catch this demon if we are slowed by wagons and cannon and horses."

One hour later he led out on his horse, followed by five hundred of his best soldiers, all of them on foot. He left behind one thousand men with all the baggage, wagons, cannon, and horses.

Ahead of him, Marion's hidden scouts silently watched Tarleton and counted his men, then moved through the swamps and trees like ghosts to report to their leader.

"Gen'l, he finally done it. Left all the wagons and cannon and such behind and lit out on foot with five hundred redcoats. He means to catch us."

Marion smiled. "Good. We'll be at the Santee tomorrow, where Elijah's waiting. We'll stop there to extend our greetings to Mr. Tarleton and his infantry."

The sun was up, promising another sweltering day among the buzzing mosquitoes and other insects and the echoing call of colorfully plumed birds in the swamps of South Carolina, when Marion and his men joined Elijah and those with him. Elijah made his report.

"We got four of them British cannon carriages somewhere's near workin', gen'l. Hid right over in them trees. We got logs cut and mounted on 'em, and we smeared black mud on the ends of them logs so's they look like sure enough cannon. We got tree limbs cut like ramrods."

"Good work," Marion said and gathered all his men around, leaning on their rifles. "Let's get ready. Go hide with the log cannon. On my signal, roll them past that open space where Tarleton can see them, and then circle around out of sight in the trees and roll them past the open place again. Do that about three times. With a little luck, Tarleton will think we have twelve cannon here, waiting for him."

Twenty minutes later, the four log cannon were poised to cross the small open space, visible for one thousand yards, down the high ground that divided the muck and mud of the swamp. For anyone approaching from the southwest, the only workable access to Francis Marion and his small band of patriots would be across that strip of high ground.

It was midafternoon when Marion's scouts trotted up the high ground to report. "He's about half an hour behind us, gen'l."

"Take your positions."

Hidden, sweating in the sultry heat of the swamp, they watched and waited. Forty minutes passed before Elijah silently raised one arm to point. Banastre Tarleton, astride a bay horse that was muddy to its belly, with his green-plumed hat unmistakable at one thousand yards, trotted forward with his exhausted column following. Marion raised his telescope and studied them intently, calculating distance, waiting.

Tarleton suddenly jerked his horse to a stop, peering across the high ground before him, then at the swamp that surrounded it, as he realized that it could be a perfect trap if the Americans were to catch his column on the open high ground, with no place to take cover. He drew his telescope from its saddle holster and extended it. For long minutes he studied the trees one thousand yards ahead, searching for any sign of the Americans, and there was none. He signaled to his men and cautiously started forward on the high ground at a walk, eyes alive, watching everything.

Marion counted their paces as they advanced—one hundred yards—two hundred yards. They had covered three hundred yards when Marion silently raised his hand and gave the signal. Within three minutes one log cannon was pulled into view, left in plain sight for several seconds, then rolled back into the cover of the trees. Moments later another followed, then another, and another.

At seven hundred yards, Tarleton hauled back on the reins, and his horse tossed its head against the bite of the bit. He jerked his telescope up and extended it, and for five minutes stared in disbelief, counting. Twelve! Twelve cannon! Hidden in the trees.

Tarleton's mouth dropped open. Where had the rebellious Americans obtained twelve cannon? His own scouts had never reported their having one cannon, not to mention twelve! Had Marion arranged to have someone else deliver them to this place? If so, how did he do it? There was no one, American or British, within fifty miles, who had twelve cannon.

Tarleton cast about wild-eyed at the place he had led his men. If they left the high ground in either direction, they would be mired in muck and slime to their elbows, unable to move. They could never reload a musket in it. They would be totally defenseless! And if they made a charge on the high ground, they would be running straight into the muzzles of twelve cannon. If the cannon were loaded with grapeshot, he would lose half his men within minutes.

Could they circle the swamp and come in behind the Americans? More than a mile in either direction? Exhausted, spiritless, dirty, hungry—could his men do it? And if they did, what would they be facing? Twelve cannon that could wipe out his entire command if Marion chose to remain where he was. And if Marion decided to disappear, they would find nothing but twelve abandoned cannon, mosquitoes, alligators, and copperhead snakes.

Tarleton saw no other choice. Humiliated, fuming, he gave the only order he could. "Fall back! Withdraw! Return to base camp."

Francis Marion, Elijah, and their tiny band of fifty patriots grinned as they watched Tarleton's column slowly back up, then turn, and start the long, humiliating, sweltering, muddy trek back through the swamps and across the rivers, to their base camp, far to the southwest.

That evening a bone-weary Tarleton sat in silence near one of the campfires, staring despondently into the dancing flames. Around him his soldiers moved slowly, wordlessly, slumped over in defeat.

A colonel stopped beside Tarleton and spoke quietly. "How does one catch Francis Marion in this trackless, swampy country?"

Ruefully, Tarleton looked up at him. "Francis Marion? You don't catch him. The devil himself couldn't catch that old swamp fox."

And overnight Francis Marion became the Swamp Fox, one of American history's most beloved and colorful heroes.

Today, there is a Francis Marion National Forest in South Carolina. There is also a Marion City, a Marion County, a Francis Marion High School, a Francis Marion University, and a famous Francis Marion hotel. The city of Marion, Ohio, is also named after the little American patriot who could not be caught by the entire British army.

SHE ATE THE MESSAGE AND SAVED THE REVOLUTION

JULY 1781
THE BROAD RIVER, NORTH CAROLINA

★ ★ ★

EMILY GEIGER, SLENDER, WITH BROWN hair and eyes and a heart-shaped face, sat listening intently to General Nathaniel Greene of the American army. They were in the general's private office, suffering in the July heat of 1781 on the banks of the Broad River in the northern section of South Carolina, not far from where Emily lived with her family. Months earlier, General Greene had been sent by George Washington into the southern states to stop the British in their campaign to subdue the south and then move into the northern states to conquer the rebellious Americans. With only a small command of soldiers to oppose the massive army under the command of British general Cornwallis, Greene had quickly learned to rely on southern patriots wherever they could be found—on farms, in mountain communities, in seaports, and on rivers.

Geene leaned forward, eyes alive, as he spoke slowly and deliberately to Emily.

"You know of the battle we fought at Ninety-Six in June. We were too few, and they were too many. We were forced to retreat by the British under command of Lord Rawdon. They followed us until we crossed the Enoree River. Then Lord Rawdon stopped pursuing us and turned back to join forces with British colonel Alexander Stuart. Those two commands came together at Orangeburgh."

He paused for a moment. "Do you understand so far?"

"Yes, sir."

"Good. They are still at Orangeburgh, and together, they are strong enough to continue north to support British general Charles Cornwallis. Cornwallis is presently attempting to find and defeat Francis Marion and then force the surrender of all American forces in the south."

Again Greene paused, and Emily Geiger nodded her head. "I understand."

Greene continued. "I have counseled with my officers and many southern patriots. It is my conclusion that our best course is to join our forces with those of General Thomas Sumter. They're camped on the Wateree River. With our combined forces, we will attack the forces of Lord Rawson and Colonel Stuart while they are still at Orangeburgh. We hope we can force them to fight us so they will not be able to join General Cornwallis. Without their added strength and support, I doubt Cornwallis will be able to catch and defeat Francis Marion, and then force the surrender of all the southern colonies. Am I clear so far?"

"Yes."

Greene cleared his throat and went on. "To do that I must

deliver a written message to General Sumter, telling him of our plan."

Emily straightened in her chair, and Greene saw the light of understanding come into her eyes as she spoke. "That is the reason you asked for a volunteer to deliver a message? You need someone to carry it to General Sumter?"

"Exactly. We cannot spare a man to do it. When you volunteered, we considered it and concluded that they would not expect such a message to be carried by a girl. That's why I invited you here today. Do you understand what we're asking of you?"

"Yes, sir."

"You recognize that if you're caught, you could be hanged for treason against the king?"

"I do."

"You know that you're going to be traveling on horseback through dense forests, and that there will be British spies all around you and loyalists still faithful to the British crown? It is possible there are spies who know you're here right now. Any one of them could have you captured."

"I understand that."

"The question is, are you willing to carry such a message?"

"I am. Yes, sir. I am."

Greene took a deep breath. "Can you leave today?"

"Yes."

"Be back here in one hour with the things you'll need to travel for four days. We'll have a worthy horse ready, and I will give you the message and instruct you where General Sumter and his command are camped."

One hour later, with the late-morning sun promising a sweltering day, Emily was again admitted to the private office of General Greene. She was wearing an ankle-length dress and high-topped shoes, with her long brown hair pulled back and tied with a leather cord. She carried a blanket rolled and tied in a tight bundle, with dried beef strips and fresh carrots and apples inside, along with the few other things she would need. She sat down expectantly, facing General Greene across his scarred desk.

"Here is the message," he said. "Read it aloud."

It was brief and direct. Greene was bringing his soldiers in a forced march to join those of General Sumter at his camp. From there they would move immediately to attack the British forces at Orangeburgh, in an attempt to prevent them from joining General Cornwallis.

Emily finished reading and handed it back to Greene, who folded it, sealed it with hot wax, and handed it back to her. "Hide this in your clothing. Do not under any circumstance let it fall into the hands of the British. Do you have any questions?"

"No, sir."

He drew a map from his desk drawer and spread it before her, then studied it for a moment before he tapped it with his finger. "That is where you will find the camp of General Sumter, on the east bank of the Wateree River. It is just about one hundred miles from here. Study the map until you are certain you can find it."

With her finger, she traced the route to the camp of General Sumter, nearly due east of them.

"I can find it," Emily said.

"Keep a keen watch for British soldiers, and for spies and those who are still loyal to the king. You must deliver that message. God bless and protect you, Miss Geiger." He escorted her to the door, and Emily walked out into the glare of the July sun where a sturdy sorrel mare was saddled, waiting. General Greene helped her into the saddle, then stepped back as she bid him goodbye. She reined the mare around and raised her to a gentle lope on the rutted dirt road that wound through the dense South Carolina forest.

She did not know that hidden British spies had secretly watched her enter the office of General Greene the first time and had seen her return an hour later dressed for a hard ride. While they did not know the purpose of her visit, they concluded that General Greene had requested her to make a journey by horseback, and if that were true, she was almost certain to be carrying a message to someone. And if General Greene was using a teenage girl to carry a message, it must be vitally important. Thus it was that the British spies sent a rider toward the Wateree River far ahead of Emily, to alert a family still loyal to the king that if they saw a lone girl riding past, they were to get word to the spy network instantly. She must be stopped and searched for any message she might be carrying.

The sun was reaching for the western horizon when Emily came in sight of a small clearing where the loyalist family lived. In the distance she saw a man standing near the road, pitchfork in hand, doing nothing. She reined the mare to the side of the road and stopped, her brow knitted down in deep thought.

On a summer's day, with crops that needed work, what would a man be doing near the road, with a pitchfork, doing nothing?

Without hesitating, she reined the horse into the woods, dismounted, and led the horse in a wide circle through the thick trees and brush, around the clearing, before she worked her way back to the road, where she remounted. She raised the horse to a lope for a half mile, then pulled her off into the trees and waited. Birds chortled and warbled and squirrels scolded, but there was no pursuit on the road. She pushed on.

Dusk settled before she rounded a curve and saw the next clearing cut out of the forest, with a cabin in the center, and a barn on one side. Lights showed yellow in the windows, and she reined the mare into the yard, tied her to the hitching post, and rapped on the door. A portly woman opened it, drying her hands in her apron.

"Yes?" she said.

"I'm traveling and have gotten lost," Emily explained. "I have no place to sleep tonight. I would be most grateful if I could stable my horse in the barn, and if you have a bed I might use. I can pay."

The woman peered at her, then looked about in the twilight to see if there were any others. Satisfied that Emily was alone, she nodded. "Put your horse in the barn. We have an extra bed upstairs. Supper will be ready in a few minutes. You can join us if you wish."

Emily led the horse to a stall in the barn, carried water to it, dropped dried grass in the feed manger, and went to the house with her blanket roll. She shared a pleasant supper with the woman, her husband, and their grown son and teenage daughter. After eating, she laid coins beside her plate, then excused herself and climbed the stairs into the loft to the bed. On one wall was a single, small window. For a time she sat on the bed in thought, uncertain if this family was faithful to the British or if they were American patriots. She blew out the lantern and lay on the bed fully dressed, with General Greene's message clutched in her hand. Soon Emily heard the family go to their separate rooms, and the lanterns were extinguished. The house became silent, and Emily closed her eyes to drift into light sleep.

The quarter moon was high when Emily shook her head and her eyes opened wide in the blackness as she struggled to understand what had awakened her. Then she heard it again—a rapping at the kitchen door beneath her. The yellow light of a lantern came from one of the bedrooms, and she heard the father, dressed in his nightshirt, raise the latch on the door.

"Who's there?" she heard him ask. "What do you want?"

A loud, heavy, demanding voice answered. "We're looking for a young girl riding a sorrel mare. Did she come past here sometime yesterday?"

Instantly Emily was off the bed and on her feet. Without a sound she stepped to the small window, lifted the latch, and pushed it open. A moment later she dropped out the window to the ground, ten feet below, and sprinted for the barn. Hastily she threw the blanket and saddle on the mare, jerked the cinch tight, buckled the bridle in place, and led the horse out of the barn and back to the road. She swung into the saddle, drove her heels into the horse's flanks, and went flying east on the road. Five minutes passed before she reined the horse in, and in the dull moonlight bowed her head and closed her eyes to concentrate. The silence held. No one was following her.

She raised the horse to a trot and moved on in the darkness. Four hours later, with the morning star fading in the east and the first rays of the rising sun streaking high in the heavens, she saw the place where the Congaree River made a line in the forest. Half an hour later she stopped at Friday's Ferry to let the horse drink while she chewed on dried beef from her supply. She was reaching for the reins to the horse when she suddenly became aware that someone was behind her. She turned, and her heart nearly stopped beating. Three red-coated British regulars stood with muskets and bayonets.

The one with three gold chevrons on his sleeve demanded, "Who are you?"

"Emily Geiger."

"From where?"

"The Broad River."

She saw the suspicion leap in their eyes. "Why are you here, alone, on a tired horse?"

"I am on my way to visit my aunt. She is sick."

"Where does she live?"

"On the Wateree River. East of here."

One soldier shook his head. "A lone girl, traveling at night through these forests, to visit a sick aunt who lives a hundred miles from her home? Nonsense. You come with us."

The burly one with the chevrons on his sleeve took the reins of her horse while the other two lifted her into the saddle to lead the horse on down the road. Twenty minutes later they came to a building in a small clearing with military tents and soldiers, and a flagpole with a British flag moving gently in the morning breeze. The sergeant took her inside the building, where she faced a British officer behind a desk. The sergeant stood at attention to speak.

"We found this young lady riding a horse on the road, just before dawn. She says she is from her home on the Broad River, traveling to the Wateree River to visit a sick aunt. That's a far distance for a girl to travel on these roads, especially in the dark of night. We're holding her horse outside. We thought you should question her."

The officer, tall, slender, sharp-faced, officious, leaned forward with his forearms on the desk. "We are aware there is a young lady carrying a message this direction." A sneer formed on his face. "Are you that young lady?"

Emily gasped and clasped her hand over her mouth for a moment. "Me? Oh, no, sir."

He stood. "Well, we shall find out soon enough." He turned to the sergeant. "Lock her in the guard house and bring Abigail Perkins here at once. Mrs. Perkins will search her thoroughly, and if she has a message, it will be found."

"Yes, sir."

The sergeant took Emily by the shoulder and marched her

back out into the heat of the morning sun to the guardhouse, locked her inside, and left to find Abigail Perkins.

Inside the small room with heavy bars on the only window, Emily peered frantically about, but there was no way she could escape. She touched the bodice of her dress where the message was hidden, aware that if she were searched, it would be found. With the message in British hands, a trap would be laid for General Greene's men coming to join those of General Sumter. British General Cornwallis would receive his reinforcements, and with them, he could force the surrender of the American forces in the south. Worse, Emily would face being hanged for treason!

She stopped, and by force of will brought her fear and her whirling thoughts under control. There had to be a way!

Suddenly it was there! She quickly seized the message, broke the seal, read it, read it again, then closed her eyes and repeated the few lines from memory. Then she tore it into small pieces, stuffed them into her mouth, and began to chew frantically. She heard footsteps approaching, and as the key was rattling in the lock, she swallowed hard, and the last of the message went down.

The door swung open, sunlight flooded in, and the sergeant walked into the dirt-floored room, followed by a large, square-shouldered woman with a huge jaw.

"This is the girl," the sergeant said.

The woman nodded and spoke to him. "You will leave while I search her."

The sergeant walked out and locked the door, and Abigail Perkins turned to Emily.

"You will remove your shoes."

Quickly Emily unlaced her shoes and handed them to Mrs. Perkins.

For ten minutes the large woman inspected the dress and the

petticoat beneath, twisting every inch of them, examining the large hem at the bottom, until she knew there was nothing hidden. Then she thrust her hands inside both shoes and felt for anything that might be a message. There was nothing. She stood behind Emily and parted her hair repeatedly but found nothing.

"You may put your shoes on," she said gruffly and waited while Emily laced and tied them before she knocked on the locked door. The sergeant opened it, and Abigail pointed at Emily.

"I have inspected everything she is wearing, and gone through her long hair. She is carrying no message."

The sergeant frowned. "You're certain?"

"Absolutely."

The frustrated sergeant, followed by Mrs. Perkins, marched Emily back to the commanding officer and made his report.

"Mrs. Perkins searched her from head to toe, and she is not carrying a message."

The officer's face clouded, and he spoke to Mrs. Perkins, standing beside the sergeant. "Are you absolutely certain?"

"I am, sir. There is no message."

The officer shook his head. "Then we have no reason to hold her. Return her horse and release her."

"Yes, sir."

Twenty minutes later Emily raised her horse to a trot as she left the small British camp, and three hours later, with the sun high overhead, came to a small home by a stream. She stopped to water her horse when an elderly man, stooped and walking slowly, approached her from the house.

"Are you in trouble, miss?"

"No. I'm traveling to visit my aunt on the Wateree River."

The wise old eyes studied her for a moment. "Just got back from the Wateree myself. Took some hams over to Gen'l Sumter's camp."

Emily peered into his face and took a chance. "Are you friendly with General Sumter?"

"Yes, ma'am."

Emily decided to take a chance. "I must find him. Can you tell me how?"

"Certainly can. Come back to the house. I got a special short-cut. I'll draw you a map." He pointed with his whiskered chin. "Your horse looks plumb weary. I got a fresh one in my stable. You can leave yours here and pick it up when you return."

The old man's map saved Emily half a day. She arrived at the camp of General Sumter the following morning and repeated the message from General Greene. The two American forces joined and attacked the combined British forces of Lord Rawdon and Colonel Alexander Stuart at Orangeburgh. The battle was fierce and ended with neither side victorious, but the British were crippled so badly they could not move north to join General Charles Cornwallis. Without them, General Cornwallis was forced to march his beleaguered command to Yorktown to re-supply and recover from their fruitless pursuit of Francis Marion.

The Continental Army under General George Washington combined with part of the French navy under command of Admiral deGrasse and seven thousand French infantry under command of French General Rochambeau to defeat General Cornwallis. The surrender of General Cornwallis at Yorktown on October 17, 1781, essentially ended the Revolutionary War, with the Americans victorious.

Today, a plaque is mounted in the State House at Columbia, South Carolina, honoring the heroic acts of Emily Geiger, and the Daughters of the American Revolution have established an Emily Geiger Chapter in Hones Path, South Carolina.

A CASE OF MISTAKEN
IDENTITY

MAY 20, 1782

BELLINGHAM, MASSACHUSETTS

★ ★ ★

Noah Taft, appointed by the colony of Massachusetts as master for enrolling volunteers from the Bellingham district into the American army, sat in his office, hunched over his large ledger, quill in hand, while he finished his last entry.

"Next," he announced and glanced up as a tall, rangy young volunteer stepped to the table, facing him. This person had a strong, jutting jaw, prominent nose, steady blue eyes, and the smooth cheeks of a youngster.

"Name and residence?" Taft said.

"Robert Shurtliff. Middleborough."

"For how long do you want to enlist?"

The answer was immediate. "The rest of the war."

Taft made entries in his ledger then turned the large book and handed the quill to the young person. "Sign here."

The enlistee took the quill and signed left-handed with a large, deliberate scroll. It was noticeable that the middle finger of the left hand had been injured at some time and would not bend.

What Noah Taft did not know was that the young, new enlistee, Robert Shurtliff, was not Robert Shurtliff, nor was he a young man. He was in truth Deborah Samson, a young woman! She had been born December 17, 1760, in Plympton, Massachusetts, the daughter of John and Deborah Samson, who became the parents of seven children. When Deborah was seven years of age, her father abandoned his family, and her mother, unable to support them all, indentured Deborah to others. She was soon taken in by a kindly but poor minister named Jeremiah Thomas, who was the father of ten sons and no daughters. Deborah was assigned to care for the boys. For more than ten years she washed and ironed their clothes, helped with their meals, shared in the harsh, unending work of maintaining the small farm, and drilled them in their school studies at night by the fireplace. With no opportunity for formal schooling herself, she became highly educated by reading their textbooks at night, by candlelight. At the age of eighteen she had served out the term of her indenture and was released.

She was a full foot taller than the average woman of her time and taller also than most men. The farm work of ten years among the ten sons of Jeremiah Thomas, dressed in the rough farm garb of a man, had given her a spread of shoulders and strength beyond most men, an understanding of how men thought, and a sense of independence that set her apart.

To the surprise of everyone, she became a schoolteacher.

Then, with the Revolutionary War coming to a close, she felt the pull of a patriot, and the question came to her mind, *Why can I not serve my country?*

What greater service than as a soldier?

She cut her hair, dressed in the common clothing of a farmer, and walked from Middleborough to Bellingham, where Noah Taft accepted her as Robert Shurtliff, a soldier.

Three days later, on May 23, 1782, Deborah Samson was one of fifty new recruits that Captain Eliphalet Thorp mustered into the Fourth Massachusetts Regiment commanded by Captain George Webb, and Sergeant Gamble marched the regiment to West Point on the Hudson River in New York. There they received their uniforms, equipment, and muskets.

In the months that followed, Deborah never complained while she flawlessly performed every duty assigned to her. She never wavered on long, sustained marches. When fortifications had to be built, she took shovel in hand and worked tirelessly, even as men around her murmured and found excuses. She became an expert with her musket and excelled at bayonet practice. She soon gained the respect and admiration of those in her company, who never once suspected that Robert Shurtliff was a woman, not a man. They wondered why young Shurtliff remained beardless, but the real reason never occurred to any of them.

With the surrender of British general Cornwallis at Yorktown on October 19, 1781, the year previous to Deborah's enlistment, the major battles of the Revolutionary War came to an end. However, the savage attacks on American targets by fanatics still loyal to King George III and England did not cease. In and around New York City, angry bands of British Tories struck without warning at American military camps, supply depots, and homes where American officers were housed. The attacks increased, with bloody, heavy, face-to-face fighting mounting.

Somehow, the bloodshed had to be stopped.

Orders were issued. The West Point Company commanded by Captain George Webb was to march to Tarrytown, near New York City, to face and stop a fierce band of Tories led by British colonel James DeLancy. DeLancy's men had repeatedly ambushed American patrols and attacked supply depots in the dead of night.

The American company arrived in Tarrytown in the early evening, exhausted after a demanding forced march. They had scarcely been assigned to their tents when the British Tories swept in, firing from ambush, charging with bayonets lowered. The fighting was instant, fierce, and bloody. Deborah shot the Tory who attacked her, then leaped to save the nearest American soldier with her bayonet. It was over as quickly as it had begun, with injured men groaning and the bodies of the dead, both American and British, sprawled in grotesque positions on the ground. Deborah laid her musket down and spent the night helping bind up the wounded.

In the next days, attacks by the British loyalists came sporadically, without warning. The fighting was often hand-to-hand, with swords and bayonets and clubs. The newly arrived Americans quickly learned to be ever alert, watching, listening, at all hours of the day or night. Deborah never faltered. Time and again she met the fanatic Tories with her musket and bayonet or a sword or anything at hand, to take a toll on them, drive them back. Many times she saved her comrades from death or injury and always, when the attack was ended, she was with the doctors, binding the wounded, reassuring them, helping. She rapidly became one of the most respected and best soldiers in her company.

It soon became clear to Captain Webb that the only way to stop the attacks by the Tories was to find them and either take them prisoners of war or destroy them. He did not hesitate. He called his company together.

"We are going to locate the British loyalists, and we are going to eliminate them. Be ready to march on a moment's notice."

The notice came within two days. Scouts and spies had located the British fanatics under the command of Colonel DeLancy. The American company was to leave instantly. The platoon to which Deborah was assigned was to lead the attack, under orders to engage the Tories and hold them in place until the entire company under Captain Ebenezer Sproat could reach them.

The lead platoon, Deborah among them, formed and left camp at a run, muskets and bayonets at the ready. They followed the winding dirt road through the dense New York forest for more than a mile before they sighted an old, abandoned log hut where they were told they would find the Tories.

The building was deserted. They circled the clearing and picked up fresh tracks of a number of men leading into the forest. Without hesitating they plunged into the thick undergrowth, moving as fast as they could. They had gone fewer than one hundred yards when the sergeant in the lead saw movement ahead. He slowed, and instantly it seemed that British loyalists came from behind every tree and bush.

"Fall back!" the sergeant shouted, as British muskets began to blast from all sides.

The fighting was a wild, deafening melee, with British mixed among the Americans, face-to-face, muskets firing, swords swinging. Quickly, Deborah sprinted forward to the side of the wounded sergeant to help him cover the retreat of the platoon. She fired her musket, then thrust with her bayonet. It was knocked from her hand by the sword of a British soldier, who swung it at her again. She felt the bite of the blade at her hairline above her eyes and staggered back, dazed as the blood came running. She seized her assailant's arm and wrenched the sword from his hand, then turned it on him and he went down. Swinging the sword on all sides, she continued covering the retreat of her platoon, moving back toward the clearing.

She felt a numbing blow midway in the front of her right thigh, and then her leg buckled, and she went down with a .75-caliber British musket ball lodged near the bone. She struggled to regain her feet, but could not make her leg move. The forest and the battle around her were rapidly becoming a mixed blur, and she realized she was losing consciousness when she heard a shout from behind.

"Follow me, men! We've got them!"

It was the voice of Captain Ebenezer Sproat, leading the main body of the company straight into the British Tories. Within seconds the Tories had disappeared in the forest with Sproat hot behind.

Deborah felt strong hands lift her, place her on a makeshift litter, and carry her back to the clearing and then on back to the hospital at camp. A French doctor carefully cleaned the sword gash on her forehead, stitched it closed, and bandaged it. He did not inquire of any other wounds, and Deborah remained silent about the British musket ball still lodged in her leg, to prevent discovery that she was not Robert Shurtliff, but a woman. When the doctor turned to treat the next patient, Deborah quietly slipped off the operating table and limped out of the hospital, back to her bunk. That night, she gritted her teeth in silence while she used her belt knife to dig the musket ball from her leg and bandage the wound the best she could.

Days passed while she recovered from the head wound, but the wound in her thigh refused to mend. Soon it began to discharge a yellow matter that had a distinctive odor, and then she developed a fever. She was taken to an American doctor who resided in the town, who quickly saw the bandage and the discoloration on the trousers of her right leg. Without hesitation he drew the trousers down to examine the wound. His mouth flew open as his head jerked forward, and he stepped back in stunned shock.

This soldier was a woman!

For several seconds he struggled to take control of his amazement. Treating the wound was one thing. What to do about a woman who had performed heroically as a man was quite another!

In silence he cleaned the wound, washed it with alcohol, closed it, and bandaged it carefully. Then he called an orderly.

"Take this soldier to my home at once. Tell my wife that he will be with us until he has recovered."

The puzzled orderly answered, "Yes, sir."

Late that evening the doctor finished his rounds at the hospital and hurried home to find his wife mystified.

"Do you have some reason to want this soldier in our home?" she asked.

"That soldier is a woman," he announced. "I cannot keep her at the hospital! What's to be done with her?"

The doctor and his sympathetic wife nursed Deborah back to health in the privacy of their own home, telling no one of her secret. Then the doctor quietly informed a general of the truth.

On October 23, General Henry Knox privately called Robert Shurtliff to his headquarters at West Point and issued an honorable discharge to him.

Following her discharge, Deborah Samson met and married a good man who was also a poor farmer. They became the parents of three children and adopted a fourth. To assist in making a living, Deborah recited her startling experience as Robert Shurtliff, a soldier, at many speaking engagements in Massachusetts, for which she was paid a modest fee. At one time she contacted her old friend Paul Revere, who admired her and understood her need and gave her some money.

After Deborah petitioned the Massachusetts legislature for pay still due and owing from her time of military service, the legislature of 1792 passed a resolve granting Deborah her request, which was approved by John Hancock. The order granting her request read in part: " . . . that the said Deborah Samson exhibited an extraordinary instance of feminine heroism by discharging the duties of a faithful, gallant soldier, and at the same time preserving the virtue and chastity of her sex unsuspected and unblemished and was discharged from the service with a fair and honorable character."

Issued much later, a report by the Congressional Committee on Revolutionary Pensions included a statement regarding Deborah Samson, which reads, in part:

"The Committee believe . . . they are warranted in saying that the whole history of the American Revolution records no case like this, and furnishes no other similar example of female heroism, fidelity and courage . . . and there cannot be a parallel case in all time to come."

The Daughters of the American Revolution organized the Deborah Samson Chapter at Brockton, Massachusetts, on January 25, 1897.

On May 23, 1983, the Governor of Massachusetts, Michael J. Dukakis, signed a proclamation declaring Deborah Samson "The Official Heroine of the Commonwealth of Massachusetts."

It was the first time any state in the union designated anyone, man or woman, to be its official hero or heroine.

THE GIRL WHO SAVED
FORT HENRY

SEPTEMBER 12, 1782

WHEELING, WEST VIRGINIA

★ ★ ★

FOR TWO DAYS, ELIZABETH ZANE, a teenaged girl, together with a small number of other Americans, had remained inside the rough log walls of Fort Henry, loading the muskets for the patriots who were defending the fort against British and Indian attackers. The fort had been under a siege of steady gunfire from the dense West Virginia forests surrounding the small enclosure. Those who lived in the few cabins and huts surrounding the fort had gathered inside to escape the onslaught, dreading the moment the enemy would storm the walls and they would all be killed or captured.

It was approaching noon on September 12, 1782, when the commander of the fort called the defenders all together. His face, stained by gun smoke, was grim as he made a fateful announcement.

"It is my duty to tell you, we have only enough gunpowder to keep firing for a few more minutes. When the powder is gone, we will have to make a decision. We can continue to defend the fort without muskets, or we can raise a white flag and try to come to terms with them for our surrender."

Surrender? To Indians? Every American inside the fort knew of the terrible things suffered by prisoners at the hands of the Indians. Instantly the cry went up, "No! No! We will not surrender! We will fight to the last before we will surrender!"

Their commanding officer nodded his agreement, then looked them in the eye. "Back to your duty posts. We will continue to fight."

"Wait!" Elizabeth exclaimed. "If we have gunpowder, can we win?"

The commander pondered for a moment. "We've held them for two days. With gunpowder, I believe we could hold them off until help comes or they quit. But that is the point. We are nearly out of gunpowder."

Elizabeth pointed. "My brother—Colonel Ebenezer Zane— is in his cabin not far from the fort. He's been there the whole time, shooting back at the British. He has gunpowder stored there! If we can get to the cabin, perhaps we can return with some of it."

Stony silence held for five seconds, and then murmuring began. Everyone knew of the cabin. How far was it from the fort? Sixty yards? Could someone cross the open space sixty yards wide, get inside the cabin, and return with gunpowder while more than three hundred British and Indian troops tried to shoot them? Who could make such a run? Who dared to volunteer?

For a moment the commander reflected. "It is possible. Is there a volunteer?"

Strong men looked at each other, then at the ground, as they searched their hearts and souls. Four young men raised their hands. "I volunteer," each of them said.

The commander shook his head. "We cannot spare four men. Only one. I will not be responsible for selecting one of you. You four must settle this yourselves, and quickly."

Then Elizabeth's voice rang out. "I can do it! I can get there and back. I can."

Everyone in the fort stared at her in shock. A girl? A sixteen-year-old girl?

The commander walked to face her. "That is a brave thing to say, but I can't let you do it. It is something for a man to do."

"No," Elizabeth cried. "They will not expect a girl to do it. I can run as fast as any man. I can be there and back in minutes."

The commander looked her in the eyes. "You know that hundreds of them will be shooting at you. Your chance of getting back alive and unharmed is very small."

"Not if I run fast and dodge their musket balls." Elizabeth planted her feet and jammed her hands on her hips. "I'm going to do it!"

Finally acquiescing, the commander led Elizabeth to the huge gates, ordered the massive bar lifted, and gave the signal. The gates opened a crack, and Elizabeth gathered her long skirt and her large, heavy apron up in her arms and darted out into the clearing that surrounded the fort. In one second she was sprinting toward the cabin, sixty yards distant, feet flying, hardly touching the ground.

In the surrounding woods, red-coated British soldiers looked twice, unable to believe what they were seeing. Indians clapped their hands over their mouths, their strongest expression of astonishment. What was a girl doing outside the fort, running like a deer for the cabin where one patriot remained?

Elizabeth reached the cabin without a single shot being fired at her. She threw open the door and flew into the arms of her stunned, thirty-four-year-old brother, Colonel Ebenezer Zane.

"I've come for gunpowder. Help me!"

She made a basket of her apron, and he dropped sack after sack of the precious gunpowder inside, until she could carry no more. Then she hurried to the door, gave him one last look, and as he called, "God bless you," she darted back out into the bright sunshine.

She had covered only five yards before it broke clear in the minds of the British soldiers. "That girl is carrying gunpowder!" They immediately raised their muskets and fired. Musket balls whined past Elizabeth and kicked dirt on all sides of her feet and tore into the trees and brush beyond her. Suddenly the Indians understood what was happening, and they also jerked their muskets to their shoulders and fired.

At thirty yards the musket fire was a continuing roar, with lethal balls singing and whistling all around Elizabeth. Dirt was jumping in all directions. Still she ran, as hard as she could, desperately clinging to her apron, holding the precious gunpowder inside.

At fifteen yards the men inside the fort swung the gate open a crack, and Elizabeth could hear their shouts: "Run, girl, run!" As she sprinted on, heavy musket balls whined past her, punching into the walls and gate, splintering the bark and wood. Then she was back inside the fort, gasping for breath and clinging to her heavy apron.

Elizabeth went to her knees, then collapsed, with the sacks of gunpowder still held tightly in her apron. Strong, gentle hands reached to lift her back to her feet, holding her while she tried to bring herself under control.

"Are you hurt? Are you hurt?"

She shook her head and panted, "No. No. I'm fine."

Then the commander was before her, shaking his head in disbelief. "The bravest thing I ever saw," was all he said before he passed out the precious gunpowder, and the patriots went back to the ramparts to defend their fort and their homes.

Throughout the day and the following night, they held the British and the Indians at bay with their steady, accurate musket fire. As the sun cleared the mountains in the east the following morning, they saw the red coats of the British regulars withdrawing and disappearing into the forest, followed by the Indians, and their muskets fell silent. British scouts had reported that help was coming to those in Fort Henry. They had had enough. The siege was over. Fort Henry and all those within were saved.

THE EYEGLASSES THAT
STOPPED A MUTINY

EARLY MARCH 1783

WASHINGTON'S HEADQUARTERS NEAR NEWBURGH, NEW YORK

★ ★ ★

THE WINDS OF EARLY MARCH WERE prying at the windows and grumbling in the chimney of General George Washington's private office in the army headquarters building in Newburgh, some sixty miles north of New York, when Washington heard the outer door open and, moments later, close. His adjutant rapped on his door and, on Washington's invitation, entered the square, austere room.

"This message was just delivered by special messenger, sir. It is marked secret and urgent."

General George Washington accepted the sealed document, then settled back in his chair to break the seal while the adjutant walked out and closed the door. In silent privacy, Washington examined the signature and recognized it as that of his former personal aide, Alexander Hamilton. Instantly, Washington sat upright and slowly read the message with narrowed eyes.

The wording was carefully chosen, exact, and terrifying.

Hamilton first stated, succinctly and accurately, that Congress was caught in a position that was just days from destroying the United States. The Articles of Confederation had made the U. S. Congress responsible for conduct of the war but had failed to give that same congress the power to levy taxes to pay for the war. The preceding summer, Congress had a grand total of one hundred twenty-five thousand dollars it had begged from the states, to pay the interest on just over six million dollars of borrowed money. The American government was bankrupt! Angry creditors were threatening to sue or worse.

One of those creditors was Colonel Walter Stewart, who had met with other creditors in Philadelphia in an attempt to organize them and approach Congress in force, demanding they be paid. Worse, most officers currently serving in the Continental Army had been promised pay and pensions if they would remain in service. The foot soldiers had been promised a bonus of eighty dollars each. None of these obligations had been met, and some of the officers and soldiers had received no pay of any kind for six years! Now, with the fighting ended, both the officers and foot soldiers were banding together to demand what they had been promised—and were threatening a total mutiny and takeover of Congress should they not get their money.

Hamilton's letter continued. There were currently certain forces working to undermine Washington's influence and power both in the army and in Congress. Washington would be well advised, as commander in chief, to use his great prestige to keep a "complaining and suffering army within the bounds of moderation" if the whole affair erupted into full-blown mutiny.

Hamilton concluded by advising that should Washington doubt all this, he could "seek to verify it with General Henry Knox."

Slowly, Washington lowered the document to the desk before him, then reached for a second letter received two days earlier from Joseph Jones, a friend and confidant presently serving in Congress. Washington reviewed the Jones letter briefly. The content was very nearly identical to that of Hamilton's letter. Joseph Jones had closed his letter with the strong suggestion that Washington would do well to conduct his own investigation of the sordid affair.

Washington bowed his head and closed his eyes while he concentrated on the dilemma he now faced.

Too well did he know that the complaints of his beloved army were true. Those men had faced starvation, sickness, British muskets and bayonets, lack of clothing, and no pay, for years, trusting in their cause and in the promises of their leader, George Washington, and Congress. Now, with the war over and the time nearing when the army would be disbanded and sent home, these men were without money to pay the debts that had accrued against their homes and families while they were fighting for their country. It was only right that they should be paid.

But how? How could they be paid by a bankrupt Congress? If they were not paid, they were threatening a mutiny that would override the authority of Congress and establish a military dictatorship—destroy the very government they had fought to establish! The great dream of a free America, for which they had paid so high a price, would be gone forever!

Where was the answer?

Torn between his love for his army and his dream for his country, Washington searched his soul for the key.

The following Monday morning, March 10, 1783, a white-faced adjutant laid an unsigned notice on Washington's desk and walked out of the office. Washington gaped in astonishment as he read it.

The notice was an invitation to all field-grade and general officers in the Honeyman to attend a meeting at ten o'clock the following morning, March 11, at the recently constructed Public Building on the military base. There they would discuss their grievances, organize, and send their ultimatum to the United States Congress, threatening that should that body fail to meet their demands, the men would refuse to disband, remove the entire army to an unsettled location to the west, leave the United States with no army, and do whatever was necessary to obtain justice. Worst of all, the notice strongly hinted that General George Washington himself was supportive of their position but could not openly declare it.

Within the hour Washington had written and issued an order postponing the meeting from Tuesday, March 11, 1783, to Saturday, March 15 at ten o'clock at the new Public Building. Then he immediately sent for General Henry Knox, his faithful and trusted general of artillery, who had been with him through the entire war.

"Quickly make a quiet investigation of all this and report back to me," Washington requested.

"Yes, sir," Knox replied.

Two days later, Knox returned to Washington's office. "Sir, it's true. There is a conspiracy, and the men involved are using your name and office to support it."

"What men?" Washington asked, eyes blazing.

"Colonel Walter Stewart started it all. General Horatio Gates joined him. Major John Armstrong Jr. has written all the letters, including the notice."

Anger flared in Washington's face. Horatio Gates! The great coward at the battle of Saratoga, and at Camden, where he deserted his own command in the midst of battle! The same Horatio Gates who had earlier created "The Conway Cabal" in his failed effort to discredit and overthrow Washington and take his place as commander in chief of the Continental Army.

By force of his iron will, Washington rose above his anger. Calmly, he said, "Thank you, General Knox. If anything else comes to your attention that I should know, you have free access to me, day or night."

Washington watched the rotund little Knox leave his office, then sat down. He squared parchment on his desk, reached for his quill, and carefully, thoughtfully began writing.

A chill rain was falling the morning of Saturday, March 15, 1783, when the officers began gathering in the Public Building. Inside the assembly hall, rows of benches began to fill. At the front of the hall, General Horatio Gates, Colonel Walter Stewart, Major John Armstrong Jr., and others took their places on the raised dais, ready to call the officers to order and begin the meeting. Not one man among them expected General Washington to make an appearance.

Then a small door to the right of the dais opened, and every head in the room turned to stare as General Washington entered. He paused to throw the rain from his hat, then unbuckled and hung his cape and hat by the door and walked to the dais.

General Horatio Gates sat in absolute shock. The last thing he had expected was to see Washington at this meeting. He stammered a greeting, then yielded control of the entire proceeding to his commander in chief, according to proper military protocol.

Washington took his position behind the pulpit and drew a document from the folds of his tunic. He straightened it, looked out at the blank faces of the officers, then began to read the remarks he had been preparing for three days.

"By an anonymous summons, an attempt has been made to convene you. How inconsistent with the rules of propriety, how unmilitary and how subversive of all order and discipline!"

Dead silence gripped the room. Washington had just ripped into Gates, Stewart, Armstrong, and all other men on the dais behind him, condemning them for their flagrant breach of military protocol and charging them with subversion!

Washington's face was like granite, his eyes piercing. He loudly declared that the author of the notice, as well as the other written documents, had in his heart "the darkest suspicion to effect the blackest designs."

No one in the room moved. Washington continued his attack on the plan that the officers seated behind him had conceived. Reading from his prepared speech, he declared the perpetrators to be "guilty of premeditated injustice to the sovereign power of the United States."

"The way is plain, says the anonymous addresser. If war continues, remove into the unsettled country . . . and leave an ungrateful country to defend itself. . . . If peace takes place, never sheath your sword, says he, until you have obtained full and ample justice. This dreadful alternative, of deserting our country in the extremest hour of her distress or turning our arms against it has something so shocking in it that humanity revolts at the idea. My God! What can this writer have in view by recommending such measures? Can he be a friend to the army? Can he be a friend to this country? Rather is he not an insidious foe, some emissary, perhaps . . . plotting the ruin of both . . . ?"

Washington paused and changed course.

He declared he was in the presence of men for whom he had a "recollection of the cheerful assistance and prompt obedience I have experienced from you under every vicissitude and fortune, and the sincere affection I feel for an army I have so long had the honor to command . . ." He reminded them that their new congress had nothing but the highest and most grateful opinion of the army, and that while they had thus far failed to meet their promises, they "will not cease till they have succeeded . . . , but like all other large bodies where there is a variety of different interests . . . their deliberations are slow . . ." However, given time, Congress would not tarnish "the reputation of an army which is celebrated through all Europe for its fortitude and patriotism."

He continued, "Let me entreat you . . . not to take any measures which . . . will lessen the dignity and sully the glory you have hitherto maintained. Let me request you to rely on the plighted faith of your country and . . . Congress."

The general concluded, promising them that if they remained true to the dream for which they had sacrificed so much, their posterity would forever remember "the last stage of perfection to which human nature is capable of attaining."

He folded the paper and raised his eyes to peer into the faces of the men before him. He saw the indecision, the frustration, the inner turmoil that was tearing their hearts. He realized he had moved them, but he sensed it had not been far enough. What could he add? What could he say? Or do?

It came to him. He drew the letter he had received from Congressman Joseph Jones from his pocket, unfolded it, and smoothed it on the pulpit. He leaned forward and concentrated on the small handwriting, indistinct and blurred. He began to read it, then stopped, held it closer to his eyes, and tried to read it again. He stumbled on the wording, paused, then laid it back on the pulpit. He reached once more inside his tunic and drew out a pair of eyeglasses. Carefully he put them on, and raised his head to look out over the faces before him.

The officers were frozen in absolute astonishment. Never had any of them seen their commander in chief wear spectacles. General George Washington? The man who could not be killed by musket or cannon? He who had survived six years of the worst that nature and war could hurl against him? Spectacles? Impossible.

For a time Washington stood without moving, looking into their faces, before he understood the profound emotions his spectacles had opened in their hearts. He looked down at the Jones letter before him, struggled to read a portion of it, then laid it back on the pulpit. Again he raised his head and looked into the faces of his officers, and in an even, quiet voice that penetrated every corner of the hall, he spoke the words that came to him.

"Gentlemen, you will permit me to put on my spectacles, for I have not only grown gray but almost blind in the service of my country."

The spirit in the hall was charged, electric. Hushed murmuring broke out. Strong men wiped tears from their eyes and cheeks. Others stared at the floor, then back at Washington, groping to understand what had swept away the purpose of the meeting and replaced it with the certainty that they must honor and support their infant government and its struggling Congress.

Washington did not speak another word. He removed his spectacles, put them back into his pocket, gathered his papers, and walked from behind the pulpit, off the dais, down the aisle that divided the hall, and out the huge double doors into the rain.

Behind him, Horatio Gates, Walter Stewart, Major John Armstrong Jr., and the other Newburgh conspirators sat behind the pulpit white-faced, shocked speechless, discredited, stripped of all honor, all respect before the officers of the Continental Army.

General Henry Knox, the round little man who had faithfully followed Washington through the entire war, strode to the pulpit, followed by others who had remained true to their commander in chief. Knox faced the packed hall and his voice rang out.

"I speak for our commander in chief, and for the United States of America! I affirm my loyalty to them, and I pledge myself to their support so long as I live! I deplore and condemn all the threats and actions taken by those who have sought to bring them down! If there are those among you who agree with me, speak now!"

The voices of the officers rang loud and long. "Hear! Hear! Hear!"

It was over. The Newburgh conspiracy had failed. The struggling young government had survived. George Washington's spectacles had played their part in the birth of America.

THE DELEGATE WHO SAVED
THE CONSTITUTION

SATURDAY, JUNE 30, 1787
INDEPENDENCE HALL, PHILADELPHIA

★ ★ ★

ABRAHAM BALDWIN, A DELEGATE FROM Georgia to the
Constitutional Convention, used his handkerchief to wipe at the
sweat on his face. Since the opening of the convention on May
25, 1787, in the East Wing of Independence Hall in Philadelphia,
it had been clear that the Articles of Confederation that had gov-
erned the United States through the Revolutionary War were inca-
pable of governing the thirteen states in time of peace because
they failed to give Congress the right to levy taxes to pay for government and they did not provide regulations to govern conflicts
between the states. In the four years since the peace treaty between
England and the United states had been signed, the states had
steadily descended into bitter disputes over issues such as the right

to control navigation on the great rivers, taxes on interstate commerce, religious conflicts, and other matters. In a last desperate attempt to save the Union, young James Madison of Virginia and a few others had arranged to have delegates from all thirteen states gather in Philadelphia, behind closed doors, to correct the fatal flaws in the Articles.

One of the worst and most basic defects was the issue of how the states would be represented in Congress. The states with the large populations insisted that they were entitled to more congressmen because they had more citizens. The states with small populations had risen in near revolt against it, loud and hot in their protest that if the large states had more power in Congress, it was only a matter of time until they would abuse it, resulting in harm to the small states.

On Friday and Saturday, June 29 and 30, just thirty-five days into the convention, the battle had become wild, hot, and loud.

"You can trust us!" the larger states shouted. "We will never abuse you."

Instantly, Gunning Bedford of Delaware was on his feet, face red and contorted in rage.

"If you possess the power, the abuse of it could not be checked. Sooner than be ruined, there are foreign powers that will take us by the hand. If we solemnly renounce your new project, what will be the consequence? You will annihilate your federal government, and ruin must stare you in the face!"

Delegates from the large states reared back in their chairs aghast! Gunning Bedford had just announced that if the larger states were given the power to outvote and control the smaller states, there were foreign powers that would be overjoyed at the notion of absorbing the smaller states; and if that happened, the United States would be cut in half! The Union would be destroyed! Everything they had fought for would be gone forever!

Then Bedford spread his feet, and his arm swung up with a finger pointing directly at the delegates of the larger states. His voice filled the hall.

"You of the large states say you will never hurt or injure the lesser states."

He paused, and for a moment the room was gripped in a tense silence as every delegate held his breath waiting for Bedford to conclude.

His voice was like thunder, his pointed finger like a sword. "I do not, gentlemen, trust you!"

Ben Franklin, George Washington, and James Madison sat staring, waiting for the convention to erupt in chaos, realizing that Bedford had just delivered an all-out assault on the honor and integrity of some of the finest minds in America. Had that insult been delivered outside the assembly hall, it could have, and in every probability would have, resulted in duels to the death with pistols.

Delegates from large states leaped to their feet and their voices rang loud and long. James Wilson of Pennsylvania, Jonathan Dayton of New Jersey, Alexander Hamilton of New York, Rufus King of Massachusetts—shouting their defiance of Bedford and his threat to lead the small states away from the convention and destroy it. Franklin, Washington, and Madison began to breathe again as they watched the delegates vent their anger in shouted rage. Some shook raised fists in their fury, but none walked out, nor did any threaten to do so.

Slowly the anger cooled and tempers were brought under control. Washington, the president of the convention, adjourned for the day, to reconvene Monday July 2, 1787, at 10:00 A.M. Every man left the hall subdued, troubled, quiet, struggling with the unbearable heat in the closed hall that left them drained and weary each day. Abraham Baldwin gathered his file and papers, stood, once more wiped the sweat from his face, and silently walked out into the oppresive heat of a Philadelphia summer day.

Most of the delegates attended a church meeting of their choice on Sunday, July 1, preoccupied, struggling in their minds to prepare for what was certain to come Monday morning. There was no question that the head-on collision between the large states and the small states would be the issue of the day, and none doubted that as the matter stood when they adjourned on Saturday, Monday would bring a stand or fall vote for the entire Constitutional Convention, and the United States of America. And since the larger states had more delegates at the convention than the smaller states, there was a great, growing sense of foreboding that when the large states dominated the vote, the smaller states would simply walk out.

Monday morning, President George Washington called the convention to order. The secretary called the roll. Unexpectedly, some delegates were absent, among them one from Maryland. Two of the Georgia delegates were absent for reasons never known. The agenda was read, the floor was opened to debate, and again the battle between the large and small states became heated.

With noon approaching, a delegate leaped to his feet and loudly moved that the debate be ended and the matter go to a final vote on the sole issue of whether representation in Congress should be based on one vote for each American citizen, yes or no. Another shouted, "I second the motion." The summer heat in the sealed room was unbearable, and the atmosphere was charged with tension. Washington asked, "All in favor of the vote being taken at this time say 'aye,'" and the great majority answered, "Aye."

The moment of reckoning was upon them.

"The secretary will call the roll and record the vote," Washington declared and took his seat while the secretary began. Washington, Franklin, and Madison sat on the edge of their chairs, scarcely breathing, fearful the convention was within minutes of disbanding, and with it, the great dream of a united America.

The vote went exactly as expected, with the large states clearly in the majority, until the secretary called for the Maryland delegation. Maryland had consistently voted with the large states, but with one delegate absent, the vote changed. Maryland voted with the small states! To the astonishment of everyone, with Maryland on the side of the small states and other delegates unexpectedly absent, the vote was in a tie when the last state was called.

There was an audible murmur on the floor, and the secretary continued.

Georgia! The last state was Georgia. The large states breathed a great sigh of relief. Georgia had voted consistently with the large states. Only then did they realize that of the four Georgia delegates, two were absent. That left only two to vote.

"How does Georgia vote?" the secretary called.

One of the two delegates present answered. "I vote aye." He had cast his vote with the large states.

The last delegate to vote was Abraham Baldwin. If he voted with his fellow Georgian, the large states would have the majority, and the convention would be doomed.

Baldwin had been withdrawn, thoughtful, quiet, throughout the proceedings, hardly noticed. Now the fate of the convention—and the United States—was in his hands alone.

Every eye was on him. The silence was deafening as Baldwin searched his soul for the wisdom to know what to do. Should he vote with the large states and be remembered forever as the man who destroyed the Constitutional Convention—and America? Or should he vote with the small states, and the survival of the convention?

Baldwin spoke. "I vote nay." Baldwin had voted with the small states! Loud exclamations erupted and continued until George Washington gaveled them back to order, and Franklin and Madison slumped back in their chairs, awash with relief.

"Mr. Secretary, total the votes," Washington instructed.

"Sir," the secretary exclaimed, "the vote is a tie."

Neither side had won nor lost. But in the process they had learned the one fundamental lesson that was to be the salvation of the Constitutional Convention throughout. Neither side was going to get everything it wanted. They must learn to listen to each other, to give and take, to sort out the best that was in them, to compromise, and move on, or face total failure. And not one man in the room could face the thought of going home to tell his people the convention had failed.

"Thank you, Mr. Secretary," Washington declared. "We will now move on to the next item on the agenda."

A PRAYER FOR KING
GEORGE III

SEPTEMBER 11, 1814

BALTIMORE, MARYLAND

★ ★ ★

THE REVEREND JOHN GRUBER, AVERAGE build, gray beard, a voice like thunder, and eyes that glowed severe beneath shaggy brows, stopped suddenly behind the pulpit in his Sunday morning sermon and cocked his head to listen. The War of 1812 was being fought, and in the tense silence that instantly filled his First Methodist Church on Light Street in Baltimore, every person in the huge congregation heard and felt the blasting of cannon at the courthouse. Three timed explosions. The signal! The great British armada that had been hovering in Chesapeake Bay for days was approaching Fort McHenry on the southern tip of the peninsula just south of the city! Fifty huge men-of-war and troop transports, intent on coming up the Patapsco River to invade and burn Baltimore!

Instantly the church was filled with excited exclamations. People stood, pointing south, gesturing, expressing their anxiety and fears. The Reverend Gruber raised both hands and nearly shouted, "Come to order! Come to order. You are in a house of the Lord! We will have respect within these walls!" The members of the congregation quieted and resumed their seats, white-faced, eyes riveted on their pastor, waiting for his counsel.

Every member in the large chapel knew that just eighteen days earlier, August 24, 1814, the British armada had landed five thousand red-coated soldiers on the west bank of the Patuxent River, near Bladensburg, Maryland. The British troops, among the best in the British army, had immediately struck the unprepared American militia in the small town, scattering them in a wild retreat. Then the British marched southwest to hit Washington, D.C., the capital of the infant government of the United States, at eight o'clock P.M. They marched methodically through the city, burning the capitol building, the president's home, the Treasury Building, and other government structures—looting, ransacking, taking whatever they wished. President James Madison had fled, coattails flying, just minutes ahead of the British soldiers who would have been most gratified to have taken him a prisoner of war. Then the British armada and their soldiers on shore moved north toward Baltimore, one of the key cities on the east coast of America.

In the days that followed, the Americans on shore tracked the British fleet and the soldiers. On September 11, from an observation tower at Herring Point on the banks of the Chesapeake, near the mouth of the Patapsco River, through a thinning fog, an American suddenly jerked his head forward, adjusted his telescope, and began the count. White-faced, he turned to his companion. "They're coming! Fifty of them! Big ones! Troop ships and men-of-war! Quick! Get word to Sam Smith!"

Instantly, his companion bounded down the stairs and burst out the door to find a small, wiry young man standing near a tall, brown gelding, saddled and waiting.

"They're here! Fifty British ships! The invasion has started! Warn General Smith."

The young man leaped astride his horse and was gone in a clatter of hoofbeats. Twelve miles later he hauled in his winded horse before the home of Sam Smith and pounded on the door. Sam Smith swung the door open and the young man nearly shouted, "They're here. Right down at the mouth of the river! The whole British navy and army!"

Sam Smith, a general in the Maryland militia, wise and experienced in battle, tough and hard against an enemy, strict but fair with his own troops, had anticipated such a move by the British and had prepared for it. Without a word he grabbed his tunic and ran out into the street, down to the courthouse to confront the twelve men assigned to the three cannon he had arranged for the warning signal to the town.

"Fire those guns," he shouted. "The British are coming up the Patapsco! The attack has begun!"

"Yes, sir!"

The three cannon crews jammed smoking linstocks to the touch holes in timed succession, and the three cannon blasted their message to the whole town. Within seconds men were running from their homes into the streets toward their assigned battle stations, carrying their muskets in one hand, pulling their tunics on with the other.

Sam sprinted toward Light Street. He turned into the

cobblestone walk to the First Methodist Church and burst through the doors into the large aisle that divided the great chapel and led to the pulpit where the Reverend John Gruber stood stock still, staring at Sam through narrowed, judgmental eyes. The startled congregation turned to stare first at one, then the other, waiting breathlessly in the intense silence.

Sam did not wait for an invitation. He bellowed, "Reverend, the British are in the Patapsco! The attack is started. We need you and this entire congregation at their battle stations. Right now!"

For a moment the air was filled with gasps and exclamations. Reverend John Gruber recoiled in his moment of decision. He was a man of the cloth, a man of peace, not war! With the British coming to burn and ravage his town and his congregation, what was his duty?

The silence became electric while Sam stood facing him, waiting.

The Reverend John Gruber took a deep breath, bowed his head, and his voice rang.

"The Lord Bless King George, convert him, and take him to heaven, as we want no more of him! Amen!"

He raised his head and loudly announced, "You are all dismissed to your duty posts!"

THE DEFIANT ROOSTER

SEPTEMBER 13, 1814
FORT MCHENRY, MARYLAND

★ ★ ★

THE FEISTY LITTLE RED BANTAM ROOSTER cocked his head and cast a beady eye toward the uproar that had just erupted inside the thick walls of American Fort McHenry. His kingdom was the large chicken yard that confined his flock of hens inside the fort. His hens provided eggs for the soldiers and civilians inside the fort, as well as an occasional meal of stewed chicken, and as long as he was king, he intended to protect his domain, oblivious to the War of 1812 then raging.

Fort McHenry was a five-sided, star-shaped fort finished in 1805 on the southern tip of the peninsula that jutted into the very northern tip of Chesapeake Bay, where the Patapsco River continued north into Baltimore Harbor. To enter the harbor and attack

Baltimore, enemy ships first had to get past the heavy cannon of Fort McHenry—one hundred of them—and none had dared make the attempt. That is, until the British navy decided it was high time to destroy Baltimore and then move thirty miles south and burn Washington, D. C., the capital and stronghold of the infant United States government.

To do this, the British had sent a monstrous armada north, up the Chesapeake waters to the mouth of the Patapsco River, to take the measure of the fortifications at Fort McHenry and bombard it to rubble. What the British failed to reckon with was one tough, hard-headed, beloved American officer named Colonel Sam Smith. When Sam heard the British fleet was sailing north to his beloved Baltimore, he thrust out his sizeable chin and started giving orders.

"Assemble the troops. Arm the citizens. Prepare Fort McHenry for battle. By Jove, we'll teach those redcoats a thing or two."

In the beauty of the morning of September 13, 1814, Admiral Alexander Cochrane sailed his British armada to less than one mile from the fort and gave his orders. "Open fire, and do not stop until Fort McHenry is destroyed."

The heavy British battleships squared with the fort and delivered a thunderous broadside. Cannonballs smashed into the thick walls. Rockets arched out, trailing fire and smoke, to drop inside the walls. That was when the little red rooster reared back in the chicken yard, bewildered and confused at the unbelievable uproar and the sight of people running every which direction, shouting, dodging, seeking shelter.

On the parapets, American officers shouted their orders, and the big cannon blasted their answer back at the British armada. American cannonballs tore into the sides of the ships, shattering rails, punching holes in the hulls, and shredding the rigging and sails of those nearest. Startled British officers glanced at the heavy damage and quickly changed their minds. It was clear that a stand-up fight between their guns and those of the Americans would be a disaster. They gave orders, and the British fleet moved back about a half mile—just enough to be out of range of the American guns, but still close enough that its big cannon and rockets could reach Fort McHenry.

On orders, the British ships delivered their next broadside. With telescopes extended, the officers saw their cannonballs blow splinters in the walls of the fort, and reach inside the walls, while their rockets arched over the parapets to drop inside.

The Americans answered the second broadside and watched their cannonballs drop into the sea just short of the British ships.

"Hold your fire, hold your fire!" the American officers shouted. "Save your ammunition."

Satisfied the battle was theirs, the British swung their ships into formation, dropped anchor, and began the deadly business of a full-out siege of Fort McHenry. Their gunnery crews began the rhythmic loading, firing, cooling the cannon barrel with sea water, and starting over again, maintaining a steady barrage of cannon-balls and rockets.

Inside the fort, buildings were being blown up, and dirt and debris were flying everywhere. The uproar was deafening. One cannonball hit the corner post of the chicken yard and blew it to kindling. Instantly the hens went berserk, squawking, leaping in the air, frantically hopping about, running out into the parade ground, absolutely certain the world and all in it had gone insane. The little rooster dutifully followed, puffing his feathers to look huge and dangerous, trying to drive them back toward the hen house; but there was nothing that could stop his brood from its headlong plunge into the wild melee.

Then a British cannonball struck the ground three feet from the little fellow and exploded. The blast knocked him fifteen feet through the air into a shallow ditch, and he hit the ground rolling, groggy, disoriented, shaking his head in a futile attempt to sort out which way was up and which way was down.

Less than ten feet away, two American soldiers had taken cover under a wagon box and were curled up in a ball, hands over their heads, desperately hoping that a kindly heaven would spare their lives. One of them opened one eye to peek at the destruction all around, and saw the smoke clear where the little rooster had been. Then he saw movement, and there was the rooster.

The little fellow struggled onto his two feet and shook himself, standing unsteadily at first, then more firmly. He looked both directions, then at the far wall of the fort where cannonballs were smashing in and exploding, then upward at the rockets, trailing their red glare and smoke. He suddenly puffed out his chest and strutted out into the open, onto the top of a mound of dirt hurled up by a cannonball. He stood there for a moment, and then he threw back his head and cut loose. He crowed, long and loud, cursing the British and their ships and their cannon and all they were doing to his kingdom and his hens and his hen house. He had had enough! He paused, then ripped out his second long, loud, raucous blast, venting his frustration and anger as he made his statement to King George.

The two Americans looked at him standing there, neck stretched up, head held high, chest puffed out, tail feathers spread, raucously defying the mightiest navy in the world, and suddenly the men looked at each other, taking courage from the little bird. One of them chuckled. Others nearby raised their heads to look.

They saw the cocky little bird and began to grin, and almost imperceptibly the rooster's feisty spirit began to spread throughout the fort.

One of the men turned back to the rooster and called to him, "Little man, if we survive this, you're going to get double grain rations for a few days."

The British bombardment did not let up. The sun set and the endless stars filled the black velvet of the night heavens, and still the great guns of the British fleet blasted while the rockets soared into the fort. Fires erupted within the walls of the fort, while the Americans frantically pumped water and formed bucket brigades to survive. In the dead of night a steady rain began to fall.

With dawn approaching, brave hands lowered the stars and stripes from the pole that topped the fort walls, while others unfolded the largest American flag in the United States and raised it proudly in the earliest gray streaks of the dawn. The flag was thirty-two feet by forty-three feet. The stars measured two feet between the points. It had been sewn at a cost of $405.90, on orders of Sam Smith by Mrs. Mary Young Pickersgill and her thirteen-year-old daughter, Caroline, who had done the work on the floor of the local brewery, the only place in town large enough to accommodate the huge flag. Smith had anticipated the attack on Fort McHenry and resolved that no matter what else happened, the British were going to see the American spirit when they raised that gigantic flag.

In the misty gray of a rainy dawn, it was there, fluttering in the morning breeze—proud, defiant, announcing to the British: "We're still here! We've taken your eighteen hundred cannonballs and rockets, and we've been through the heaviest bombardment in naval history, and we've been hurt, but we're still here, beneath the biggest flag in the country!"

Twenty-six hours after the siege of Fort McHenry began, the British commanders understood the Americans were never going to surrender the fortress. The invaders were not going to reach Baltimore. Their hope of destroying that city was not to be.

They issued orders. "Cease fire. Withdraw. Withdraw."

It was over.

Inside the fort, jubilation was rampant. A half dozen men repaired the chicken house and yard and herded the squawking hens back inside. The two men who had first seen the feisty little rooster vent his wrath on the British navy caught the little fellow and delivered him back inside also, once again to be king of his domain. Then they went to the granary and carefully measured out a double issue of mixed grain and tossed it inside, smiling as the beady-eyed little fowl began pecking.

ENDNOTES

★ ★ ★

1. THE PETTICOAT THAT SAVED PAUL REVERE. See David Hackett Fischer, *Paul Revere's Ride* (New York: Oxford University Press, 1994), 103 et seq.

2. HARD TO KEEP A GOOD MAN DOWN. See Allen French, *The Day of Concord and Lexington* (Boston: Little, Brown & Company, 1925), 193–264.

3. THE CRIMINAL WHO SAVED WASHINGTON. See Carlos E. Godfrey, *The Commander-in-Chief's Guard: Revolutionary War* (Boston: Genealogical Publishing Company, 1972), 21–34; Henry P. Johnston, *The Campaign of 1776 around New York and Brooklyn* (N.p.: N.p., 1878; Reprint, New York: DeCapo Press, 1971), 129–30.

4. ADMIRAL SIR PETER PARKER'S DRAWERS. See Robert Leckie, *George Washington's War* (New York: HarperCollins, 1992), 228 et seq.

5. SEVEN WOMEN AND THE STATUE OF KING GEORGE. See Leckie, *George Washington's War,* 257; Johnston, *Campaign of 1776 around New York and Brooklyn,* 93.

6. THE WOMAN WHO SAVED GENERAL PUTNAM AND THE AMERICAN ARMY. See Johnston, *Campaign of 1776 around New York and Brooklyn,* 39–40.

7. THE WOMAN CANNONEER. See Charles F. Claghorn, *Women Patriots of the American Revolution* (Metuchen, N.J.: Scarecrow Press, 1991), 55–56.

8. THE WOMAN WHO SHAMED THE MEN. See Mollie Somerville,

Women and the American Revolution (Washington D.C.: National Society, Daughters of the American Revolution, 1974), 36–39.

9. WASHINGTON'S SECRET SPY. See Richard M. Ketchum, *The Winter Soldiers* (New York: Henry Holt & Company, 1997), 239–42; Leckie, *George Washington's War,* 258–59.

10. THREE WHO STEPPED FORWARD. See Henry Steele Commager and Richard B. Morris, eds., *The Spirit of Seventy-Six: The Story of the American Revolution as Told by Participants* (New York: DeCapo Press, 1995), 519–20; Douglas Southall Freeman, *George Washington: A Biography,* 4 vols. (New York: Charles Scribner's Sons, 1951), 4:332–33, n. 44, 45; Ketchum, *Winter Soldiers,* 278.

11. WHEN SIX HUNDRED STOPPED FIVE THOUSAND. See Ketchum, *Winter Soldiers,* 286–91.

12. WHEN KING GEORGE II LOST HIS HEAD. See Ketchum, *Winter Soldiers,* 309–10.

13. THE RIFLE SHOT THAT TURNED THE WAR. See Don Higginbotham, *The War of American Independence* (Boston: Northeastern University Press, 1983), 193–97; Leckie, *George Washington's War,* 389–426; Piers Mackesy, *The War for America, 1775–1783* (Lincoln, Nebr.: University of Nebraska Press, 1993), 130–41.

14. BENNINGTON. See Higginbotham, *War of American Independence,* 191; Richard M. Ketchum, *Saratoga* (New York: Henry Holt & Company, 1977), 291–319; Leckie, *George Washington's War,* 397–99.

15. THE WEAK-MINDED ENEMY HERO. See Ketchum, *Saratoga,* 34–35; Barbara Graymont, *The Iroquois in the American Revolution* (New York: Chelsea House, 1988), 144–45; Leckie, *George Washington's War,* 394.

16. THE QUAKER LADY WHO SAVED WASHINGTON. See Claghorn, *Women Patriots of the American Revolution,* 60–61; Henry Emerson Wildes, *Valley Forge* (New York: Macmillan, 1938), 142–44; Somerville, *Women and the American Revolution,* 56.

17. VON STEUBEN—PROFANITY AND SALVATION. See John W. Jackson, *Valley Forge, Pinnacle of Courage* (Gettysburg, Pa.: Thomas Publications, 1992), 124–26; John F. Reed, *Valley Forge, Crucible of Victory* (Monmouth Beach, N.J.: Philip Freneau Press, 1969), 38–39; Leckie, *George Washington's War,* 438–39; Wildes, *Valley Forge,* 170.

18. LADY WASHINGTON. See Noel F. Busch, *Winter Quarters* (New York: Liveright, 1974), 71, 94–95; Leckie, *George Washington's War,* 142;

Reed, *Valley Forge, Crucible of Victory,* 34; Jackson, *Valley Forge, Pinnacle of Courage,* 171.

19. THE UNKNOWN SAILOR. See Dudley W. Knox, *A History of the United States Navy,* rev. ed. (New York: G. Putnam and Sons, 1948), 26–32; Joseph Jobe, ed., *The Great Age of Sail,* Trans. Michael Kelley (New York: Crescent Books, 1967), 151.

20. THE CROSS-EYED WOMAN PATRIOT. See Somerville, *Women and the American Revolution,* 42.

21. THE OVERMOUNTAIN BOYS. See Mackesy, *The War for America, 1775–1783,* 342–45; Leckie, *George Washington's War,* 582–97.

22. THE IMMIGRANT WHO SAVED THE AMERICAN REVOLUTION. See Shirley Milgrim, *Haym Salomon, Liberty's Son* (Philadelphia, Pa.: Jewish Publication Society of America, 1979), 6 et seq.

23. SUSANNA'S DESPERATE RIDE TO SAVE GENERAL LAFAYETTE. See Claghorn, *Women Patriots of the American Revolution,* 30.

24. HOW THE SWAMP FOX GOT HIS NAME. See Hugh F. Rankin, *Francis Marion: The Swamp Fox* (New York: Thomas Y. Crowell Company, 1973), 1 et seq.; Leckie, *George Washington's War,* 518–19.

25. SHE ATE THE MESSAGE AND SAVED THE REVOLUTION. See Claghorn, *Women Patriots of the American Revolution,* 85.

26. A CASE OF MISTAKEN IDENTITY. See Somerville, *Women and the American Revolution,* 28.

27. THE GIRL WHO SAVED FORT HENRY. See A. B. Brooks, *West Virginia History* 1, no. 2 (Charleston W. Va.: West Virginia Archives and History, 2007), 110–18.

28. THE EYEGLASSES THAT STOPPED A MUTINY. See Douglas Southall Freeman, *Washington* (New York: Simon & Schuster, 1995), 368, 498–501; Richard B. Morris, *The Forging of the Union, 1781–1789* (New York: Harper & Row, 1987), 47–49; Higginbotham, *War of American Independence,* 409–12.

29. THE DELEGATE WHO SAVED THE CONSTITUTION. See Bill Moyers, *Report from Philadelphia* (New York: Ballantine Books, 1987), page dated July 2, 1787.

30. A PRAYER FOR KING GEORGE III. See James A. Whitehorne, *The Battle for Baltimore 1814* (Baltimore, Md.: The Nautical and Aviation Publishing Company of America, 1997), 159–94; Scott Sheads, *Fort McHenry* (Baltimore, Md.: The Nautical and Aviation Publishing Company of America, 1995), 33–43; Donald R. Hickey, *The War of*

1812: A Forgotten Conflict (Urbana, Ill.: University of Illinois Press, 1989), 202–3; Garry Wills, *James Madison* (New York: Times Books, Henry Holt & Company, 2002), 140; J.C.A. Stagg, *Mr. Madison's War* (Princeton, N.J.: Princeton University Press, 1983), 427–28; Richard V. Barbuto, *Niagara, 1814* (Lawrence, Kans.: University of Kansas Press, 2000), 270–71.

31. THE DEFIANT ROOSTER. See Whitehorne, *Battle for Baltimore 1814,* 159–94; Sheads, *Fort McHenry,* 33–43; Hickey, *War of 1812: A Forgotten Conflict,* 202–3; Wills, *James Madison,* 140; Stagg, *Mr. Madison's War,* 427–28; Barbuto, *Niagara, 1814,* 270–71.

INDEX

★ ★ ★

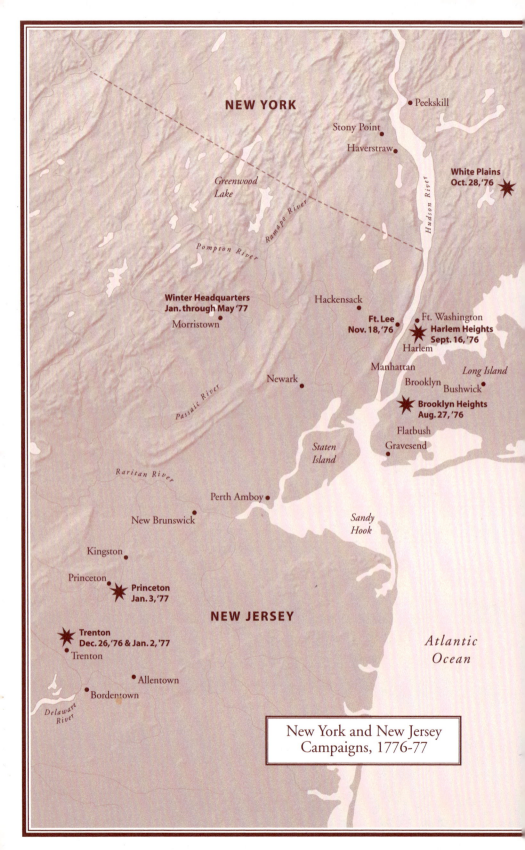

NEW YORK

• Peekskill

Stony Point •

Haverstraw •

Greenwood Lake

Ramapo River

Hudson River

White Plains
Oct. 28, '76 ✸

Pompton River

**Winter Headquarters
Jan. through May '77**

Hackensack •

**Ft. Lee
Nov. 18, '76**

Ft. Washington •
✸ **Harlem Heights
Sept. 16, '76**

Morristown •

Harlem

Manhattan

Long Island

Passaic River

Newark •

Brooklyn •

Bushwick •

✸ **Brooklyn Heights
Aug. 27, '76**

Flatbush •

Staten Island

Gravesend •

Raritan River

Perth Amboy •

Sandy Hook

New Brunswick •

Kingston •

Princeton •
✸ **Princeton
Jan. 3, '77**

NEW JERSEY

Atlantic Ocean

✸ **Trenton
Dec. 26, '76 & Jan. 2, '77**

Trenton •

• Allentown

Bordentown •

Delaware River

New York and New Jersey
Campaigns, 1776-77